Praise for Omar Tyree and *Welcome to Dubai*

"With this second installment of *The Traveler* series, Omar Tyree's transition from urban to mainstream fiction is complete. In *The Traveler: Welcome to Dubai*, Tyree moves the setting from the back streets of big-city America to Dubai, where, like the ancient Egyptians, poor laborers work on massive construction projects for men of unimaginable wealth. It is there his protagonist, Gary Stevens—the Traveler—is caught in the middle of an immigrant insurgency that places the lives of hundreds of hostages at risk. *Welcome to Dubai* is a well-plotted, riveting tale of Stevens reaching his potential as a highly trained operative. Tyree uses his unique voice to bring his characters to life, from the incomparable beauty and innocence of Ramia to the effervescent personality of the taxi driver Johnny, the characters are real and captivating. The next installment of *The Traveler* series can't come soon enough. Wherever Tyree decides to take his readers, I want to be along for the ride."

—RON MCMANUS, award-winning author of *Libido's Twist* and *The Drone Enigma*

"Omar Tyree's characters pull you in and the action-packed plot does the rest. It's a nonstop thriller. Tyree keeps us up reading way too late."

—WILLIAM ELLIOTT HAZELGROVE, best-selling author of *The Pitcher* and *Tobacco Sticks*

Welcome to Dubai
by Omar Tyree

© Copyright 2013 by Omar Tyree

ISBN 978-9-38467-49-3

Published by

◤ köehlerbooks™

210 60th Street
Virginia Beach, VA 23451
212-574-7939
www.koehlerbooks.com

Publisher
John Köehler

Executive Editor
Joe Coccaro

THE TRAVELER

WELCOME TO DUBAI

VIRGINIA BEACH
CAPE CHARLES

October 2012

Chapter 1

A DELTA JUMBO JET from the United States passed over Saudi Arabia, heading east for the United Arab Emirates. The descending flight, full of passengers, made its way into the airspace of the city of Dubai in the early afternoon, passing over an inspiring landscape of new and still developing properties. The opulent construction of Dubai included five-, six- and seven-star hotels and resorts, the largest shopping malls on the planet, and the tallest building in the world, along with an advanced transportation system of high-speed rails. There were state-of-the-art sporting complexes, international gold, diamond and clothing markets, an inside ski resort and hundreds of tourist attractions. Scores of new apartment buildings and villas housed the hundreds of thousands of immigrant citizens of the world who had traveled there to help design and build this paradise in the sand and live in its splendor.

Abdul Khalif Hassan breathed heavily with anxiety as he

stared out of his large office window at the steady stream of flights arriving and departing from Dubai's international airport. He stood at the corner window in his office on the twenty-seventh floor of an elaborate downtown building near the waterfront of the Persian Gulf and Dubai's famous man-made Palm Islands. An Arabian businessman of royal lineage in his late thirties, Abdul wore a fine designer suit with a striking white shirt and a colorful silk tie. He was a wealthy and confident member of the *Emirati*, the ruling class of local families of the Middle East, who had benefited from their ownership of abundant oil property. The Hassan family and many other Arabian businessmen had now moved into the tourism, hotel and retail industries, where Abdul's recent plans were not proceeding as scheduled. Construction of his new hotel had fallen nearly a year behind completion.

Abdul's smooth, light-brown forehead tightened with concern as he ran his hand through his dark mane of thick, wavy hair. He sighed in frustration.

"When will we have the next genius design robots to do the work of construction on time?" he asked rhetorically.

In the advertisements, brochures and worldwide promotions of Dubai, every building was complete, where in reality, many of their grand-scale projects remained in feverish construction, with cranes atop buildings and unfinished streets below.

Hamda Sharifa Hassan, Abdul's regal wife, stood in his office not far from him. Hearing her husband's impatience, she walked over to comfort him, placing her hand in the small of his back.

"You cannot rush time, Abdul. Everything will happen when it is supposed to, Allah willing," she told him calmly. In her mid-twenties, Hamda wore a knee-length white dress with tiny, vertical red stripes. Around her neck was a thick gold necklace and seashell amulet that held a large ruby. With it, she wore matching gold-and-seashell earrings. She was a stunning young queen with dark, straight hair past her shoulders, and she was college educated and mature beyond her years.

"We should go out to eat at the Promenade," she suggested.

"It will take your mind off your worries about construction."

Abdul nodded in response to her proposition, but he could not take his mind off of his projects.

"Anything you want," he grumbled. He leaned forward and kissed his wife on the cheek.

Hamda frowned and eyed her husband, knowingly. "Your stress will not make anything better. Relax, and leave it all up to Allah. The Magnificent will see all of your plans through. Has Allah ever failed you before?" she challenged him.

"Of course not," Abdul objected fiercely. Such a charge was considered dishonorable and blasphemous.

His wife reached forward to hold his hands in hers and to face him, taking his attention away from the landscape outside the window.

She told her husband with conviction, "Abdul, you will be successful at everything you do, and so will our children. So stop wasting my visit with you, and let's go do lunch." She continued to stare into his dark-brown eyes to settle him.

Finally, he grinned and loosened up. "Hamda, don't you know we cannot rush time?" he mocked his wife.

She tapped his arm gently and chuckled at his sarcasm.

"Come on, let's go," she demanded. "Call for the car."

She moved to cover herself in a white *abaya*, the traditional Muslim garb for public viewing, and added a royal, red-trimmed *khimar* to cover her head and shoulders.

Abdul stepped quickly away from his wife and toward his desk.

"First, let me call my management."

Hamda eyed him again in irritation. *Men will be men,* she thought. *My husband has the heart of a bull.*

Abdul picked up the phone from his desk and made a call to the management office of his various developing properties. His young wife watched him and took a seat with patience.

* * * * *

At one of the hundreds of construction sites owned and financed by the *Emirati* of Dubai, a project manager, wearing a red turban over his traditional white *throbe*, nodded with a cell phone to his ear.

"Yes, praise be to Allah."

He hung up his phone with urgent new orders to speed up his crew, moving immediately to inspect a group of workers who had taken their lunch break on the dusty ground floor of a rising skyscraper.

"How many minutes have you been on break?"

The sandy-brown men with thick, dark hair, dressed in identical light-blue uniforms, were startled. The imposing man in the long white garb seemed to have appeared out of nowhere.

"We, we just took our break," a well-respected worker responded for all of them. He was a soft-spoken native of India.

"Are you sure?" the manager questioned.

The Indian man nodded respectfully. "Yes."

Some of his co-workers were not as cordial. They looked at the Emirates overseer with disdain, tired of the disrespect they received as immigrant workers. The large population of multicultural immigrants did the majority of the building in Dubai—immigrants from India, Pakistan, Sri Lanka, China, Taiwan, Egypt and Ethiopia, with architects and engineers from Germany, France, America and Australia. They had come from all around the world to work and live there. These hardworking men with wives and families felt they should be allowed to eat at work in peace, especially on a job where many of them had been bused in to give their all from sunup to sundown.

"What are you looking at?" the manager asked a particularly stern-faced worker. He was a tall and rugged Pakistani, who leaned against an iron pole with his bowl of rice and bread. The Pakistani could care less about respecting a man who did not respect him. Nevertheless, he needed the job, so he looked away to avoid a confrontation.

The manager attempted to bully him anyway. "You heard me. What are you looking at?"

The Indian co-worker spoke up to support his crewman. "He

is okay. He is just tired and hungry. A man gets cranky when he cannot eat," he joked with a chuckle.

The manager continued to stare down the rugged Pakistani, unafraid of his superior size. He even walked in closer, crowding his space.

"You tell him not to look at me like that again," he informed the Indian to translate. The manager assumed the Pakistani worker could not speak English.

When the Pakistani looked into his Indian co-worker's eyes, the Indian man became hesitant to relay the message. Instead, he turned back to the Muslim overseer.

"Yes, I, I will," he stammered.

"You tell him what I said *now*," the manager demanded.

Suddenly, the tension between them all became apparent. The Pakistani man met the overseer's ire and refused to back down. He stepped forward against the restraints of his co-workers, who frantically jumped in between the two men to hold him back.

"No, no, stop it!" the Indian peacekeeper pleaded.

A serious altercation seemed inevitable.

"You dare to hit me?" the Muslim man challenged the Pakistani. "Hit me then. You will be fired. You are already *fired*!"

The Pakistani man cursed him in his native tongue and no longer cared about the job.

As the scuffle continued on the ground, a crowd of workers watched the commotion from the floors above, which had not yet been enclosed with walls. One of the workers standing on a steel beam slipped and lost his balance.

"AAAHHHHH!"

The worker fell headfirst from twenty stories up.

The Indian peacekeeper rushed into action as if he were a superhero, attempting to catch the falling worker in his arms. But as he ran to predict the landing of his free falling co-worker, he tripped over a water bucket and fell to the ground himself. By the time he had climbed back to his feet, his co-worker had met a ghastly ending.

The shocked Muslim manager fell to his knees in the dirt and immediately began to pray.

"Oh, Merciful Allah ..."

The Pakistani man and his co-workers looked on and shook their heads in disbelief. Some of them covered their eyes from the horror. As the overseer continued to pray, the Pakistani had seen and heard enough. He cursed the spiteful overseer and spit to the ground in front of him before walking away from the job.

"Saleem, what are you doing?" the Indian peacekeeper ran from behind to ask.

Saleem stopped and stared at him incredulously. "What are *you* doing, Rasik?" he responded in English, and added, "I no longer work here." He had chosen to fake ignorance to save himself from the daily defacement, but it was too obvious that he could no longer work with such disrespect from his bosses without killing the man in authority. And as he began to walk away from the scene of the tragedy, a number of his co-workers followed behind him. The men could no longer ignore the contempt of their imported services.

Chapter 2

IN THE WOODS OF Northern Virginia, less than an hour away from Capitol Hill in Washington, Gary Stevens hustled down a dirt road trail toward an open grass field, wearing long gray sweats. Over six feet tall and well-built, the thirty-one-year-old reached the open field, where four shooting stations awaited him with loaded pistols. Paper targets stood fifty feet away in front of him, shaped like fugitives and carrying assault weapons.

Gary grabbed the black nine-millimeter pistol at the station and aimed with sharp green eyes, firing two shots that zipped through the knees of his target. He then slammed the gun down and ran toward a finish line to his left.

Special Command Officer Howard Cummings waited behind the line with his stopwatch in hand. A stout military veteran in his fifties, wearing camouflage hunting gear and a matching cap, the officer grinned.

"You're twenty-seven seconds behind your record," he stated.

Gary kneeled over to catch his breath in the frost of Octo-

ber. He chuckled and said, "Yeah, I got a little too comfortable."
Beads of sweat dripped from his four-day-old mustache and
beard. Combined with his short-cropped, light-brown hair, the
beard and mustache made him appear more rugged and man-
nish than he had looked in his younger college years.

Cummings nodded and told him, "You would have made a
great military man, Gary."

"Not while my mother was still alive," Gary countered. "She
wouldn't have allowed it."

The officer continued to grin. "Well, you've come a long way
since we first met." He had expressed his confidence in the young
man more than a dozen times in the three years that he had gotten to know him.

"Thanks to you guys," Gary admitted. "I have no idea what I'd
be doing right now. I'd probably still be running a record store
and chasing tail in Louisville."

"You mean, as opposed to chasing tail in Virginia?" Officer
Cummings quipped. "You're still unmarried, right?"

Gary smiled sheepishly and didn't bother to answer.

"Yeah, I know, you're gonna try to hold out for as long as
you can."

Gary chuckled. He appeared sharp and determined, with the
maturity of life experience behind him.

"I don't want to hurt anyone's feelings until I'm really sure,"
he said.

Before Cummings could respond, they both looked back at
a second man and a woman, racing out of the woods toward
the shooting station. The man was slightly in the lead, but only
slightly, with less than two hundred yards to go to the finish line.

"Fox is gonna catch him at the end," Officer Cummings pre-
dicted.

Gary grinned and watched as his mentor, Jonah Brown, a
nearly forty-year-old African-American woman dressed in black,
ran behind the slightly younger guy in dark green. They reached
the shooting station simultaneously and aimed their pistols to
fire at their targets. With three rapid shots to the stomach, chest

and forehead, Jonah was off and running again toward the finish line. However, the younger man struggled to control his gun with weary arms and shoulders. He needed more time to steady his aim. When he finally shot the pistol, connecting with a single shot to the chest of the target, Jonah had crossed the line.

"Great comeback," Gary told her.

Jonah hunched over, her hands on her knees as her thick dark-brown ponytail fell over her right shoulder. She gasped for air as she rolled her eyes.

"Are you kidding me? I was trying to catch you."

Officer Cummings laughed. "Yeah, well, get in line."

The third runner crossed the finish line and said, "You two need to try out for the Olympic pentathlon team for Brazil."

"Maybe *he* can, but I'll be too old in twenty-sixteen," Jonah huffed.

"You can do anything you put your mind to, Fox," Officer Cummings interjected.

Jonah looked at Gary and nodded with an approving smile. She was proud of him.

"So can he," she responded in reference to Gary. "He's come a long way now."

"I tell him that every day," Officer Cummings said.

"Yeah, but I see he still won't shoot to kill," their third runner commented. "He shot the target twice at the knees."

"And he hit 'em both," Jonah argued.

Gary smiled. "I think it's much harder to target different parts of the body."

"Of course it is," Officer Cummings agreed. "That's why you're the *Eagle* and he's the *Beaver*; you're *sharper*."

"Yeah, but a beaver still gets it done," the man retorted.

"It just takes you a little longer," Jonah joked.

The Beaver looked back into the woods at a fourth man, dressed in dark blue, who was just making it out into the open greenery.

"Yeah, but I'm not as slow as him."

They all shared a laugh as Cummings shook his head, concerned about his latest recruit.

"That's what happens when you allow yourself to get out of shape."

* * * * *

Later that evening, Gary strolled into a downtown Arlington, Virginia, bar to meet up alone with Jonah. Dressed comfortably in a long black-wool coat, the wandering eyes of young women followed Gary, just as they always had. His handsome mystique begged for attention, even though he no longer asked for it.

Jonah sat at the bar in a conversation with a tall black man in his late twenties who stood beside her. He looked huge and well groomed, like a professional athlete with money to blow. But when Jonah spotted Gary approaching her, she dismissed the young man.

"All right, I may call you. But my business partner just walked in, so you'll have to excuse me."

"You *may* call me?" the well-groomed man questioned. He didn't budge. After buying her a drink at the bar, he felt slighted.

Jonah eyed him with measured authority. "That's what I said," she told him. "Now have some respect for your elders. As I told you earlier, I have a business meeting."

The towering man paused and grabbed his drink from the counter. He nodded and said sarcastically, "You have a good night," before walking away.

"Did I just break up something important?" Gary asked Jonah, picking up on the tension.

Jonah smiled. "Not at all. You know my dilemma with men. There are other things that are more important."

Gary grinned, marveling at how young and vibrant she continued to look. Dressed professionally in a black skirt suit with her hair done, she didn't look a day over thirty.

"Well, they never stop lining up for you," he commented with softness in his eyes. Any man would line up for a woman as attractive, professional and confident as Jonah, if only they could handle her intimidation factor.

Having been trained in the military's Special Forces Unit, Jonah was no-nonsense. She had been sent to guard Gary by her employer, an affluent and mysterious international business-man—Gary's father, in fact, who Gary knew only through Jonah.

Gary had been raised in Louisville, Kentucky, where his over-achieving and beautiful young mother, Gabrielle Stevens, had pampered him alone, having never married Gary's father. The all-American boy with no father grew to become a charmer who was super-smart, with movie star looks and natural athleticism. Gabrielle often viewed him as her overgrown puppy of a son.

When Gary was in his twenties, his mother died, a victim of a carjacking, followed by the cold-blooded terrorist murder of his best friend, Taylor. Gary was forced to grow up quickly, and it became Jonah's job to prepare him for the world, then safely usher him through it, with the perks of Gary's father, who had financed his son's military training and livelihood.

At the bar, Gary took a seat next to Jonah. "Anyway, getting back to our business, because no one gets more attention than you do," Jonah commented lightheartedly.

"Tell me about it. I need to get away from one right now," Gary hinted. "I'm thinking about taking a much-needed trip out of the country. It's been a while."

That idea gave Jonah a moment of concern. The last time Gary was out of the country, he had lost his friend Taylor to murder at point-blank range.

"Are you ready for that yet?" she asked.

Gary sighed. "I told myself years ago that you have to face your fears to live the life that you ultimately want to live. So after spending the last five years of my life to finish school and complete military training, I need to figure out who I am and what I want out of life. What am I even here for, you know? I still haven't answered those questions of myself ... and I still haven't met my father."

Jonah looked away momentarily, feeling some guilt. She said, "You've been great about that. You've really shown a lot of patience and maturity."

"Yeah, too bad I can't say the same about the old man," he jabbed.

As the intermediary between a father and his estranged son, Jonah was leery of the waiting game as well. How much more did Gary have to prove to show that he was trustworthy enough to meet his father? Maybe Gary's acceptance of the matter had only served to prolong the issue. Nevertheless, Jonah was the consummate professional who would continue to carry out the orders of the man who had hired her, no matter how close she had become to his son.

As usual, Jonah quickly changed the subject. "So, where would you plan on going?" she asked him.

Gary shrugged. "I'm thinking I'll fly to Dubai," he answered. "The place looks awesome, and I understand it's the biggest tourist haven in the world now."

Jonah nodded and thought about it. Dubai was considered safe ground as an international tourist destination in the middle of the desert. The Middle East connected Africa, Europe and Asia.

"Good choice," she said, thinking of Gary's safety. "Are you taking your lady friend from DC?"

She took a sip of her drink, anticipating an interesting answer. She knew that Gary would have one. In the five years that she had watched over him, the young man had been as elusive with the opposite sex as she had been in her own personal life.

Gary paused and grinned. "That's where the problem is," he answered. "I really need to get away and find myself before I can really commit to anyone like that. I don't think it would be fair to have a man who's obviously still searching to find himself."

"I bet she wouldn't agree with that, especially after you tell her you're traveling there alone."

"Yeah, well, at least I'm going to a place where all of the women are covered in sheets," he joked.

Jonah chuckled. "Not all of the women. I'm sure they have enough tourists over there who are not in sheets."

"Well, that's not what I'm going there to look for. I just need to clear my mind for a minute. And I haven't done that in a while."

"You *sure* have the money to do it," Jonah hinted with another sip of her drink. "Are you gonna stay at one of their seven-star hotels?"

Gary was very fortunate, but he had barely touched any of the money he had inherited from his mother's estate—she had done well as a political consultant for the local government in the state of Kentucky—let alone millions more that he would soon receive from his father. Money would never be an issue, and he never liked to talk about it. But Gary had definitely been spoiled by his parents' wealth, and he knew it.

He shrugged. "I may spend one or two nights at a fancy hotel just to see what it feels like, but for the rest of the time, I'll just stay at a three- or four-star."

Jonah chuckled and joked, "Yeah, a Motel 6 in Dubai, right? As if that even exists over there."

Gary laughed along with her. He joked back, "Maybe they call theirs a Motel 16."

Jonah asked him, "Does this girl know how well-off you are?"

Gary frowned. "Of course not! Look at how I'm dressed."

Jonah looked over his typically casual dress code and grinned.

Gary was more embarrassed and apologetic of his windfall, especially in light of the recent economic struggles in America and around the world. He never once bragged about fortune, and he had contributed more than a million dollars to different foundations for charity. After the tragic deaths of his mother and his best friend, Gary thought constantly about ways to help others. His humility had been strengthened by his painful losses.

Jonah said, "Well, whenever you want to buy a top-grade suit and shoes, you just go do it. That's definitely how your father would want to see you."

"Yeah, when he finally agrees to meet me."

Jonah changed the subject again. "Okay, so let's get to the hard part. Do you want to change your name for this trip? I can help you do that if it'll make you feel safer."

After what happened to Gary and Taylor in Medellín, Colombia, Jonah was very cautious of his travel out of the country. But now that Gary had years of military training and instruction in mixed martial arts, he was more than able to protect himself.

Gary joked and said, "What, you want me to become Jared Heath or something?"

He laughed out loud at the idea.

"If that's the name you want," Jonah responded seriously. "Of course, we would have to do a name search first to make sure there's nothing crazy attached to it."

Gary frowned and said, "Yeah, but I'm not a spy or anything. That would be more of a hindrance than me using my own name. What if someone asked me some hard questions?"

"I'm only trying to protect you," Jonah said. "I wouldn't want anything to happen to you." She paused then added, "It's my job."

Her comment forced Gary to think back to his painful trip to Colombia five years ago. His exploration there had been a spur of the moment idea that was definitely ill-advised. Gary could still hear the Colombian man's voice in his head, *Now you can travel alone in pain and fear*, followed by the blow of the single gunshot to his best friend's head.

Gary had often shot at targets during his military training with the Colombian terrorist in mind. His unfortunate torture in South America had been the reason for receiving military instruction. He wanted to learn how to protect himself in the future from any situation. He also realized that it was time to move on and let it go ... unless he ever came face-to-face with the Colombian again.

Shaking off his thoughts of pain, fear and revenge, Gary imagined a beautiful time of healing, discovery and wonder in Dubai.

"All I have to do is mind my own business and behave myself like a respectable tourist, and I'll be all right," he stated. "So I'll book a room at a normal place and do what every other tourist does to stay out of trouble."

Jonah nodded, agreeing with his strategy. "You do that. So when are you planning to go there?"

Gary shrugged, thinking spontaneously. "I don't know, in the next few weeks, maybe."

Jonah nearly choked on her drink. "In the next few *weeks*?" she repeated. "Well, that's not enough time to—" She stopped herself, thinking about her own spontaneous travel. The military life had its travel perks, and Gary could afford to do whatever he wanted, whenever he wanted.

Jonah smiled and said, "I hope your friend doesn't mind the short notice."

Gary smirked and didn't respond to that. Instead, he joked, "If you need to fly over and save me from something, don't hesitate to do it."

"That's not funny. And if I have to fly anywhere to save you, your butt's not going anywhere but Disney World from that point on. So stay out of trouble and leave the exotic women alone."

Gary chuckled, attempting to keep it light. "Yeah, I'll do my best."

Chapter 3

ABDUL KHALIF HASSAN AND his wife climbed off of the executive elevator at the garage level of their building, flanked by three armed Muslim guards in white *throbes*.

The guards were serious and experienced men with the important duty of executive-level security. Abdul was a tremendously wealthy businessman and was always full of activity, but he was with Hamda, who had talked him into a lunch date.

As they stepped forward and away from the elevator, a white Rolls Royce with gold trim awaited them inside of the parking lot. A large driver sat behind the wheel. More armed security men drove a white Cadillac Escalade in front of the Rolls Royce, with a second white SUV behind it.

Hamda took a deep breath. She was used to it all, nevertheless, she continued to fantasize of less protective measures with her husband. It would have been nice to go out for a change without need of a full security team. Anything was better than nothing. But as soon as they climbed into the luxurious backseat of the car, Abdul's cell phone rang at his hip; it was his business line.

Hamda noticed it and sighed. *Here we go again ...*

Abdul quickly held up his right index finger before his wife could announce her usual displeasure. "One minute," he told her as he answered his phone.

Hamda looked away and shook her head as the three cars drove off toward the garage exit and the streets of Dubai.

"Merciful Allah. I can never have his undivided attention," she complained.

Abdul frowned and ignored the remark. *The woman just doesn't understand business,* he thought. His management knew not to call him on his cell phone unless it was urgently important, so he answered it with alarm and curiosity.

"Yes, this is Abdul," he spoke gruffly. His threatening tone hinted of irritation. It was also his way of maintaining the necessary business edge when needed. At the same time, he reached out to caress his wife's soft hand. But it only took a few seconds for the dire news to rattle him.

"What?!" he exclaimed into the phone. He released his wife's hand immediately and brought his fingers up to his temple. "This just happened?"

A frown of concern brought new wrinkles to his forehead.

Hamda turned to study him, knowing that their lunch date was now out of the question. A serious issue was upon them.

"How did this happen?" Abdul continued to question. "Every week now there's something new. Merciful Allah!"

As Abdul raised his voice and ranted into his cell phone, Hamda casually placed her hand on her husband's thigh for comfort and support. But he removed it, in need of focus.

When their caravan of white vehicles hit the bright and sunny streets of Dubai, Hamda looked out of the window at the beautiful, tall buildings that surrounded them. The construction of the city of Dubai was indeed impressive. But what was it all worth without the peace of mind and the uninterrupted love of your husband?

Hamda had witnessed Abdul's violent reactions to disappointments in business many times in the past, and she had learned to avoid probing because it only inflamed him more. *He always overreacts,* she thought. *He always shows his temper.* She felt her husband should model himself after the more aristocratic men in his family, who carried themselves with poise.

"Is there a report? Who saw it happen?" Abdul asked.

Listening to his turbulent conversation, Hamda decided that her husband's questions did not sound like the usual business talk. So she turned again to face him.

Abdul began to shake his head and breathe deeply.

"Who was up there with him?" he asked. "Have the police come yet with an ambulance?"

Hamda froze and looked concerned herself. The news began to sound graver by the second.

"Okay, I am on my way to the site myself. I will be there in twenty minutes."

Hamda looked on with horror and was speechless. *What is going on?* she thought.

Abdul hung up his cell phone and spoke first to his driver. "Take us to the new construction site." He then addressed his puzzled wife with the news.

"What is wrong?" she asked him.

"An Indian worker fell from the construction building today and died."

Hamda covered her face with her hands, in shock. "Merciful Allah."

The driver quickly called the security team to inform them of their new destination, speaking to them in Arabic.

"Did someone push him?" Hamda questioned her husband. She could not imagine it as an accident. There had to be more involved.

"They don't know yet," Abdul snapped, as if the matter was none of her business. "That's what I want to find out. The management said that many of the men walked off from work."

"He let them walk *off*? Why did he let them do that?"

Hamda imagined that anyone there could have been a suspect.

"I don't know," Abdul answered her. He was peeved, and he would ask his men every question once they arrived.

* * * * *

The caravan of white vehicles pulled up to the construction site in the heat of the desert. Shade from the afternoon sun was one of the many blessings provided by the tall new buildings of Dubai. But wherever construction was incomplete, the sun seemed to beam down even harder on the naked steel, pipelines, plaster and the busy bodies of hundreds of immigrant workers.

At the scene of the tragic accident, UAE police officers had already arrived with an ambulance to try and piece together the needed information. They had questioned six construction workers who had been on the same floor or in the vicinity of the Indian man who had fallen to his death earlier. The men all confirmed that it had been an accident with no foul play. More than a hundred immigrant workers, the overseer and several site managers milled around in the background of the dusty ground floor, awaiting their turns to be questioned in the hot afternoon sun.

Abdul jumped out of his car and headed toward the site before his security team could flank him. He had no fear of his surroundings. His security was only there for precautions and to serve as a warning to those with ill intent.

As he approached the scene through the dust and dirt of the construction, Abdul looked back momentarily and noticed his wife had climbed out of the car behind him.

Conflicted by her actions, he paused and wondered if he should stop to address her or continue on with his business of joining the police and his site managers for questions and answers of his own.

What is she doing? he asked himself.

Abdul decided to return to his car to promptly address his wayward wife.

"Hamda, why did you not remain inside the car?" he asked. "You do not need to be here when I question these men. Filthy construction sites and sweaty men are not the proper place for a wife. These men do not deserve the right to see you. They will be fortunate to lay eyes on me."

Hamda grimaced and said, "Abdul, what about the wife and family of the man who died today? Are you telling me he does not deserve my sympathy and prayers?"

She figured she could lend her husband additional sympathy through her presence. It would be a generous gesture. And she was already there with him. But Abdul remained against it.

"You can pray for them just fine inside of the car, and without these men having to see you. And if you like, I can send for his wife and family to meet us both in private."

"That would be fine. But it is even more selfless of me to pray for him out here amongst the other men," Hamda countered. "That would show that you are indeed gracious and a true follower of Allah."

She was a wife of steel and iron will herself. Maybe she should have been a man.

Abdul shook his head and continued to resist her as his security men waited to escort his wife back to safety, but they dared not to touch Hamda without a direct command from Abdul. Even then they would be superbly gentle with her.

"This is *not* a good idea!" Abdul was now sorry that he had even taken his wife.

"Abdul, imagine the loyalty these men will have for you when they know your lovely wife can feel their loss and pain."

She took his smooth, clean-shaven face into the palms of her hands and eyed him gently, like a mother to a child. But Abdul pushed her hands away, embarrassed.

In a whisper, he told his wife sternly, "We are *not* in privacy. Now *please*, go back to the car. We will discuss this later."

Hamda finally began to see her husband's point as the men all stared at them. It was Muslim custom for a wife to obey the wishes of her husband and to refrain from the affairs of men.

Even the police officers were staring. So she nodded in submission and spoke to him in Arabic.

"*En sha Allah*," she responded, and she returned to the car with his security.

Abdul took a deep breath, swallowed his pride and returned to his business.

"And you did not see him walk to the edge before he fell?" an investigating officer asked one of the immigrant workers. The officer wore a policeman's uniform of an olive-green short-sleeve shirt, long matching pants, a black officer cap with red trim and black boots. He was a light-brown Arab man, clean-shaven and roughly thirty-five years old.

The darker brown worker in front of him shook his head and mumbled hastily with pretty good English, "No, it was sudden. It happened very fast."

"And no one else was near him?" the officer asked.

Hakim, the Muslim overseer, stood nearby, listening in on the interrogations. He continued to speculate what *he* thought might have happened. But as he continued to eye the number of immigrant workers in question—Indians, Pakistanis, Bangladeshis, Sri Lankans, Somalians, Ethiopians and Egyptians—he realized that few of them struck a chord. They were mostly unfamiliar faces.

Hakim shook his head and thought solemnly, *We have too many men working here who I do not know.* He then looked toward one of his hiring managers.

"Khalid," he called.

A small, medium-brown man of Yemish descent walked over to respond to him.

"Who are these new men? I don't recognize many of them at all."

Khalid held up his hands and shrugged. "They have left other construction sites that have been shut down or delayed because of the economy. So, Abdul told me to hire these new men to finish our building faster."

Once Hakim discovered that his boss had sanctioned more

hiring, apparently without his advice or notice, he decided to back away from his reprimand.

However, he did question the manager. "Does Abdul not know how many problems these new men have caused us on the job? We are hiring far too many of them."

Khalid looked at him in confusion and shrugged again in defeat. He asked, "And what would you have me to do: tell him that it's a bad idea? Even though I thought so myself, he had this idea that the loss of other construction business would be our gain."

Hakim listened and shook his head, feeling powerless.

"And now this is what we have—a bloody mess."

In haste, Abdul walked into the fold with his security team and was visibly upset. "Okay, what happened?"

The UAE police, Hakim, and Khalid, all eyed each other to see who would speak first. It was the policemen's job to report their findings.

"The man leaned over from one of the higher levels of the building and fell to his death. That is all that we have and all that the men have told us," the investigating officer explained. There were five more officers on the scene with more on the way.

Building code officials arrived at the scene to comb over the safety provisions of the construction site. They showed up in their uniforms of hardhats, clean white shirts and official badges. Apparently, someone had made an urgent call for them to investigate the site, with perfect timing.

"Aren't there more safety measures for the workers on the higher levels?" the officer asked Abdul right as the building code inspectors arrived.

Abdul was embarrassed and looked toward Hakim and Khalid, who immediately answered the officer's safety question.

"Of course we have our safety provisions," Hakim spoke up. "But sometimes all of the men don't use them."

It was not the best answer, and it was surely not what Abdul wanted to hear at the moment.

He shouted at both of his men, "You *make them* use more safety! That is your *job*!"

The minor managers remained out of Dodge and allowed their two leaders to take the heat, just as the building inspectors began to introduce themselves.

"Abdul Khalif Hassan? This is your building?" the lead inspector asked him. He was a tall Muslim man with fair skin, lighter than Abdul's and the rest. His question was a mere courtesy. The inspectors already knew who Abdul was and that he owned the building. They had been around and had spoken to Abdul on plenty of his previous projects. However, where there had been a silent understanding of unsafe practices at construction sites before, the impact of a slower economy on incomplete, hurried and stalled developments around Dubai had forced the inspectors to be less lenient. Developers were becoming increasingly desperate and too willing to cut corners in efforts to complete their financed projects on time.

Realizing as much, Abdul addressed the officials accordingly. "We will make sure that this kind of tragedy never happens again."

Nevertheless, the inspectors had to at least appear as if they were being more diligent on the job, especially in front of the UAE police officers. So they pressed him with questions while filling out reports.

"How many men work here?" the lead inspector asked. His team began to search through the area with their official notepads and pens in hand.

Merciful Allah! Abdul thought to himself. He didn't know the answer—and didn't want to know. The truth was that they were doing whatever they could to finish the building sooner rather than later.

Sensing trouble, Khalid spoke up, "We have several shifts of men, so we don't overwork them."

"How many men and how many shifts?" the inspector asked.

Khalid did not want to reveal it. He already knew they had hired too many men. But in his books, he had falsified the information; hundreds of men were being paid secretly.

"I will show you the books," he answered.

The lead inspector nodded to another member of his team to follow Khalid to the main trailer office. "Alim, you go check." He then nodded back to Abdul. "We are sorry for the tragic loss today."

Abdul wondered how they had found out so fast, but he would not ask the inspector in front of the officers. Instead, he nodded back. "All prayers be to Allah." He figured he would have a chance to speak to the inspector alone later, as they always did.

* * * * *

In sync with the modern world of media exposure, a camera crew of Dubai news and events reporters showed up in trucks, loaded with equipment. They were a part of the new, young regime of camera journalists, capturing the people, places and things of the United Arab Emirates. They usually covered only the positive news and rarely strayed into more tragic or political stories, unless it was sanctioned by the Emirates. But right as the emergency ambulance zoomed away from the commotion with the Indian man's dead body inside—headed toward the closest hospital—the young camera crew moved into action at the scene.

Obviously, another phone tip had been made that day.

Through the dark-tinted windows of the Rolls Royce, Hamda noticed the eager camera crew excitedly pulling their equipment from the back of their trucks, and she immediately thought of the impact a bad media story would have on her husband's building.

Oh no! she thought.

She looked back toward the construction site, where her husband had disappeared into the interior of the debris and the office trailers, and she decided to divert the camera crew's attention with a spontaneous interview.

She climbed out of the car, forcing the remaining security team to surround her, diverting the attention of the camera crew, just as she had hoped and expected.

A young Arabian woman wearing uncovered blue jeans and a black designer T-shirt, recognized her instantly. She had noticed the white Rolls Royce and Hamda's opulence before in the shopping areas of Dubai.

"Guys, that's Hamda Sharifa Hassan," she alerted the rest of the crew.

They stopped and looked dumbfounded as Hamda approached them.

"Please, return to the car," one of the security men begged her. He was terrified that Abdul would fire them all because of his wife's defiance. But Hamda ignored him and motioned for the camera crew.

"Would you like an interview?" she asked them.

"No, no interviews. *Please!*" the security men pleaded. They even revealed their guns to scare the young camera crew off.

Nevertheless, Hamda insisted, "No, they're harmless; just kids. Put those away." Actually, a few members of the camera crew were older than Hamda.

As the security men reluctantly lowered their weapons, the brave young reporter in jeans and a T-shirt led the interview. "Yes. *En sha Allah*," she spoke out of respect. "We would love to interview you. Would you tell us what happened here?" she asked with a microphone and cameras rolling.

The security men all looked toward the construction site, where their superior had accompanied Abdul. They had no idea how to stop his strong-willed wife from speaking, so they sent one of the men to run and inform their superior. Hamda paid it no mind and went on with the interview. She was thrilled by every opportunity to speak out and reveal her astute education in worldly affairs. She was a proud communications graduate from the University of Dubai, and she planned on using her degree.

"There has been an unfortunate accident today involving one of the workers," she said. "And I would like to send a blessing of my prayers to Allah for the loved ones, wife and family of the deceased."

The young reporter stood there, astonished for a minute before she remembered to ask her next question. She couldn't believe they had the opportunity to interview one of the most respected young wives of the *Emirati*.

Hamda Sharifa Hassan was already revered and celebrated amongst the young Muslim women who idolized her. She was a majestic wife with a strong sense of fashion and confidence who was politically aware and outspoken. An updated interview would make her more celebrated for her bravery and eloquence— the young reporter was sure of it. The interview would go viral and inspire hundreds of Muslim and Arabian women to acquire the education, poise and confidence that they needed to speak out on the affairs of Dubai and all of the United Arab Emirates.

"Will this be another hotel or—"

"Yes. My husband hopes to employ thousands of new workers with all of his hotels and developments. It is the work of Allah to provide opportunity for all. So as we pray for the safety of the men who work here, we also pray for the employment of the many people who will benefit from tourism and the new income of Dubai."

Before the young reporter could ask her another question, Abdul and the head of his security team came rushing back to stop them.

"What is going on here?" he asked. He looked toward the camera equipment. "This is private property, so anything that you film is now *my* property."

In a flash, his armed security men seized the cameras and ejected the tapes to keep for themselves.

"Hey!" the young reporter protested. But there was no fight as the police watched closely. The construction site was indeed private property. As far as the UAE police were concerned, the camera crew was trespassing and had no reason to be there.

"Move along before we arrest you. This is a private matter and not of your concern," the police warned them.

As the crew moved on without their tape, of course there was frustration, but the thrill of interviewing Hamda Sharifa Hassan for even a minute had been worth it.

* * * * *

Abdul, looking agitated, climbed back inside of the car with his wife. "Hamda, what is wrong with you? Why would you do that interview? I told you to remain inside the car."

"I saw these kids ready to film the property and the commotion, where they could have made up their own incorrect story, so I offered them an interview of the truth."

"For what? They don't need to know *anything*. You know how many news reports we could have while building a new hotel? *Thousands*! But no one cares until it is done. Then we do our stories of grand openings. But you don't do stories like this. There is nothing good that we could gain. We can settle up with this man's family in private with a *Diyat* of blood money. And his Indian family will be satisfied with that."

Abdul shook his head and continued, "Unbelievable! You are too pressed to use your education for the wrong reasons. When there is no reason to speak, you do."

Hamda snapped, "Well, what do I use my education for then, only to speak to our children?! You won't allow me to teach. You won't allow me to do interviews. You barely allow me to speak at events. And you do not allow me to develop my own business ideas. And yet, you always tell me how intelligent I am."

"You *are* intelligent," Abdul insisted. "But there is a time and place for everything, and this is not it."

Merciful Allah! he thought. *She makes me feel more like a father than a husband. Maybe I should have married a less ambitious woman who would not be bothered to speak so much. Now I have no choice but to treat her with more reservation.*

"Take her home with the security," he told his driver. "Then come back for me later."

He leaned over the seat to kiss his wife on the lips only for her to turn away and deny him.

"I did it only to help you," she told him.

Abdul softened. "Thank you. Now you can go home and help me again. My nerves will be much calmer here, knowing that you are safe at home with our son."

"Knowing that I am silent," Hamda snapped back at him.

Abdul sighed and shook his head. *She has far too much Western woman in her,* he thought. And although he had been attracted to her strong will initially, it was now becoming a problem.

"I will see you later at home," he told his wife of three years. He climbed out of the Rolls Royce with no response from her. He then watched as his driver sped away in the dust with half of his security team; then he returned to his business at the construction site.

Chapter 4

ANOTHER DELTA JUMBO JET from the USA entered into the airspace of the United Arab Emirates. Inside the roomy aircraft, Gary Stevens sat in window seat 26A, headed to Dubai International Airport. He had reclined his chair all the way back while falling asleep listening to his Beats headphones. The fifteen-hour flight from Atlanta had been exhausting, and he was only awakened by the loud bells of landing preparations as the passengers stirred and became excited.

"We're lannndinnggg," the blond-haired boy sitting beside him hummed. He was eight years old and traveling with his parents and older sister, who sat in the middle seats across the aisle to their right.

Gary pulled his chair back up and stretched out his chiseled arms in a dark-blue T-shirt. He then massaged his weary eyeballs with his fingertips and grumbled, "Yup, we're here all right." He took off his headphones, prepared to put them away inside of his carry bag.

"What hotel are you in?" the boy asked him. His big brown

eyes contrasted with his bright-blond hair.

Gary was hesitant to answer. "I don't know yet."

The boy looked confused. "You don't know yet? You didn't make your reservations?"

Obviously, he had traveled enough to know the process.

Gary smiled at him. "I wanted to see everything first."

"Then you'll buy a hotel?"

Gary continued to grin. "Ah, I don't know if I'll buy a hotel. I'll rent a room, maybe."

"Yeah, that's what I meant—a room."

"Richard, would you leave him alone," his older sister barked at him across the aisle. She was a teenager with two-toned blond and brown hair and the same deep-dark-brown eyes as her brother's. "He'll talk your ears off if you haven't noticed."

"Yeah, I see," Gary said, grinning. "So where are you guys all staying?"

"At the International Suites."

Gary nodded. "Good choice. You can never go wrong at the International Suites."

The girl's mother and father woke up beside her and glanced at Gary.

"How are you doing?" her mother asked.

"I'm good," Gary said. "I just needed a little getaway."

"Don't we all," her father grumbled.

* * * * *

Gary walked out of the airplane bridge in the city of Dubai. He was taller than most and lighter complected and would stand out in this country filled with more diminutive, darker men. He was sharp looking, with his hard-body, full head of hair and taut skin. Even his two-day old beard looked good. Gary often went without a shave for a few days. He found that the scruff kept him out of trouble, serving as a warning sign of toughness. It said, *Don't mess with me.*

Nevertheless, the happy-go-lucky American boy and his

family were hardly intimidated. Gary's eyes showed nothing but peace and friendliness.

"Byeee," the blond-haired boy hummed in his direction while being pulled away to claim his luggage.

Gary smiled and waved again, needing to claim his own luggage. The first thing he noticed about the airport of Dubai was the huge shopping advertisements behind bright lights and glass.

It looks just like America, he told himself, *only it's in Arabic.*

But once he claimed his luggage and followed the crowd to the long immigration lines, armed guards with assault weapons and guard dogs were everywhere. It had been a similar scene in Colombia. Only the Middle Eastern guards looked friendlier.

"Where are you staying?" the immigrations desk asked him at the front of the long lines.

"The Hilton," Gary lied. He still hadn't made up his mind on a hotel yet, but he knew that the Hilton was in the middle of downtown. So was the International Suites. However, he shied away from getting a reservation there. The place catered to tourists, whereas the Hilton was more businesslike.

"Which one?" the immigrations officer asked him.

Gary shrugged. "I guess the biggest."

The Arabian man in a white-shirt uniform smiled at him. He stamped the American passport and said, "Welcome to Dubai."

"Thank you."

The man nodded. "Enjoy your stay."

"I plan to."

Once Gary walked out of the airport exit to catch a taxi to downtown Dubai, the diversity of the culture became immediately apparent. There were Arabs, Indians, Asians, Americans, French, Italians, Africans, Latinos, Canadians and Europeans all vying for taxis and rental cars. Instead of rushing his movements, Gary relaxed and took it all in. He watched the new sights of dusty foreign cars, listened to the sounds of different languages and sniffed the late-afternoon air.

By the time they had arrived, it was after six o'clock in the evening. And eighty-five degrees ... in October.

"Amazing," Gary mumbled to himself. "I'm here in the Middle East." And he felt no fear at all, only curiosity.

As he continued to stand there on a cement platform for passenger pick-up, Gary looked to his right and met the eyes of a Muslim woman covered in white garb from the ground up. There was a red veil over her shoulders adorned with red rubies. She was surrounded by a pair of shorter women, who were much older and wearing similar white garb without the red. They appeared to be assisting her with three small children, who climbed into the back of a black Mercedes SUV. A second Mercedes SUV pulled up behind it and gathered up the older women.

Gary stood there hypnotized by the scene. *They must be important,* he assumed.

"It's the *Emirati*, the royal class of locals from Dubai," a man told him from his left. "Although most of them live in the finished city of Abu Dhabi."

Gary turned to lock eyes with the man. He was young and tall himself, although not as tall as Gary. He was brown like a paper bag with thick dark-brown hair that was combed back like silk. He looked late twentyish and spoke with quick and clear English that was definitely British. And his clothes were well fitting and fashionable.

"You never want to stare at the locals like that," the Brit said. "They might think that you're trying to kidnap them." Then he chuckled.

Gary grinned and kept his poise, taking another look at the pair of black Mercedes SUVs as they drove away in front of them.

"You're American?" the man asked.

Gary continued not to speak as he thought things through. He hated that his nationality was so obvious. Maybe he should have worn something different from his usual blue jeans and T-shirt. But it was comfortable and unassuming. Or so he thought.

He asked the man, "Is that a good thing or a bad thing here? Are you from London?"

The man smiled and nodded. "Yeah, how did you know?"

"You sound very British and your clothes are tight."

"Ahhh, and you sound very American," the Brit responded, laughing. "And your clothes are too loose. Americans can all use a good tailor." He reached out his hand in friendship. "My name is Johnny Napur. My family's originally from Sri Lanka."

Gary took his hand and remained apprehensive.

"I'm just a lonely traveler. I'm nobody from nowhere."

Johnny smiled. "Okay, Mr. Nobody From Nowhere, where are you going? Are you waiting for a ride or catching a taxi?"

"I was. I'm headed downtown."

Johnny nodded. "I can take you there. Have you converted your money yet? One U.S. dollar is worth more than three and a half *dirham*. So for one hundred *dirham*, I can take you downtown."

Gary did his own translation. "That's about thirty dollars."

"Roughly, yes. But if you had British pounds, they would be worth more than five and a half *dirham*, and I would only charge you *twenty* pounds for downtown."

Gary chuckled. "Sure, rub it right in. So where's your car? It's not a dump, is it? My luggage is sensitive."

Johnny laughed back and mocked him. "Sure, rub it right in. But no, it's a Mercedes." He paused and added, "It's just an *old* one. But I have plenty of trunk space for one bag."

Gary chuckled again; he liked this guy. Johnny was dressed cool enough to hang out with, and he would be easy to kill. Gary had learned to think that way for years now. It was a basic survival measure. He constantly asked himself how easy or hard would it be to kill a man if he needed to ... or a woman. And poor Johnny would offer him little resistance.

Then again, I have no idea who he knows over here, Gary mused.

"My car is right this way," Johnny told him, and walked to the right. "So how long are you staying?"

Gary pulled his wheeled luggage and carry bag behind him. He asked, "Can I see everything in a week?"

Johnny laughed and said, "You have a very dry sense of humor, friend. But if you have the right tour guide, anything is possible."

He was obviously offering more services than just a ride.

"Tour guide?" Gary questioned. "Is that your business here?"

"It depends on who's asking and what they want."

Gary nodded. *Okay, this guy is into things,* he mused. *And maybe I don't want to be that involved.*

"I'll just take a ride downtown for now."

Johnny nodded and grinned. "Yeah, for now," he hinted. "But you take my card for anything else you need."

Johnny continued, "You're over here with no girlfriend or a family? Well, it gets lonely at nights."

"But not for you, right?" Gary hinted.

Johnny grinned and turned to face him. "I know a lot of beautiful women here who would love to hang out with you. You're an American rock star? What do you play, baseball or something?"

He was sizing Gary up as Gary sized him up.

"Not quite. I played some lacrosse in college and a little bit of basketball on the side."

"Oh yeah. I played some cricket."

Gary grinned and told him, "It's not the same."

"Yeah, yeah, I know. Americans are better at everything, right?"

He sounded patronizing.

"No, I wouldn't say that. You guys still have soccer and polo."

"That's fútbol," Johnny corrected him.

"Yeah, whatever."

When they reached his car at the temporary parking area, it was indeed an old black Mercedes, but it was very dusty on the outside.

Gary joked, "I guess a car wash would make a ton of money over here."

Johnny frowned and snapped, "Not here. That'd be a waste of your money. With the dust and sandstorms, you'd have to wash your car every three hours. Only the *Emirati* does that. They have the money and water to waste."

Inside, the car was not bad. His black leather seats were nice and clean, and there was refreshing incense in the car.

Gary nodded. "Okay, this is better than a taxi. So tell me, what's the best hotel for me to stay at downtown?"

"It all depends on how much you want to spend. The Hilton Dubai Creek is one price, Jumeirah Beach is another, and Burj Al Arab is only for true rock stars. You can't even look inside unless you have serious money. They have a small bridge with security for you to even enter."

Gary smirked. "I heard about that one."

"Yeah, it's one of the most famous hotels in the world."

"And what if you just wanted a cheap place to stay for the night?"

As they hit the dirt roads on their way to downtown Dubai from the distant airport, Johnny eyed his no-name American passenger and said, "There are plenty of hotels for that. But you wouldn't come to Dubai just to stay in one of the other cities. Abu Dhabi is way too political and expensive, and Sharjah—that's where I live—is just not the same as Dubai. That's where every-thing is."

Gary grinned. "I get your point. I guess that would be like staying in New Jersey instead of New York."

"Yeah, or staying in Kensington instead of London. That would be a waste. But if you stayed at the Hilton, that's right in the middle of everything," Johnny said. "You would love it around there. It's walking distance from many of the shops and downtown restaurants."

Gary nodded and was ready to commit. Johnny was only confirming what he already knew. "All right. That sounds like where I need to be then," Gary agreed. He planned to try out the more expensive hotels as well, but Johnny didn't need to know that. The man knew enough already.

"So, what's the big deal with the ah, family in the Mercedes jeeps?" Gary asked.

"Oh yeah, if you ever see a Muslim woman dressed like that, with the red designs on their veil or on their shoulders, that prob-ably means they're local royalty, especially if you see a whole gang of them like that. And the older women without the red were probably maids and housekeepers."

"What's up with the color red? I thought *purple* was the color of royalty."

Johnny shrugged. "Each country chooses its own color. And in Dubai, it's red. So that family with Mercedes SUVs were definitely locals."

"*Locals?*" Gary questioned.

Johnny continued to smile, enjoying his history lesson. "Locals are like the indigenous Arabs who were here before the massive immigration started. But some of them also come from the other Arabian countries: Saudi, Qatar, Oman, Kuwait ... They're all referred to as *locals* here. They are original descendants from the Middle East."

Gary nodded, taking it all in. He noticed how cracked and gnarled the roads looked. "These roads look like they cut them out of the desert last week."

"My friend, it's the dust and the heat. Just like with the cars, it's hard to keep any new roads looking fresh here. But in London, we have fog, rain and bitter cold to keep everything cooled down. I'm sure in America you have the same. But in countries like this, where it's always hot and dusty, road construction is a waste of time and money. So they focus mainly on the downtown areas."

The downtown area, stuffed with tall hotel buildings and office towers, seemed to explode out of nowhere, with paved streets and elaborate walls to protect the residential housing from the dust storms.

"They respect the locals here," Johnny said. "They have no other choice. It's similar to the respect that Americans have for Hollywood stars and superstar athletes, like you," he teased with a grin. "Only in Dubai, that respect is for *life.*"

Gary nodded, enjoying the information he was getting.

"Nevertheless, thousands of immigrants come here each year to work and to earn money for their families back home," Johnny continued. "Dubai is the new playground of the world, and I'm here to play too."

By then, they had entered the busy nighttime traffic of downtown Dubai, which looked very similar to the density of New York, Chicago and San Francisco. There were buildings, cars, sidewalks, shops, restaurants, bright lights and multicultural people everywhere. One of those buildings was the Hilton Dubai Creek, where Johnny pulled up in front of the busy parking attendants.

He placed his car in park and handed the no-name American his card. "Again, anything that you need, you just call me. I know of some parties tonight, where you pick out a girl, and I'll see if I can go get her for you. But if not, you just come out and enjoy yourself. No pressure."

Gary could imagine the smooth British playboy enticing the international women of the Middle East. He had the look and confidence to pull it off with ease. He even wore a few pieces of expensive gold jewelry.

Gary was tempted to ask the precocious young man if he supplied recreational drugs. He suspected that he did—only he would make you ask him for them first. Maybe pushing women instead was much safer in Dubai, particularly for a young American stud. Johnny imagined that several women he knew would agree to hang out with Gary for free.

To test his hunch, Gary asked, "Are exotic women all that you have to offer? I've been in too much trouble with women already," he hinted and laughed. "I'm trying to stay loyal to my girl back at home. I just want to get in a mood to enjoy myself for a moment, you know."

Johnny kept his cool and nodded. "You tell me what you need ... but it'll cost you."

Gary grinned. "Sure, it will." Then he took out a fifty dollar bill. He had separated it earlier. He handed the currency over to Johnny and said, "That's about a hundred and seventy-five dirham, *right*? Is that a good tip?"

Johnny laughed. "Yeah, that's about right. It's pretty good. So I'll see you later on tonight then, or maybe tomorrow if you're too tired. Those long airplane rides can take a lot out of you."

"Yeah, we'll see," Gary told him with no promises.

"What's your name again?" Johnny asked him on the sly.

Gary grinned it off and said, "I told you, I don't have a name. Just call me 'The Traveler' for now."

Johnny smiled back and conceded. "Okay, The American Traveler."

Gary didn't like that idea either. He wanted to lose the "American" part. But for the moment, he left it alone and climbed out of the car as the hotel attendants grabbed his luggage from the trunk.

"Welcome to the Hilton in Dubai."

Gary felt weird. It was his first trip overseas alone, and without his mother or his best friend around. He had not traveled outside of the U.S. since his mother was kidnapped and killed and his best friend murdered. He still missed them both, dearly.

Gary took a deep breath as he headed toward the registration desk inside of the hotel.

There's no turning back now, he thought. *It's time for me to grow up.*

Chapter 5

TEN DAYS HAD PASSED since the tragic accident at the hotel construction site on the far west side of Dubai. The building inspectors had turned in their reports, the UAE police officers had turned in theirs, and the family of the deceased back home in Pune, India, had agreed to accept an offering of twelve years in wages for the loss of their productive husband and father. The rapid construction of Dubai continued.

Abdul was in his office on the twenty-seventh floor of his building when he was paid a late-afternoon visit by the UAE building commissioner. The calm, experienced and gray-haired official sat across from Abdul's ornate desk in a comfortable chair, wearing a fine-tailored suit. He spoke slow and deliberately, with his hands folded in front of his chin, right under his thick, gray mustache.

"Abdul, we must all learn to reevaluate the speed and caution that it takes to complete these buildings. In our haste to finish them all so rapidly, we have put far too many men in unnecessary danger, particularly with so many inexperienced workers."

Abdul responded respectfully from across his desk, "We cannot prevent all accidents. There are a lot of people on a construction site and an accident can happen to anyone."

"Yes, but these accidents and rumblings from immigrant workers will only continue to increase if we do not proceed with more prudence," the commissioner countered. "I fear that you younger developers, in your love for Western capitalism, have pushed construction to the point of breaking. But these are *humans* and not machines. So I have held on to this position, well past my time, so I can continue to negotiate better practices, not only for the commercial buildings of Dubai, but for all of the new construction of the United Arab Emirates, including new residential housing."

Abdul was well aware that there had been constant reports of faulty apartment buildings for low-income workers and families who lived in and around the poorer districts of their wealthy nation. He also realized that the commissioner was approaching ninety years old, and that new and younger commissioners might not be as tactful or as responsible as he had been for more than thirty years.

Abdul was not even born in the early era of Middle Eastern development, where the commissioner had first made his mark. He had learned much about building from Europeans and Westerners himself. So Abdul respected the man immensely. The commissioner held an expansive wealth of knowledge.

Abdul nodded. "Yes, I understand." And he thought again of his outspoken wife's plea to slow down.

The commissioner added, "*En sha Allah*, we will arrive where we ultimately want to go, as one of the greatest nations on earth. But we must understand, as great as the pyramids are in Egypt, none of them were built overnight."

There was nothing more that Abdul could argue. The commissioner had made himself perfectly clear, so all that was left to do was offer him an evening meal.

Abdul bowed in his chair as a show of respect. "May Allah be Merciful of my bad judgment and hear my blessings for His forgiveness."

The commissioner smiled. "I'm sure He will. Allah is the Magnificent. We are able to do all through His blessings."

Abdul stood from his desk chair and asked, "Would you allow me to invite you to dinner this evening?"

The commissioner stood gingerly from his own chair and extended his old hand. "I would love to, but my grandson has chosen his first wife, and we are going to eat with her family tonight."

"Ahhh, Merciful Allah!" Abdul cheered him. "How old is he?"

"He is twenty-one, and far too young," the commissioner joked and laughed.

Abdul kissed his hand and showed him to the door, where the commissioner's own security team awaited.

"Give my blessings to your feisty wife," the commissioner continued to joke to Abdul. It had become common knowledge that the young real estate developer had chosen an overzealous woman who loved to speak in any setting.

Abdul laughed it off. "And you give my blessings to yours."

When he closed his office door behind him, Abdul continued to think about his wife. He had watched the interview that she had given the day of the accident, and he had agreed that it was good. She was much better with her words than he was, but her excellence did nothing to improve his image amongst other Muslim men.

In Western society, Hamda would have been a fabulous asset, professionally as well as a wife. But in the Muslim world, he was forced to continue to negotiate how much she could do before it was acceptable.

Or maybe she will be the first to do great things for all women of Dubai, he mused often. He already realized how much the younger women revered her. Nevertheless, many of the *Emirati* and Muslim men didn't see it that way. They viewed Hamda as one of Abdul's many weaknesses. So he remained conflicted about his wife's strong will and spirit.

He sat back in his chair behind his desk and thought of calling his wife to announce that he was on his way home, as he had always done. But then he stopped himself and contemplated everything.

Is it possible for me to love my wife too much? he asked himself. *Maybe it's time for the balance of a second wife.*

But he didn't want a second wife. He loved Hamda too much to share his time, his heart and his wealth with anyone else. So he picked up the phone and called her anyway.

* * * * *

After the construction site incident, the news of Abdul's handling had reached the older and more established real estate developers of the UAE, as well as the *Emirati* council. A trio of wise men decided to hold a private meeting to discuss their shared concerns about their country's most recent obstacles. Sheikh Al Rashid, Sheikh Al Naseem and Abdul's uncle, Sheikh Al Hassan, all met at the latter's villa home in the capital city of Abu Dhabi for dinner and dialogue. And in the privacy of Sheikh Al Hassan's home, they were free to eat and socialize at the large marble dinner table without need to wear their public headdresses.

"How many more buildings in Dubai do we have yet to complete? Five *thousand*?" Sheikh Al Rashid asked the other men. He pulled a piece of bread in half to eat. He was the oldest of the three distinguished council members, but he was the smallest in physical stature.

Sheikh Al Naseem, the youngest and the largest of the three, chuckled at his elder's exaggeration.

"We don't have that many. Or at least I don't believe so," he commented. "But I do understand what you mean. We have had a lot of overproduction."

Sheikh Al Rashid became insistent. "We have been overproducing for *years* now. So much, in fact, that we will soon cease from being recognized as an Arabian nation."

Sheikh Al Hassan smiled and spoke casually. "We are still an

Arabian nation, my friend. No amount of immigrant workers or tourists will change that. But you must also remember that we are still a very young nation—less than fifty years old. So we are still establishing ourselves around the world."

After hearing the younger council members' comments, Sheikh Al Rashid pounced on them with vigor.

"Yes, and in less than five more years, it will be the youth, like your nephew *Abdul*, who will undo our establishment as a respectable nation through too much *greed*," he blasted. "We do not need to open up our country to *everyone*. For the Mercy of *Allah*, how much tourism and immigrant workers are enough?"

Sheikh Al Hassan sighed deeply and bit into the white breast of his sesame chicken. His overly ambitious nephew had caused him a lot of heartache and embarrassment through many impulsive decisions. Nevertheless, Abdul had been the only Hassan kin to apply himself through business and enterprise, where Sheikh Al Hassan's oldest son, Talib Mohammed Hassan, had only managed to waste several opportunities before abandoning the Middle East and moving with his young wife and family to London.

Sheikh Al Rashid continued, "Now I know that Abdul is your favorite nephew, and that he has many talents in business. But his ways are just too—" He stopped and shook his head in search of a word. "They are just not *humane*, or in the honorable methods of Allah. We should not submit people to human sweatshops, like the businesses of China and Southeast Asia. It is an *abomination!*"

Sheikh Al Rashid had always been passionate in his words. Maybe it was his older age and his desire to outpoint his younger council members. But the younger men each found it hard to match his ire.

"The ways of international business have always been complicated," Sheikh Al Hassan responded. "Without thousands of immigrant workers, the best foreign engineers, equipment, finance and urgency, the great cities of Dubai and Abu Dhabi, as we know them today, would have never existed."

"This I know," Sheikh Al Rashid admitted. "But if these methods of international business do not adhere to the ways of Allah, then how closely should we follow them?"

Sheikh Al Naseem ate his rice, chicken and salad, while he watched and listened to the two older men as if he were a spectator at a tennis match. After their conclusions, he nodded in concurrence with the elder council member.

"I agree with Sheikh Al Rashid. Even your nephew's wife, Hamda, has taken on more of a Western woman's aspiration to speak out in public places and in business affairs. Did you not notice how often she addresses business officials and reporters without first seeking permission to speak? She is setting a bad example for the next generation of Muslim women."

Sheikh Al Rashid grunted. "She has already done so. And your nephew has not managed to control her."

Sheikh Al Hassan had been guilty of admiring Abdul's wife himself. Hamda Sharifa was very impressive. She represented a new wave of Arabian woman, and one who was unafraid to find her voice. Sheikh Al Hassan even viewed her as a strong example of courage and achievement for his own young daughters and grandchildren. So he held his tongue from more slander and decided to defend her ambitions.

"So, what am I to say to my eight daughters and grand-daughters if they are not allowed to speak their minds in the twenty-first century?" he responded artfully. "More women are getting educations and qualifying themselves to speak, more so than some of the men who speak out unwisely."

Sheikh Al Naseem admonished, "You may tell your grand-daughters to utilize their education and ambitions to speak out when they are *asked* to do so."

"And when may I ask is that?" Sheikh Al Hassan countered quickly.

As Sheikh Al Rashid prepared to add his own views to their argument, Sheikh Al Hassan's youngest daughter, Sara Mumia, entered the room, wearing her covered garb and veil, to inform her father in Arabic that she would be on the way to the library.

He responded in Arabic for his daughter to be careful and to take an escort for security. He also told her to call her mother after she arrived.

"Yes, I will," she promised her father in English.

As soon as his daughter had left the room for her outing to the royal library of Abu Dhabi, Sheikh Al Naseem questioned, "Is that basic respect too much to ask of a wife or a daughter? I believe it is *not*."

Sheikh Al Hassan continued to grin while enjoying his meal. He said, "There will come a time when we will be forced to recognize the value of a woman who is much *more* than just a *wife* or a *daughter*. Like *Aishah*, the Prophet Muhammad's youngest and most gifted wife, there will be women amongst us who will be destined to rule, whether we are prepared to accept it or not."

Both Sheikh Al Naseem and Sheikh Al Rashid began to laugh out loud.

Sheikh Al Rashid conceded as much as he devoured his fruit and garden salad with light dressing.

"You are probably right, my friend. But at my old age, I may not be around long enough to see it," he commented. And the *Emirati* council members shared another laugh.

Chapter 6

THE SAME YOUNG REPORTER who had been fortunate enough to interview the honorable *Emirati* wife Hamda Sharifa Hassan, continued to reflect on an opportunity that could have made her famous amongst the Muslim and Arabian women of Dubai. Ramia Farah Aziz dreamed as she watched old footage from a year ago, presenting the grand opening of a downtown hotel where Hamda was allowed to cut the ribbon and congratulate her husband as one of Dubai's top young developers.

Ramia watched the old footage on a small television set in a cramped apartment room on the man-made island of Palm Deira, where she had moved in with her cousin Basim. And she found herself having a hard time letting the excitement of the unexpected interview go. They had arrived there to find footage of unsafe immigrant worker conditions at various construction sites, not to capture a Muslim icon in a one-on-one interview. But now that the *Emirati* government was onto them, the police pressures had forced their camera crew to lie low for a while, leaving Ramia with idle time and a need to find other work.

"Ugh, we were so close to something *great*," she fussed to herself while slapping her face with both hands. Ramia was determined to lead a life of courage and enlightenment, while taking destiny into her own hands, which was why she had challenged herself to leave home in Jordan and to room with her cousin in Palm Deira three months earlier. Showing fearlessness and exceptional presence in front of a camera, a group of guerilla newsmen and film producers dared the young Jordanian to help them report the many current events and cultural happenings in and around Dubai. And with the blessings of her big cousin, Ramia jumped at the opportunity. But after more than a week of the group's inactivity, she became eager to find something else to do to occupy her time. She and Basim began to job hunt.

While waiting for callbacks, she sat inside of their cramped apartment room. Basim already had a job, leaving her to battle boredom. Despite her cousin's warnings about the worker-class area that they lived in, Ramia was anxious to explore. She wanted to speak with strangers and ask questions just like the men were able to. She was impatient, anxious and fearless, emboldened by the growing women's rights movement. "Why should I have to remain inside all day?" she huffed. "I'm not a child."

Ramia left the apartment defiantly and as soon as she walked outside of the building to stroll the hardened streets of the area, she realized why her cousin was so nervous about her being out and unattended. Without an *abaya* or a headdress to cover up, or Basim there to protect her, the Palm Deira district was definitely not a place for a young and beautiful woman to sightsee.

The blue-collar area was largely populated by unmarried immigrant workers. Pakistan, India, Sri Lanka and Southeast Asia were all represented there, including many immigrants from North and West Africa—Egypt, Ethiopia, Sudan, Somalia and Kenya. The area's construction of gray cement buildings and seedy, dark streets was not the bright and photogenic images the young nation chose to show the world in its advertisements, websites or brochures of tourism. The working-class districts of the UAE represented the hard realities of thousands of hopeful immigrants desperately seeking income and a fresh start. But most of them had fallen into positions of long hours of sweat work.

Ramia could have been a *Victoria's Secret* model. She had soft skin, bright-hazel eyes, thick, auburn hair and the slim, curvy frame. That was why Basim had been so insistent that she not wander around unattended. She surely would attract lots of attention—possibly dangerous attention. Lustful eyes were everywhere, and she was worth every second of a desperate man's lust. She could feel their penetrating stares as soon as she hit the sidewalks in her casual blue jeans and T-shirt.

Basim had begged his cousin not to come live there with him until he could afford to move to a better area in Sharjah and away from the overcrowding near the interior of Dubai. But Ramia refused to wait. Everything was immediate and urgent with her, as if the world would run out of time. She had been willing to do anything to move away from the farmlands of her home in Jordan as quickly as possible, and away from her nation's strict Muslim code for women. Men in her home nation continued to practice "honor killings" each year against dishonorable wives who dared to disobey or embarrass their husbands. Ramia wanted no part of that, so she refused to marry, and at the legal age of twenty-one she left her immediate family in Jordan to try her luck in Dubai, which was more liberated.

As the sun began to set in the early evening, Ramia walked a couple of blocks from the apartment building and passed by two Indian men at the curb who were smoking cigarettes and conversing in Hindu. With loud, mocking laughter, they startled her and forced her to pick up her pace. Although she was not fluent in Hindu, she could easily assume that the men were talking about her. She could read it through their eyes, darting in her direction as well as through the suddenness of their snickering. So she wasted no time in moving away from them, while quickly turning the corner to her left.

"Hey, watch where you're going," a man warned her in gruff

English. In her reckless haste, Ramia had bumped into him.

"Oh, excuse me," she responded nervously.

The man paused and nodded. He stood tall and imposing on the sidewalk. It was Saleem, the Pakistani worker who had walked off from Abdul Khalif Hassan's troubled construction site after the tragic accident. But Ramia did not know him. Two brown workers stood beside him, all wearing casual clothes.

"Why are you walking around by yourself?" Saleem asked the girl with authority. He could read the bewildered innocence in her face that marked her as a newcomer. And he felt that she should have been forewarned about the dangers and illegal activities of certain areas, particularly after sunset.

At first Ramia ignored him, projecting irritation and bravery. But since the man seemed sincere, she was respectful enough to answer him.

"I'm waiting for my cousin."

"You should wait for your cousin *inside*," he snapped at her.

The two men at his side began to chuckle before Saleem silenced them.

"Enough!" he snarled in their direction.

The men swallowed their pride and stopped their chatter immediately.

"You find your way back inside to wait for your cousin safely," Saleem advised the girl. He added, "This is not the place for tourism."

Recognizing the man's honorable position and power, Ramia backed down from her tough stance and decided to heed his warning. She nodded and was embarrassed, heading silently and quickly back toward Basim's apartment building. She knew that a tough-minded and principled man was watching her back. Even the two mocking Indians fell silent as she returned past them.

Who in the world was that? she asked herself as she walked. She then noticed the pickup of aimless energy out in the streets as the sun set. There was random car traffic, human transactions and the noise of menace that came with any overpopulated area.

Oh, my God! she thought in a panic. Suddenly, she couldn't wait to get back to the building.

Up on a fifth-floor patio in a building directly across the street, a stern-faced Egyptian man watched Ramia's entire short-lived walk to the corner. When she made it back to safety inside of her building, he smiled and grunted before walking inside himself.

Ramia rushed back inside to wait for the elevators in her building, only to find Basim waiting.

"Basim, when did you get home?" she asked her cousin excitedly.

Basim looked back in alarm and frowned at her. "Where did you go? And why are you out of the room?" he barked. With thin-rimmed brown reading glasses, Basim looked more like a student, and he was still dressed in the yellow-shirted uniform from his job at the gas station and convenience store. The twenty-eight-year-old was usually calm and caring. But at the moment he was irritated by Ramia's defiance.

"Basim, I can't just sit in there all day and night. I need something to do."

"You will have something to do as soon as a job calls," he told her. "Then you can start school at the university."

The plan was for Ramia to attend the Women's University of Dubai or even American University of Sharjah. But without the money to afford it, they realized that their plans would have to wait.

In frustration, Ramia pouted. "I know, I know. But I just get so tired of sitting around and reading in the heat. Your room does not even have a patio."

"Because I don't want to waste the money," he snapped. "I have no intentions of staying here, so why would I pay extra for a room with a patio? I told you I wanted to move to a new place before you even came."

"You were just taking far too long," Ramia snapped back. "So I just wanted to take a walk."

She stepped past him and climbed onto the opening elevator as the other tenants overheard their argument. In her extra week of idleness, she was really beginning to irk her cousin. They did not even speak as they rode the elevator up to the third floor.

"What are you going to do—drag me back inside the hot room?" Ramia added sarcastically as they climbed off the elevator. "I didn't even stay out there long."

Basim shook his head, exhausted from his day. "Don't you see what kind of people are out there?" he asked her. Surely she wasn't blind. Basim did not like the area at all.

Ramia ignored him and used her key to reopen the door to the room.

"I just wanted to get out," she repeated.

"And when I get home, you can," he insisted.

Ramia turned to face him at the doorway. She was so bothered by her cousin's chauvinistic tone that she wanted to hit him. Instead, she growled and balled up her fists.

"Argh! You sound like a Muslim *husband,* and I am not your *wife,*" she shouted.

"Yes, but you are a guest in my house, and so you are my responsibility," Basim argued. "Do you realize how much trouble I would be in with our parents and your brothers if something were to happen to you here? So stop acting inconsiderate. You have not been here long enough to know this place like I do."

Again, Ramia felt squeamish. She closed the door behind them and said, "But I feel like such a *slave* in this little room. Look at this!"

The apartment was so small that Basim used curtains to separate the rooms with no walls. Only the small bathroom had walls.

"Why do you even bother to give me a *key*?" Ramia pouted.

"Because you will go back to work next week, and you will need to use it," Basim responded supportively. "This place is only temporary for *both* of us."

Understanding how supportive Basim had been, Ramia calmed down and took a seat at his tiny kitchen table.

"What makes you so sure they will call next week?" she asked doubtfully.

"Because I have faith in Allah."

Ramia listened and refrained from engaging in a social religious argument with him. She no longer followed the Muslim faith. Outside of women's rights, she didn't know what to believe in anymore.

"We will see," she told him.

"Yes, we will," Basim concluded. "In the meantime, I only want to protect you."

Basim was not an imposing man at all. Unless he had secretly trained in the martial arts, or owned a loaded gun—neither of which was the case—Ramia could not imagine him being able to protect her anyway. He was nowhere near as threatening as the Pakistani man she had bumped into at the corner.

"What if the man who tried to harm me was much bigger and stronger than you?" she asked him hypothetically, imagining the man at the corner.

"Then I will pray to the all Powerful Allah to give me the strength and skills to beat him."

Ramia shook her head and could no longer take it. "Allah will not help you with everything. There are thousands of people in this neighborhood, and even in this building who pray to Allah, and nothing happens."

"You take that back," Basim warned her.

"I will not."

"Then I will pray to Allah for your forgiveness."

Basim was unwavering. Ramia could see now how he had been able to survive for so long on his own. In her mind, it was not Allah at all—it was Basim. He had faith in his own belief that he would succeed in anything no matter how long it took. So she finally gave into him.

"Okay, forgive me. Now let's fix you something to eat." She immediately went to his pantry with ideas of cooking her cousin a good meal. Basim Yaqoob Zahir was indeed a good man, and he deserved it. She really appreciated him. So she rubbed his back and smiled at him.

"I'm sorry, Basim. I can still act like a brat sometimes."

Her cousin chuckled and remained silent. He loved her anyway. She was family.

"You are your own woman," he told her. "And I respect that. Maybe you should even go to Britain or America *after* you become educated."

Ramia smiled and chuckled. Britain and America seemed a long way from home. Nevertheless, she refused to back down from anything.

"Maybe I will," she teased. Then she opened the refrigerator for eggs and meat to fix the meal. "I will also help you to move into a new place."

He took a seat at his kitchen table and waved her idea off. "Just worry about your money for college. I will take care of my own. I'll just make sure to send enough money back home to my mother and family."

Ramia nodded. She remembered that her aunt in Jordan had been fighting different physical ailments off and on for years.

"I still have a little bit of money to help."

Again, Basim waved her off. "Everything costs money here. You save it to buy some things for yourself." Then he looked her over and grinned. "After all, you're still a very pretty girl. You deserve to pamper yourself."

"Stop it," she told him. But it was true. Ramia could have easily become the pampered wife of a wealthy man, yet she would never allow herself to be kept, especially as a second or third wife. She treasured her independence.

Chapter 7

IN THE GRAY CEMENT building that was directly across the street from Basim's, an important meeting of the minds was ready to take shape between Saleem and a much wiser man. Saleem arrived at the fifth-floor apartment with his two followers and walked into an apartment in the building across the street from Basim's. The apartment was much larger than anything Basim would pay for or could afford. Inside, several immigrant men sat in a circle on the floor. They were from various nations, and many of them had become construction workers like Saleem. These were men who believed that working in Dubai would greatly benefit them and their families back home. But now they knew better.

The practices of cheap labor, dishonor and negligence in Dubai had unnerved them all to the point of vengeance. These laborers felt exploited and demoralized. They had become perfect followers of the radical Mohd Ahmed Nasir, an Egyptian man in his sixties who held some serious intentions.

A group of Mohd's loyal guard were in the apartment, standing armed and against the wall, while the laborers sat cross-legged on the floor complaining about dangerous working conditions and the poor pay. At the moment of Saleem's arrival, there was disciplined silence inside the room. Out of respect for their worshipful elder, none of the new recruits dared to speak unless they were asked to do so. Mohd often made men wait in dead silence for long stretches at a time before he would even make eye contact with them, let alone allow them to hear his speech or his impressions of them. Such was his way of discipline, because men who spoke without being asked were not to be trusted.

Silence was a methodology of determining the anxieties and temperaments of those who claimed to desire leadership. An honorable student would not rush the teacher, and Mohd only desired to teach honorable men. So after nearly an hour of silence, reading the impatient stares and the stormy emotions of the men who sat inside of the candlelit room, Mohd stood from his seat inside of the circle and walked toward the window, where he stared down at the activities on the streets below them. Finally, he decided to speak.

"Even in righteous land, the selfish and individual pursuits of wealth allow poverty and want to eventually turn us all into victims of greed or criminals who succumb to our own desperate opportunities."

His first words to them were well worth the wait, although some of the men could not follow his astute English and needed translations from those who could speak the various languages inside the room. So Mohd awaited their detailed translations before he would continue.

The man spoke as if he were an international dignitary, with a worldwide address to heads of nations. His delivery alone held the men captivated without even having to look at them.

In contrast to his armed and rugged guards, who wore dark, non-distinct clothes, Mohd was clean-shaven and noble in a plain white T-shirt and blue jeans. He looked at peace and was very casual. He was not short, nor tall. He was not thin, nor stout. And he had no particular features that would distinguish him from the thousands of light-brown men who populated the various nations of the Middle East. Even his low-cut salt-and-pepper hair was barely noticeable. However, when he spoke, the man became magnificent.

He turned and looked into their faces to ask them all a question. "How many of you here will die in Dubai, or in your homelands, as old and beaten men without ever reaching your full potential as fathers, husbands, brothers or sons? How many of you will die without having a chance to leave something of encouragement and hope for the families around the world?"

They were rhetorical questions with no need for an answer. So Mohd awaited the translations and continued with his deliberate address.

"*We*, in this room, are all *brothers*, not because we are *Muslim*, or *Christian*, or *Jew*, or *Hindu*, but because we are *human*. So even if we do not all follow *Muhammad*, or *Jesus*, *Moses* or *Abraham*, or even *Buddha*, we must learn to protect and guide each other as twenty-first century *humans of poverty* on this earth. How long are we willing to *wait* before we decide to rise up and protect *ourselves* and claim our *own destiny*?"

Again, he awaited the translations. And at that point, some of the men inside the room, who were lost in much of Mohd's zeal, looked to their friends for an evaluation. Were they to believe in no religion at all? Mohd allowed them all to contemplate his meaning before he went on.

"That is why I choose to remain in the working-class slums of the Emirates, so that I may remind myself *always* of the conditions of the less fortunate and not be blinded by the promotions or *illusions* of progress. We must ask ourselves the question, 'Progress for *whom*?' Can we even imagine owning *anything* that we have already *built* and continue to build in this wealthy nation? You ask yourself *that* question?"

Mohd paused once more to allow the men time to translate. And in the middle of the group of twenty, Saleem, the defiant

Pakistani, was rock solid in his focus, and he did not have a need to translate. He listened and marveled with full concentration, and he was glad that he had agreed to come.

Recognizing his intensity and interest, Mohd eyed Saleem individually from the group. He then spoke as if singling him out.

"There are those among us who desire nothing more than to be treated like the honorable *men* that we are. So I heard a week ago the news of another of our poor *brothers* who lost his life for the benefit of those who care nothing about *him* or his *family*. I told myself that *vengeance* will come, but only those who are willing to live and *die* in not only *hope,* but in the courageous decisions that we must make as *men* and as *brothers* to earn our respect as equals on this earth!"

No longer awaiting the translations inside the room, Mohd concluded, "And if that means that we are to become *serious* enough to take matters into our *own hands* and create the re-spect that we deserve as men on this earth, then so be it."

Instinctively, the agreeable men inside the room began to nod with much enthusiasm, but they were still acutely aware that any exuberant celebrations would not be warranted, tolerated or desired within such small and unsecured quarters. Mohd's speeches were to be internalized and contemplated, not exalted. He was not interested in their reverence, but in their focused actions for the future. He wanted men who would be less moved by him and what he had to say, and would be more moved by the contemplation of their own thoughts.

As he continued to survey the group of men who were eager to become his new recruits, Mohd had already decided on those amongst them who he would trust with his plans, and those that he would not. In the Pakistani soldier, Saleem, Mohd imagined a brave combatant of integrity and loyalty, who was strong and steady enough in his own will to lead a group of mercenaries who would be capable, willing and ready to announce their presence and mission to all of Dubai and to the international tourists of the world.

Chapter 8

AFTER SPEAKING TO HIS wife, Abdul remained at the office after hours. It was approaching nine o'clock and it was dark out, but he was still there trying to decide on his next plan of execution. Although he had not met with the *Emirati* council members yet, he knew that he would have to explain himself to them soon. Not only would he need to explain himself to the *Emirati*, who he was sure had been discussing his latest error, he would also need to discuss the recent setback with his investing partner from Russia, who had flown in on an unexpected visit. So Abdul called him over to meet in private that night instead of during the busier daytime hours.

A buzz from his office phone signaled the arrival of his evening appointment.

"Abdul," he answered.

"Yes, Mr. Daniel is here."

"Send him up."

As soon as Abdul hung up the line, he called out, "Al-lahhh!"

with open palms from his desk. He had been a young shining star of city development. But now he needed strength and guidance in his time of despair. So he prayed to remain calm and in control of his emotions.

When the security detail knocked on his office door, Abdul pushed a buzzer to allow them in. Daniel Hovska was a short, thick-built man of thinning blond hair and crystal-blue eyes who was fast approaching fifty. He was an ambitious Russian who had partnered with Abdul on his latest property to share some of the risks and definitely some of the windfall. But over the past few months, the new construction work had not gone well.

Daniel waited until he sat alone with Abdul before speaking. And once the security had left them, he asked his Muslim partner, "Abdul, what is going on here?"

Although Abdul was a considerably younger businessman with less experience, Daniel had allowed him to take the lead on their deal in the United Arab Emirates. He had no choice in the matter—it was either Abdul's way or no way. The Emirates government had been strategically strict on any and all foreign investments. They did not want their tourism playground in Dubai to get away from them with outsider control. But lately, Daniel had been very concerned about his lack of say-so, enough to pop up at short notice to assess the recent troubling developments at the newest construction site.

Abdul maintained his poise across the desk, while Daniel sat in the office chair in front of him, filled with apprehension.

"There is nothing to be concerned about. Our construction will still be completed ahead of schedule," Abdul assured his partner with confidence.

"Well, if this faster pace is not safe for workers, then maybe we don't need to rush ahead of time. I would much rather we keep a normal schedule with men who we know and trust, than have so many new men that we don't. That is why we are having so many new problems," Daniel commented.

Obviously, he had done his research, and his assessment was in agreement with Hakim and Khalid, who both worked the construction site daily.

Nevertheless, Abdul repeated nonchalantly, "Accidents will happen."

"Well then, maybe we should find more ways for them *not* to happen," Daniel suggested boldly.

Abdul considered his agitation and remained calm. He realized that if he did not push to complete his various construction properties ahead of schedule, he would become worried himself about how the volatile economy might affect the business climate and their ability *to* finish. Completed buildings were much easier supported by incoming revenue. But while the buildings were still in development, Abdul projected that they would run out of capital beforehand, and he had far too much pride to ask his uncle for another bailout of a business loan, nor was he willing to offer up a larger stake of the ownership with Daniel. But now his Russian business investor was becoming more distressed about their partnership.

"So, you are not concerned with how a slower pace may affect the original schedule of business, even if we were to fall behind?" Abdul asked.

Daniel thought before he spoke. He then answered the question philosophically. "Sometimes, the slower building is built to last much longer. And although I, like anyone else, would desire to be finished on time or even early like you, if it is not to be, and it must take a while longer to complete, then so be it."

Once Abdul was fully aware of Daniel's disposition on completion, he decided to cater to the man's ego. So he nodded, as if finally able to see the situation with better judgment.

"My friend, you do understand that my decisions are always made with your generosity and business support in mind. I was only attempting to please *you* as my partner, first and foremost, by making certain that no bad economy would stop us in our goals."

Daniel held up a massive right hand of caution and began to shake his head with wisdom. He understood patronization when he heard it. "Abdul, I understand that. I *do*. And I respect you immensely for it. But you would please me more by delivering a building in due time that does not cause your president and countrymen so much irritation and strain, not to mention the workers. Because I do plan to do more business here. And I would not want to wear out my welcome because of bad business experiences."

Abdul nodded again and smiled, loosening up behind his desk. "I'm glad we were able to have this conversation and understanding. It has taken a great amount of weight off of my shoulders."

"I can imagine," Daniel told him. "But at the same time, that does not mean that we slow construction down to a turtle's pace."

"Of course not," Abdul responded. "But enough talk about business. Have you seen Irina since you arrived here yesterday?"

Abdul had introduced his partner to a beautiful woman from the independent nation of Ukraine, who had previously worked in his international accounts office. She now worked in a banking office.

Daniel smiled wide and answered the question before even speaking. Abdul had already realized the Ukrainian beauty had cast a lustful spell on his partner—a bewitching spell that was hard to break.

"She was ah, waiting to go out with me for this evening. But she knew that I needed to meet and speak with you first," Daniel responded.

Irina Kievla was nearly half his age and was quite smitten by his class and wealth. But the divorced father of four was not yet ready to commit to a new marriage with her.

"Well, now you've met with me, and we have come to a new understanding," Abdul said. "So I guess now you can go out and enjoy yourself with Irina. I'm sure that she continues to enjoy your company."

The Russian laughed. "Indeed, she does." Then he stood from the office chair to make his exit. "And how have you been with your wife?" he asked Abdul while standing.

Abdul took a deep breath of honest reservation. "I think that she has had far too much influence from Western culture."

He was certain that Daniel had heard the many opinions about his outspoken wife around Dubai and the UAE, so it made no sense to dodge the question. It was what it was.

Daniel countered, "But what is so wrong with a woman having her own thoughts? Irina speaks out with me all of the time about everything."

"Yes, but would you allow her to speak out in public on the concerns of your business, while the entire Russian nation watches and listens?"

Daniel shrugged. "If she were able to speak with as much intelligence and confidence as your wife, Hamda, I would. But Irina is not quite there yet, nor does she desire to speak out on business at this time. She just wants to keep *me* busy showing her a good time."

Abdul laughed. "Well, enjoy another great dinner tonight from the lookout of the Burj Al Arab."

"I just might do that," Daniel said.

Abdul stood and enjoyed another laugh with him as his Russian partner headed back toward the office door. Abdul showed him out.

"Remember to take your time, Abdul. Don't worry. Everything will get done in time."

Once Daniel walked out with the security team, Abdul returned to his desk and spun his chair around to face the night skyline out the window. Dubai's skyline was beautiful at night. And the Burj Khalifa, the tallest building in the world, was always in view, soaring far above the nearby Emirates Towers and Dubai World Trade Center.

Abdul studied the tremendously tall building and used it as an inspiration. *There is nothing in this world that man cannot do when he is Blessed with power and wisdom of Allah,* he thought. He then rubbed his eyes in exhaustion. It had been a very long day.

He mumbled, "Merciful Allah. What have I gotten myself into again?"

The lightning-fast development of Dubai was extremely tax-ing. But after Abdul had challenged himself with the question, he stood at his office window with the vigor of his youth.

My work must continue to be done. For it is the will of Allah alone who drives me.

Chapter 9

GARY STEVENS USED HIS bathroom at the Hilton Dubai Creek for the first time and felt squeamish about the toilet douche. He had noticed the two-foot long water pipe that was placed in a holder to the right of the toilet when he first inspected the room earlier, but to actually use the contraption was another story.

He laughed, feeling self-conscious, as if it would be unclean *not* to use it. *I guess they're serious about being spic-and-span here in the Middle East,* he thought, grinning.

He had gotten in a couple of hours of sleep before feeling rejuvenated. It was nine at night in Dubai, an eight-hour time difference from his home in the Washington, DC, area. *Time to check in,* he thought.

A worldwide access code from Jonah made it easy to connect with her at all times

"The U.S. military has all kinds of perks if you can afford it," he mumbled while dialing the coded number. He figured speaking to Jonah first would be quicker and less stressful.

"Hey, Gary, how's Dubai? Have you checked into a hotel already?" Jonah asked.

Gary began to smile, feeling comfortable with the familiar sound of her voice.

"Yeah, I decided to crash at the Hilton at Dubai Creek."

"But you're still in Dubai as soon as you walk out that door," she said. "And getting a room at the Hilton was a safe decision. But have you called to check in with your lady friend yet?"

Gary chuckled, guilty of nervousness. "Not yet. I wanted to talk to you first."

Jonah chuckled back. "Another good decision. You're batting two for two. You're getting close to home base. Get all of your words together first," she teased him.

"Yeah, so what exactly do I say to her? I haven't been in this position for a while now."

"What did you say before you left?"

Gary smiled even wider. "I kind of told her that I couldn't tell her," he commented. "You know, I made it sound like I had a secret mission or something."

Jonah broke out laughing and said, "Oh, my God. So you totally went James Bond and CIA on her?"

"I didn't know what else to say. I mean, she knows that I've been training with you guys out in Northern Virginia."

"You told her that?"

"Not exactly. She kind of assumed it. She grew up around military men. I told you, she's a Navy brat. Her father was a lieutenant commander. So she kind of insinuated that I was buff and fit like a military guy."

"Oh, my Lord," Jonah stated. "Guys and their egos. You should have just told her that you like to work out and left it at that."

"What, you wanted me to *lie* to her?"

"Well, isn't that what you did when you flew over to Dubai? Does she know you're over there to ah, find yourself?" Jonah hinted.

Gary continued to laugh. He said, "I just told her I had an ah, errand to run for a couple of weeks that I couldn't really go into too many details about."

"And she went for that?"

"She said she trusts me."

Jonah paused, contemplating it all. "Okay, well, keep on going with what works."

"Yeah, but what if she asked me where I am now?"

"Ah, that's not my problem. You're the one who got yourself in it, so keep playing Mr. James Bond."

Gary laughed, feeling totally comfortable with her. "Wait a minute, I thought you're supposed to be my protector and mentor."

"And where does that say relationship expert? You're on your own with that. I'm not Dr. Phil."

"Yeah, what good are you?" Gary retorted playfully.

"Just don't lose your phone out there, or it'll cost you a lot more to call. The code I gave you is very specific."

"What, like digitized to my iPhone?"

"Something like that. I don't know how it works, I just know that it's awesome."

"So if someone stole my phone, I would be able to track them down?"

"In a heartbeat."

Gary paused and looked at his iPhone. He asked, "What did you do to it? You like, bugged me or something?"

Jonah paused herself. She said, "If I tell you, are you gonna act like a kid or a grown-up?"

"I *am* grown," Gary responded.

"Okay, well, that phone is able to tell me a lot of things. I switched it for you a long time ago."

Gary looked at the iPhone again and didn't see anything different about it. He asked, "Can you ah, hear everything I do or say, even when I'm not using it?"

"Knowing *you*, I wouldn't want to do that," she joked. "But it's a possibility, yeah."

Gary said, "So I am like James Bond then."

"I'm just trying to do my job and protect you," she told him.

"Shit, I'm thirty-one years old now," Gary snapped at her. He felt disrespected.

"And how old is the president? Age has nothing to do with it."

"Okay, well, if I'm so important to Mr. *Unknown*, then how come I still can't meet the guy? This is ridiculous! What kind of life is this?" he stated in reference to his father.

"It's your life," Jonah told him calmly. "That's why you're over there in Dubai. You have a right to live it, and no one is stopping you."

"Yeah, while being *spied* on," he countered. "So, what else did you swap? My luggage? My wallet? What?"

Jonah paused in silence. "So ... are you gonna act like a kid or a grown-up if I tell you?"

Gary could hear the sarcasm in her voice and imagine her mischievous grin without even seeing it. He said, "You know what? I don't even want to know anymore. You have a job to do, and I have a life to live." And he hung up the phone on her.

Then he said, "I guess you can hear me now too, right? And you know what floor I'm on. Well, what if I just left this phone right here in the room?"

He tossed the cell on the bed, while having a full tantrum.

Then he thought about his wallet. He couldn't leave that inside the room. And what about his shoes? Or his belt buckle? Jonah could have bugged and swapped anything.

Gary stopped and shook his head, realizing how unreasonable he was acting. But he loved his freedom, so to be traced everywhere he went as a grown man, and without him knowing about it, was hard to stomach.

"I don't believe this. I'm not a damn kid," he snapped. He imagined that Jonah could still hear him. Then he thought about his overreaction. He hadn't snapped out like that in years.

Shit, I am acting like a kid, he thought. He expected Jonah to call him back soon, but she didn't. So he called her back.

"Okay, I apologize for overreacting, but this is just weird."

"And what part of our relationship has been normal?" she asked him. "You'll just have to get used to it. That's why I told you. I didn't want you to be blindsided. And if it'll make you feel any better, I will never listen in on your private conversations. That's not what it's there for. It's only an emergency mechanism. And you should be glad that you have it."

"But what if someone steals it or I misplace it or something? I don't want anyone overreacting."

Jonah calmly told him, "If someone steals that phone, we can call it and signal for it with a very loud and irritating alarm, and then tell them to return it to the nearest lost-and-found before it explodes in their hand."

Gary looked at the cell phone again and panicked. "Oh shit, it can do that? I could have been arrested on the plane with this thing."

"Gary, calm down," Jonah said with a laugh. "Your phone is very safe. Just don't worry about it. Act normal."

"Yeah, that's easy for you to say."

"Okay, so what's the weather like over there? Is it still hot in late October? What are you plans for the night?" she asked him to change the subject.

They had talked about his hi-tech phone for long enough.

"I don't know yet." Then he grinned. "Maybe I'll get into some trouble and see if this thing works," he joked.

"It's not a weapon," Jonah warned him.

"Yeah, but I am. You're making me *feel* like a weapon now. I even have gadgets."

Jonah sighed, noticeably.

"Yeah, I know, am I a kid or a grown-up, right?" Gary quizzed.

Jonah didn't respond, instead she told him, "Go ahead and call your girlfriend ... so I can see what you come up with." She laughed and added, "Gary, you're making it real easy to toy with you."

"Yeah, whatever." She had the last laugh. Gary just had to deal with it. So he hung up and immediately called his significant other back in Washington. He didn't even know what to call her.

He wasn't sure if he wanted to be that serious yet.

"Hey, Karla, it's Gary."

"Hey, I know."

Gary stopped himself, still thinking about the phone. He didn't know if his normal cell phone number would pop up or not in America.

I guess she sees my normal number there, he told himself. So he moved on.

"Yeah, I just wanted to call and say hey."

"Are you allowed to tell me where you are?" she asked him.

Gary hesitated. "Ahhh ..."

"You don't have to if you really can't," Karla said. She was letting him off the hook way too easily.

Melissa Weddington would have never gone for any of this, Gary thought of his last serious fling back home in Louisville. He felt guilty about his relationship with the Navy brat already. He knew that she didn't have the mettle to keep him. Or maybe Karla's abundant trust in him would be her saving grace to hold on.

"Give me a few days to work that out, okay?" he negotiated.

"Well, is it warm where you are?" she asked instead.

Gary nodded and grinned. He couldn't help thinking about Jonah being able to listen in on him, whether she bothered to do so or not. He knew that she could if she wanted to, and she never had to admit it to him.

He said, "Yeah, it's pretty warm here."

"Are you in another country?"

"Ahhh ..."

"Okay, you don't have to answer that."

Gary chuckled and imagined that Karla was getting a kick out of the guessing game.

"And what are you doing tonight?" he asked, to get her away from questions about him.

"Umm, I'm probably gonna hang out on Fourteenth and U streets with my girls again."

The hub of 14th and U streets was the popular Washington

strip where Gary had first met her at Po'boys restaurant and café. They held regular poetry nights there, and the popular area was flooded with new-blooded Washingtonians, who all loved the urbaneness of redevelopment.

Gary nodded and patronized her. "I wish I was there with you."

"When will you be?"

"In another week or so. You can never really tell sometimes," he added.

"I know, right? My father was like that all of the time. So I just learned to be patient."

Listening to the syrupiness of it all, Gary began to curse himself. *This is all bullshit! I should just tell her the truth already. But it is more complicated than normal,* he thought. *Maybe I'll tell her everything when I get back.*

"Yeah, I'll have to have a long talk with you, face-to-face, when I get back there."

"Okay. Are you well fed out there?"

"Ah, I don't know. I haven't eaten the food yet. But I'll tell you about it."

"Do you a busy schedule for tomorrow?"

Her conversation was so bland and inconsequential, that Gary didn't want to talk to her long.

Are you kidding me? Is this how she's going to be whenever I'm away? I don't know any girls like this. Or maybe I just went out with all of the jealous ones, he mused.

"Yeah, my schedule's loaded. I have a lot to do tomorrow. But I need to get myself ready for it, so I won't talk long."

"Okay, well, call me when you can. A week's not long at all."

Are you kidding me? he wanted to tell Karla. *Have some more backbone about you. You're making this far too easy for me to respect.*

He could imagine Jonah grinning from Dubai to California about how gullible this girl was.

"Have you been this understanding with other guys that you've dated?" She was twenty-six, originally from New Mexico, and she now worked in the federal government office of Veterans Affairs. And she was definitely *hot*, with dark bountiful hair, a tight body to die for, passionate brown eyes and rich skin tone. Her mother was mixed with Irish and Native American, and her father was Italian and Polish, creating a beautiful mixture named Karla Marchetti, with just enough freckles in the right places to add to her flavor. But she was so bland, sweet and trusting, that it was all but killing him not to break her heart into a thousand pieces, like he would have done five years ago.

"Sure," Karla answered. "I mean, I've had my share of assholes who took advantage of it, if that's what you mean. But I'm not gonna change who I am because you want to do what you want to do. And if a guy appreciates me for being me, then he gets a dedicated girl. But if not then ... I mean, I can't change who you're gonna be. Why, are you trying to tell me something?"

Gary froze. It wasn't the right time. There was far too much distance between them. Their detailed conversation would have to wait.

"No, I'm just ah, not used to it."

"Why, because you've had jealous girlfriends in the past? I mean, I can understand it. You're pretty hot. I can feel it in the room whenever I'm with you," she admitted candidly. "But I've just never been the jealous type like that."

"Yeah, because you're hot too," Gary told her with a chuckle. "It's not like you lack any attention." He was actually impressed with her easiness. Karla was liable to say anything as easy as water. She was that comfortable in her gorgeously toned skin. And she was quickly reminding him why he liked her. She had no vanity about her.

"Thank you. I just thought I was always one of the girls."

"No, you're more than just one of the girls," Gary told her. "You're *my* girl now."

In his mind, he could imagine Jonah bursting at the seams in laughter. The swagger of the jock and spoiled slacker from Louisville, Kentucky, was still there beneath the surface, and it could jump out at an unsuspected moment.

Karla chuckled. "Is that right? You're claiming me now?"

Their relationship had been pretty loose and unspoken for months, but lately, it seemed on the edge of getting more serious.

Uh-oh! Gary panicked in the heat of it. *What the hell am I saying?*

"I've already claimed you, haven't I?"

Karla paused. "Not exactly, but getting there. I mean, we really haven't talked about it like *that*."

Okay. Back up out of it, Gary advised himself. *Put it in reverse.*

"We'll have plenty of time when I get back," he hinted quickly.

"Okay."

"Well, have a good time out with your girls."

"I always do."

When Gary hung up his cell phone, his thoughts overcame him. *She's just ... she's just, cool man. And she's fucking gorgeous. I've never had a girl like this. Girls are always out to prove something to me, but Karla's not like that at all. That's why I like her.*

Chapter 10

THE HILTON DUBAI CREEK was only walking distance away from the dense downtown business district, where the Thursday night life was in full buzz by ten. Gary walked out of the busy hotel lobby on the bottom floor amongst dozens of local and foreign guests, wearing a pair of tan khaki pants, brown loafers and a plain black T-shirt. He was trying his best to blend in as a nobody and remain low-key. He was no longer Mr. Excitable, searching for validations of his reckless youth. Gary had hurdled over the age of thirty and only wanted to enjoy the sights, scenes and sounds of Dubai, like an old ghost.

But as soon as he hit the sidewalks and swung a left away from the docks and boats that littered Dubai Creek behind him, the exotic cars of the night zoomed by in the streets, blasting festive music that came alive, sounding like the radiant Caribbean energy of dancehall, reggae and calypso.

Gary smiled, eyeing the flashy Mercedes, Porsches, Beamers, Range Rovers and Cadillac SUVs that zoomed by while reflecting on his music shop back home in downtown Louisville. He hadn't been home in a few months, while spending time in Northern Virginia to train and visit his new lady friend in the capital of Washington. However, the music in the air of Dubai reminded him of the good old times back home on Main Street and the party district of Louisville.

Caribbean music is everywhere, he mused as he strolled through the tranquil night. That music also reminded him again of his best friend, Taylor, who had helped him to manage his downtown music shop, and his mother, who wrote the check to secure the property.

"Shit," Gary cursed. The memories of his dead loved ones would never fade.

Approaching the curb at the street corner, he stopped and snapped back to the present. He was prepared to cross a busy street in another foreign country, where many of the retail shops remained open for business along with the restaurants and pubs.

Looks like they want every dollar they can get here. Or dir- ham, he thought.

The scene was very American to him, like a night in New York around Christmas, but without the snow or freezing weather. The only truly unfamiliar scene was the many Muslim women, dressed in white or black *abayas* with *hijab* face and head covers. Gary had only seen a few fully cloaked Muslim women in America, but in Dubai, they were everywhere. Only their eyes showed.

Gary imagined that their eye shapes, sizes and colors were all very important to differentiate them. And as he walked through the downtown streets of Dubai, he found himself looking too intently upon the only part of the Muslim women he could connect to—their eyes. Some of the women wore red embroidered designs in their head dressings.

This is weird to feel so compelled to look into their eyes like this, Gary told himself. *It feels incredibly personal, as if I'm not supposed to.*

I may get myself arrested over here for reckless eyeballing, he joked to himself. *But why come out at night at all if you're*

*so concerned about men looking at you? Is there really a need
for them to be out here this late at night?*

It all seemed hypocritical, even Gary's thoughts of liberating
the seemingly oppressed women. *Should a woman be forced to
remain in the house just because she's a Muslim?* he debated
to himself. *If they're all covered up, it's like wearing a house
outside with you anyway.*

He shook it off and mumbled, "To each his own." While
walking the busy streets of the night, Gary remained alert to
everything, including a diligent watch of the various foreign men
who strolled along the sidewalks with him. They didn't look as
friendly as he figured the people of a tourist nation would be.
Obviously, they all had their own lives on their minds.

Who said you had to smile and be nice to every tourist? Gary
reasoned. *New York doesn't do it and neither does Washington.*

There was also an abundance of jewelry stores in Dubai—or
maybe just in the downtown area that he was in—with flash-
ing lights of golden designs and gaudy diamond watches. He
was thinking so much about Dubai, he nearly forgot that he was
hungry—until his stomach growled again.

Up the street and to the right of the intersection in front
of him was a McDonald's with its famous golden arches. Gary
looked up at them and laughed.

"I didn't travel halfway around the world to eat at McDonald's," he mumbled. But as he neared the intersection, thinking
more about food, an Applebee's popped out from his right. Then
he spotted a Red Lobster across the street and an Olive Garden
farther up.

Gary laughed harder and said, "Are you kidding me? Wow!"

However, in between the familiar American brands were traditional Arab and Asian restaurants. Gary followed his nose and
senses and looked inside of the large twenty-foot window of Ali
Rashid Cuisine. The decor was beyond elaborate, with tall designer chairs, large tables and booths, dim lighting, rich curtains,
golden-framed artwork and attractive servers wearing all black.

The place looked plenty expensive, but the price of a first-rate meal was not an issue for him. Gary could afford it all, deciding to walk right in.

"You have a reservation?" the hostess asked him from her booth inside the door. She was a tall and slender Asian woman, with her hair slicked back into a small ponytail. Her naturally tanned skin hinted of Southeast Asia, from Taiwan to the Philippines. The dark, slick hair, height, body size, ponytail and professional poise told him everything. She looked like a well-traveled model who would fit right in on a catwalk in Milan. He could smell the stimulating perfume that she wore and could only imagine how many languages she spoke.

But before he answered her question about a reservation, Gary pulled out his wallet and handed her a black credit card that spoke for itself.

"I could find a seat at the bar if you like, but I'd rather have a small table in a corner where I can see everything. If one is available," he added politely.

Using his black high-limit credit card with confidence was another one of the many tricks that Gary had picked up from Jonah. But she only used the card in emergencies, and it was his first time trying it.

The hostess looked at the card and nodded. "A table for only one?"

Gary stopped himself from flirting with her. "Yes," he answered.

"One minute," she told him, prepared to seek permission.

"Ah, can I see a menu before you go?"

He was starving and didn't want to waste any time with his order.

"Oh, sure." She handed him a menu from behind her station.

"Thank you," he gushed.

She smiled back at him and held up her right index finger. "One minute."

When she walked away, Gary looked at the twelve-page menu covered in plastic and was overwhelmed by his choices. The food was all listed in Arabic and English, with beef, roast, lamb, steak, salmon, fish, chicken, rice, potatoes and vegetables all served with dozens of different spices.

Wow, what a menu, he thought. He had no idea where to begin. He decided to ask the hostess once she returned.

She handed Gary back his card with a smile and said, "Follow me," with her index finger.

Gary followed behind her as she led him through the room of money. At every table sat businessmen, significant others, and high rollers who could afford to splurge. But none sat alone until Gary was shown his intimate table with two chairs on the far side of the restaurant, where he could indeed see everything.

"Is this good?" the hostess stopped and asked him.

Gary nodded. "This is very good. But what's the best meal for me to eat?" he hinted with the menu in his hand.

She grinned and said, "Whatever you like?"

"Well, what do *you* like to eat?" he asked her pointedly.

The hostess continued to grin. "Moroccan beef. And your server will be right out."

Gary could feel the tingles of flirtation running up and down his spine and landing at his sweet spot, while he forced himself not to stare at her ass as she walked away.

"Man, it's good to be rich," he mumbled and grinned.

He imagined that Jonah could still hear it all through his cell phone in the holder at his hip. But so what? He would simply have to deal with it. And so would she.

"Like you said, it's my life," he said out loud.

Then his server walked over, an alluring Russian brunette in her early twenties. Her hair was pulled back into a ponytail too, only longer.

"Anything to drink?" she asked him in heavily accented English.

Gary looked straight up into her pert breasts from his chair and thought, *Jesus! She has them right in front of me.*

He gathered his poise and said, "Yes, I'll have a glass of Merlot. And I'm ready to make my order."

"Oh, okay. What will you like?"

She pulled out her pen and pad.

"Ah, the Moroccan beef, chicken, lamb, shrimp—let me try a sample of all of it, with the rice and bread."

The server grinned and said, "Really? Wow, you have an appetite."

"Yeah, I had a long plane ride in."

She nodded and asked, "From the States?"

"Yeah, Atlanta."

"Is that where you're from?"

"No, I'm originally from Louisville. That's in the state of Kentucky. Where are *you* from?"

"The Ukraine."

"Oh, a break-off from Russia."

She smiled again. "Yes. I'll go put in your food and bring your drink."

"Thank you."

When she walked away, the rest of her curves were undeniable. Not only was she stunning, but there were two other young women of Indian and Spanish heritage who were just as noticeable. And they were all extremely tactful.

Gary grumbled, "Man, if I don't watch myself, I'll get into all kinds of trouble over here."

He was so intrigued by the professionalism and beauty of the women who worked inside the restaurant that he wondered what the parties of Dubai would look like. In case he had any leftover energies after dinner, Gary had brought along the card of his Sri Lankan driver, Johnny Napur, and decided to use it.

"Johnny," the excitable driver answered.

"This is Mr. No Name, The Traveler," Gary said. "You still wanna take me around to a couple of parties tonight? And nothing extra, just a normal music party."

He didn't want the guy going out of his way to hook him up with anything; he just wanted to see more of the culture.

Johnny got all wound up immediately. "Oh yeah, definitely. I was just getting ready. I could pick you up in less than an hour."

"Okay, but what should I wear?" Gary asked. Jonah had ad-

vised him to pack a variety of clothes for the trip, including two
sports jackets and a pair of black dress shoes for more professional attire. "You never know what you may be invited to over
there," she had told him.

Now, Gary waited for Johnny's response. "Wear whatever
you want," Johnny said. "They'll still treat you the same, especially if you're with me," he boasted. "No one's really into dress
codes here, unless you're going to a formal affair with the *Emirati*."

On that note, Gary liked what he had on already. "Okay, well
you can pick me up from downtown. I walked out of the hotel to
grab a bite to eat. So call me back when you get close."

"Oh yeah? What restaurant did you go to?"

Gary didn't want to tell him. He didn't want the guy sizing up
his income based on his expensive taste in food.

"Ah, I don't even know the name of it," he lied. "I think it's
a Moroccan place. But just call me when you get close, and I'll
wolf down my food."

"All right. You're not at the Ali Rashid, are you?"

Gary froze. It was a hell of a guess. "Why, is there something
wrong with that one?"

Johnny broke up laughing. "Not at all, my friend. Ali Rashid
is a great place to eat. I know a few girls who work there. It's very
international. That's where I would eat if I was a single guy."

Gary had no idea he'd chosen a hot spot. "Well, I won't do it
again. This place looks like it'll break my budget," he joked. "So
call me when you get close."

"All right. I know exactly where you are. Give me forty-five
minutes."

"Make it an hour so I can eat."

"Yeah, and enjoy the view," Johnny joked back.

Gary smiled and said, "Exactly."

As soon as they hung up, his server from the Ukraine brought
back his drink and set it on the table in front of him. She smiled
and said, "Enjoy," while lingering there for an extra second, as
if waiting for him to say something else.

"Thank you," he said. He promptly took a sip of the dark Merlot to keep his mouth shut. He didn't want to say anything else. *I guess I'll find out how ready I am to settle down with my girlfriend.*

Chapter 11

BACK IN THE HARDENED working-class district of Palm Deira, pacifist Indian laborer Rasik sat at the bar in a local pub, drinking away his recent pains. He had not been right since the death of his co-worker at the construction site more than a week ago. He continued to have his doubts about how to respond to it. Should he quit, revolt or continue working there without anger or any suspicions?

Recently, Rasik had gained some inside information on what may have happened that day. After being asked a few questions about his work and what seemed to be troubling him, he began to blab away to a man who offered to pay for his drinks at the bar. And Rasik began to tell him all that he thought he knew about the tragic accident.

"I keep asking myself, how did everyone know so soon what had happened? The police, the ambulance, the news cameras— they were all there in a matter of *minutes* when sometimes it takes hours and *days* for anything to happen at our site," he explained to the stranger. "All of it was very unusual."

"So you believe that someone informed them all in advance?" the man asked. "But this accident happened in broad daylight in the afternoon. Of course they would all arrive there quickly."

The light-brown man showed an extreme level of calmness and understanding. He had noticed Rasik wearing his light-blue construction uniform from work, and he decided to befriend him by asking about his day on the job. He too had worked as a laborer. And as one question led to another, Rasik began to tell him everything. He nodded with his right hand around his fourth small glass and said, "I've heard a few things about a vendetta."

The stranger frowned. "A vendetta?"

"Yes. A few older workers who have been here for a number of years ..." Rasik stopped momentarily to gather himself as the strong drink began to throw him off balance at his barstool. Even the bartender gave him a knowing look from behind the tall counter.

On cue, the stranger told him, "I believe you've had enough drinks, my friend. Will you be able to make it back home?"

Rasik nodded profusely. "Yes, I can make it home." But he was on a roll with his story and wanted to finish it. He felt compelled to complete his statement of what he knew, and the drinks had blocked his better judgment to remain silent.

"What I was saying was that I was told by some older workers that—"

"Excuse me, are you certain that you've not had too much to drink?" the man interrupted him.

As Rasik became frustrated, his imbalance was more noticeable. He nearly fell off of his stool as the man moved to catch him. That heightened the bartender's attention.

"Are you all right?" the rugged man behind the counter asked him.

"No more drinks for you, my friend," the stranger concluded.

"I'm fine," Rasik protested to both of them.

"You are not fine," the bartender argued. "And you have had enough drinks for one night." The rugged man was over six feet

tall, with a knife scar across his left cheek. If Rasik objected again
or became unruly, he was prepared to alert his staff to show the
man out, or he would do it himself. He even took the intoxicated
man's drink away.

"That is enough."

Rasik was in no position to argue, and he was not unruly. So
he nodded and accepted his fate without telling the rest of his
pressing story. He then stood from the barstool and wobbled.
The friendly stranger moved again to catch him.

"Let me help you out," he offered.

Rasik accepted and walked gingerly with him to the exit. The
bartender continued to watch.

"Are you sure you can make it back home?" the friendly
stranger pressed him.

Rasik smiled and answered, "Slowly," with a chuckle. He was
suddenly embarrassed that he had had so much to drink. "I just
need to get home and lie down."

The two men shared a laugh as the man opened the door
wide for him.

"Thank you for the drinks and your kind ear," Rasik told him.

The man placed a kind hand across his back. "Don't mention
it, my friend. Anytime."

As Rasik made his way outside and back into the streets of
Deira, the friendly man returned to his barstool and secretly signaled to a companion across the room who casually stood and
walked out behind the drunken construction worker.

"I feel sorry for the man," the stranger commented to the
bartender. "He seems to have had a rough couple of weeks."

The bartender frowned and was unconcerned. "We all have
our rough weeks," he said as he filled another drink order at the
bar. There had been plenty of immigrant men with bad days at
work who had chosen to drink too much. And their drinking had
paid the bartender's rent.

* * * * *

As Rasik headed gingerly down the street toward his small apartment building in the night, the second man from the bar easily spotted him meandering down the sidewalk. The Indian laborer had not gotten very far in his drunkenness. The second man from the bar then signaled to three more men to follow. They had been waiting outside for their instruction for close to an hour. The second man then returned to the bar and was done with it.

"Okay, you two watch the streets," the lead voice of the three men commanded. He was in his thirties and dressed in a heavy, dark jacket to hide his weapon. The two younger men in their twenties wore plain clothes to blend in with the normal pedestrians. They then separated into three different directions. One walked left, the other walked right, and the leader followed behind Rasik.

After ten o'clock, there were still people, cars and taxis out on the streets of Deira, but not as many as there had been an hour or so earlier and fast decisions and actions could now go undetected. So the man followed the slow-moving and wobbly laborer up the sidewalk, while watching for his cues of his young cohorts, with one in front and behind him. When it appeared there were no onlookers, the man wasted no time in running up and jamming his six-inch hunting knife several times into Rasik's back.

"Unnhh!" Rasik squealed. The pain was excruciating and sudden, even with numbness from the alcohol.

The man quickly stuffed Rasik's mouth with a rag to keep him from screaming too loudly, while cutting open his pockets to take his belongings. The assault and robbery all took less than twenty seconds before the man ran off into the night.

Rasik crumbled to the ground and squirmed, bleeding on the sidewalk. By the time five minutes had passed and the first person found him there in a pool of fresh blood, the three assailants were long gone.

As the Indian laborer slowly slipped into the afterworld, he thought of his wife back home in India and mumbled his last words in Hindu, "Sunita … I'm sorry."

Chapter 12

FROM THE EARLIER GATHERING with Mohd Ahmed Nasir, there were a few men of a certain character who were invited to remain behind for one-on-one discussions. Saleem, the rugged Pakistani, was one of them. He was told to wait and be patient, while Mohd conducted conversations with several men before him in a private room. In fact, Saleem was called in last.

"He wants to see you now," he was told by Mohd's personal bodyguard. Bakar, a thick-mustachioed Algerian, was one of the biggest men inside the room; Saleem was sure that he would be a handful in any form of combat.

Saleem stood from where he sat on the floor and had to stretch out his legs to avoid stiffness. The armed guards showed him into a bedroom to the right of the kitchen that had been converted into an office. There was a small desk with a tall leather chair behind it where Mohd sat, and a much smaller chair in front of the desk where Saleem and the rest of the men were shown to sit. Behind Mohd's desk were a small cot and a pillow for him to rest.

Saleem sat in the chair across from the desk as a lone guard stood behind him with an assault weapon cradled in his arms.

Mohd looked directly at the Pakistani and smiled. "You are a military man," he stated.

Saleem nodded. "Yes."

"But now you want to make a civilian living for your family." Mohd spoke as if he knew everything. That was his way.

Saleem paused and thought out his words before responding. "It was a very difficult decision."

Mohd nodded back to him. "I understand. I had to make difficult decisions as well. How many children do you have?" he asked next.

Again, Saleem paused. He didn't want to discuss it, but he had lost much of his family from the constant warring in and around Pakistan, including his young wife and children. It was a reason he had left his homeland, deciding to live a civilian lifestyle. If only that civilian lifestyle could be more profitable and respectful, he would have no complaints.

"So you no longer have children or a family?" Mohd assumed.

Saleem was surprised by this, and he remained hesitant.

"I have lost loved ones as well," Mohd told him calmly, "and my war was an economic one. I had a decision to make between my family and modest wealth, which was no decision at all. Every family must eat and have shelter; otherwise, you will have no family.

"Do you know the man you used to work for?" he asked Saleem next. His questions were rapid and continuous, as if he had a lot to ask.

Saleem shook his head, uncomfortable with not knowing. But he hadn't come to Dubai to know all of his employers; he was there to work, provide a new living for himself and create some peace of mind.

Mohd continued, "His name is Abdul Khalif Hassan. I used to work for him myself, when he was far too young to know his influence. I served as his first overseer on the construction of the

International Suites hotel."

Saleem nodded. He knew that hotel. It was very popular with international tourists. He had imagined what it would feel like to have a room there for a night.

"He owns that hotel?" he asked Mohd.

The wise old man grinned momentarily. "Abdul owns many things, but he lacks the ownership of a strong *conscious*. In his world, the completion of a task overrules all of humanity. So the construction of his buildings will go on, regardless of who pays the price with death."

Mohd paused, then added, "Including my wife, Faiza, of thirty years, who needed money for an operation."

Saleem narrowed his hardened dark eyes, sharing Mohd's pain. Men of pain could relate. It was spiritual. Even the armed guard flinched with irritation inside the room, and he had heard the story several times before. "You did not have enough for your wife's operation?" Saleem asked him. He was immediately sympathetic. Deprived men lacked the monetary resources for many of the needful things of life, let alone the extravagances that men and women desired. Poor men had been trained to do without.

Mohd smiled and remained calm. "I did. And my wife was able to have the operation. But I was not allowed to return home to be with her in the hospital, nor during the time of her recovery. I was asked by the *Emirati* child to keep it all in the hands of Allah. Not because of his faith, but because he needed my experience here in Dubai to finish the job of construction.

"But I should have told him to keep his *construction* in the hands of Allah, and gone back home to Egypt to be with my wife and family during her operation and recovery," Mohd added sternly. Then he paused again and breathed deeply. It was his moment of revelation. His armed guard breathed deeply as well.

"There were complications with my wife's recovery, where she came down with a life-threatening fever. So I told the *Emirati child* that I was returning home to Egypt immediately to be with my ailing wife and family. And at that time, he told me that if I left my post, I would no longer have employment in Dubai when I returned."

Mohd stopped and shook his head, looking down at his dark wooden desk. He peered back into the sympathetic eyes of Saleem. "I had a moment of hesitancy, where I thought about how much money I could lose. As an experienced engineer from the Egyptian Army, there were not many here who were in my position. The majority of the building engineers of Dubai, Abu Dhabi, Sharjah and the surrounding Emirates were European. So there was a lot for me to lose, not only for my family, but as a representative of Arab professionals here in Dubai. Nevertheless, I eventually made the decision to go home, where my wife, Faiza, died in my arms."

He stopped and shook his head again, gravely.

"My personal dilemma should not have been such a difficult decision. It would have been honorable and gracious for an older and wiser developer to allow me the time I *needed* back home with my wife. And although there is no way to guarantee that my wife would have lived had I been there earlier, there is no argument that the *ignorance* and *youth* of Abdul Khalif Hassan was in complete negligence, as he continues to be today.

"He is driven by his insanity to complete each and every building *yesterday* instead of today or *tomorrow*. It is an insanity of *youth* and inconsideration that must be dealt with. *He* must understand, and all those who have allowed him into power, that there is a penalty, not only for poverty, but for *wealth*.

"So yes, I *too* have had a difficult and painful loss in which to deal with, my friend," Mohd added. "And I can no longer sit idly by and allow thousands of good men and families to lose their lives, their dignity and their human spirit through the continuous practices of greedy and inconsiderate men. Do you agree?" he asked Saleem with opened palms.

Saleem grinned and nodded. "Yes, I do."

"Good. Then we will leave it at that," Mohd said. "One day I will hear your story. But for now, I am tired, and a man must rest," he joked.

Saleem smiled back and stood from the chair to leave. But

before he could reach the door to walk out, Mohd told him, "You are a good man, Saleem. And you are loyal to justice. But smart men must also be loyal to their intelligence. And it is not intelligent to speak about everything that you know. I can sense that in you, that you understand what information is yours to *keep* and that which you are allowed to share."

He looked into Saleem's eyes again to make sure that they understood each other.

Saleem nodded. "I understand."

"Good," Mohd said. "Foolish men do not. And they will not be allowed to breathe amongst us."

As Saleem turned to walk out, he was sure to comprehend the seriousness of their conversation. The assault weapons carried by Mohd's personal guards were there to remind him that their talks were not to be repeated. However, Saleem had no fear of most of the guards. As Mohd had already noted, he had been a militant man himself—and a good one.

With a confident and lightning-fast maneuver, Saleem could easily disarm the guard and use his weapon against every man inside of the apartment. Bakar, the huge Algerian, would be his only concern—but there was no need to have any. From what he could read inside of Mohd Ahmed Nasir's eyes—promising the softness of tears—he was a man of deep thought, peace and regret. As Saleem walked out of the gray cement building after hours of gathering vital information, he still did not feel that he had enough.

That man does not seem like he is ready for war, he told himself as he paced the sidewalk and crossed the street. *Yet his men are all armed and ready to go. Interesting.*

He had not been used to peaceful men leading revolts. Pakistani men who spoke of war would show it. However, Saleem was quite respectful of Egyptians. They were old and revolutionary fighters with a very proud history. And they demanded respect in Dubai, even as laborers. So maybe Mohd could inspire a group of men to revolt.

Maybe ... or maybe not, he contemplated.

* * * * *

As Saleem walked the streets of Deira through the night with deep thoughts, there was a commotion of police cars and an ambulance up ahead of him. He was then rejoined by his two comrades from earlier.

"What is going on?" he asked them.

"It was Rasik," one of the men stated in a low tone. "They found him stabbed in the back and robbed."

Saleem looked to the second man to confirm it. The second man nodded.

"There was a pool of blood on the sidewalk. Someone stabbed him in his back."

Saleem took the information in and nodded back. He had never liked Rasik much anyway. But the man was harmless and penniless. He sent every dime he made back home to his wife and kids in India.

Saleem frowned and asked, "Who would want to stab and rob him?"

"They said he was also drunk," the first man added. "He threw up on the sidewalk and peed his pants from his drinks."

Saleem looked more confused. Rasik had not been a heavy drinker. And it was too late at night for him to still be out. The dedicated Indian man continued to work at the same construction site from sunup to sundown, while many others had quit.

Saleem wanted to get a better look for himself at the crime scene, so he walked toward the crowd that had gathered out in front of him.

Sure enough, the blood, alcohol and urine stains remained on the sidewalk after the ambulance and police had carried the body away.

"Move back! Move back!" the police continued to shout at the crowd. The authorities had roped off the area on the sidewalk.

"You see?" Saleem's comrades asked him, confirming it.

Instinctively, Saleem began to look around at the faces of the men in the crowd. Who could have done it or knew more about it?

This was not a robbery, he told himself. *It was an assassination made to look like a robbery. I wonder what Rasik did? And who did he offend?*

Saleem kept silent. None were trusted enough to know his thoughts. But just as the investigating police would do, he would start by returning to the bar where Rasik had bought his drinks earlier to find out who was there with him and who he had spoken to.

* * * * *

In an apartment building not far from the crime scene, two older immigrant men cowered from a pair of masked assailants who had broken into their apartment. The attackers wore black ski masks and long dark clothes, while wielding blades that were larger than the one that was used to kill Rasik. They had broken into the apartment with a master key, like professionals. And they knew exactly who they were after.

"What have we done?" the first older man asked the attackers. He knew that it was an assignment. The masked men were there for murder and for murder alone. So he protected himself with raised hands in front of his face. He and his roommate had been inside of the kitchen, cooking when the men broke in.

But there was no answer to his question, only a forceful grab of his arm, a forward twist of his body and a swipe across his aged throat with the sharpened blade. The fatal move of the assassin was so brisk that it hypnotized the second older man. And as the murderer carefully cradled his dear friend and roommate's body in his arms to stop it from crashing loudly to the floor, the second older man froze and stared in disbelief at what he had just witnessed. So did the second assassin.

"Don't stare, *do it,*" the first assassin ordered. He was obviously the more experienced leader.

Suddenly, the second older man broke out of his stupor and moved to grab a frying pan from the stove that was filled with fish and hot grease. He tossed the contents toward his attacker.

When the hot fish and grease caught the masked man flush in the face, he began to yell in pain, but he was silenced immediately with a towel that his leader cleverly wrapped around his mouth, tying it into a knot around his head. The lead assassin, with his large blade still out, then faced off with the second older man.

"You know why we are here, Shyam. You have been telling secrets that don't need to be told."

The older man grabbed a kitchen knife from the stove behind him and held it up to defend himself.

"But why now?" he asked.

The masked assassin took a position of attack while his companion continued to recuperate from the shock and suddenness of his burns.

"That is not of your concern," the assassin answered.

"So it is time then? You have set your vengeance for Abdul?" The older man had a hunch who his attacker was. In fact, he was sure of it. That only made him more nervous.

"You know too much already," the masked assassin responded. "And you will never tell another soul."

As he faked forward to strike the older man with his blade, the poor man swung his kitchen knife with all of his might, and missed. That was all that it took for the masked assassin to find the angle he needed to slash the man's throat. He then grabbed his arm with the kitchen knife to restrain him long enough to take him slowly to the ground while allowing the fresh blood to run out of his severed neck as he died.

When it was done, the assassin looked to his companion and scolded him. "If you had not fallen asleep on the job, you would have never gotten yourself burned. But now you'll have a souvenir for the rest of your life to remind you of this moment. And you will never hesitate again," he assured him.

He then leaned the dead man's body up against the kitchen stove and asked for the first one.

"Drag the body here and place it beside him."

The burned man did as he was told and pulled the first kill to the stove to lean him next to his dead friend. The lead man then walked to the door and looked out of the peephole. He checked to see if anyone was in the hallway before they would make their exit.

"You follow right behind me, and we will deal with your burns later."

His burned man nodded and prepared himself to leave, while still in obvious pain. He hoped that the mask he was wearing had protected him from most of it, but it surely didn't feel that way. He felt as if his skin was peeling off.

But once the hallway was clear, they made their move for the exits, while leaving the dead men positioned with their slashed throats against the stove inside the kitchen. And their message was clear: Do not talk to anyone.

Chapter 13

JOHNNY PICKED UP GARY outside the Ali Rashid Cuisine restaurant in the business district of downtown Dubai, and he promptly teased the American about the beautiful international waitresses who worked there.

"So, how many phone numbers did you get?"

Gary chuckled. "None. They were busy doing their jobs."

Johnny looked at him from the driver's seat and grinned, knowingly. "You have a lot to learn about Dubai, my friend. And you've found the right man to teach you."

Gary didn't know about all of that. Maybe he had found the *wrong* man. Johnny seemed to be into a lot of things that were "extra."

"So, where are we off to first?" Gary asked, changing the subject. He wanted to get out into Dubai and see the people.

"Well, this early, we'll go to an after-work bar that has a hot DJ. It's called The Beach. They have a nice mix of young professionals there that you'll like."

Gary frowned. "An after-work party? At eleven o'clock? Well, what time do the regular parties start?"

"Around this same time. As The Beach winds down, the other parties are just starting up. That's why we'll go there first. Then we'll catch everyone leaving out and see where they're going next."

The plans sounded makeshift to Gary, but he didn't complain. He allowed Johnny to be the host. And when they arrived at the Jumeirah Beach Resort, he was impressed with the wide-open splendor of the bar, which had a large dance floor. The location was right off of the Persian Gulf. It reminded Gary of the beach clubs in Miami.

"Yeah, this is nice. Right off of the water," Gary commented.

Johnny smiled. "I know what you like," he bragged.

The confident Sri Lankan man walked right in past the security, with his American friend on his heels, and acted as if he owned the place. All eyes were on them as Johnny introduced Gary to a dozen people around the room, including several gorgeous young women. They all spoke over the pounding dancehall music.

Gary shied away from most of the introductions though, preferring to keep his conversations light. He had a hard time stopping himself from having flashbacks of Colombia, so he continued to eye the men inside the room to make certain that they were not offending anyone.

I don't need to make any extra trouble for myself if I can avoid it, he thought. Nevertheless, he refused to be afraid of the international social scene. He could protect himself much better now. And he felt safer without having any family or loved ones there to worry about.

I can handle myself anywhere, he insisted. *That's what I've been training for. I have nothing to fear.*

"Gary, this is Saeeda. She's Lebanese," Johnny said, snapping him out of his thoughts. The traveling man had finally broken down and given his name. So Johnny introduced him to a curly- and dark-brown-haired beauty, who looked like a

Mexican-American siren straight out of Los Angeles. Gary even joked with her. "You're Lebanese? You look like an American movie star from LA."

She laughed with perfect white teeth. "I wish. You wanna put me in a movie?"

Gary looked at Johnny before he answered her. Johnny nodded his head feverishly behind the young woman's back. But Gary shot the idea down.

"No, I'm afraid I'm not into movie productions."

"Really? You look like a movie star to me." She even reached out and rubbed his three-day-old beard.

Johnny grinned and interjected, "We could shoot a local movie. I know some guys with cameras."

Gary continued to deny the idea. "You're kidding, right? We don't even have a script."

"We can make it all up," the young woman told him. She had a positive glow about her that was infectious. Her enticing cleavage was right in his face too, but Gary failed to go for it.

"No, I'm not here to make any movies."

"Awww," she whined playfully.

"Where are you gonna be later on?" Johnny asked her.

"I don't know. Around, I guess."

He nodded to her. "I'll call you then."

"Will Gary be with you when you call?" she asked. The tall, boyish American looked old and young at the same time. And she mentioned his name as if she had known him for years.

"We can arrange something. I'll call you."

As soon as they left the young woman, Gary asked, "What was that all about?"

Johnny shook it off. "She's a big flirt, man, but if she likes you and ..." He shrugged. "Who knows? But I like the Hollywood line you gave her. I have to use that."

"But it wasn't a line. She does look like a star. She reminds me of Jessica Alba."

"Who?"

"Ah, don't worry about it."

"You want to get a drink before we leave?" Johnny asked him.

Gary thought about the man driving and declined. He also wanted to remain alert.

"Maybe at the next party."

They had only been there for thirty minutes, but they had rushed through the place like a whirlwind, collecting several party invites along the way.

"All right, fine with me. We got a few more places to hit."

As they walked back out into the parking lot to fetch the car, Saeeda had gotten herself into some type of trouble. A huge bodybuilder of a man was pulling her arm, and he was not with security.

Gary noticed immediately as the young woman struggled to free herself.

"What's going on there?" he asked Johnny.

Johnny looked and froze. "Shit. She's always getting involved in something. She probably had too much to drink."

Gary disagreed. "She didn't have too much to drink. She's just bubbly by nature."

Regardless of nationality, he knew the type. Bubbly women tended to attract overzealous guys who wanted to control them. Gary also doubted that she had spent much time in Lebanon. She didn't have the seriousness for it. She seemed more like a free-flowing British girl. Even the guy who harassed her looked British—big, white and rigid.

To confirm his hunch, Gary asked Johnny, "Do you know her from Britain too?"

There seemed to be a lot of British citizens who traveled back and forth to Dubai. Johnny had been telling him all about it.

"Yeah, how'd you know?"

"Well, she doesn't seem like she's local. And I've never been to Lebanon, but I don't picture them being so ah ... *poppish*, I guess I could say. You know, she seems like a person who watches a lot of television."

Johnny laughed. "I know what you mean. I think she's only been to Lebanon twice. And she said she was bored there."

In the meantime, she cursed the brute of a man who mis-handled her.

"Look, would you leave me alone?!" she shouted.

Gary looked around for the security guards, but they were not in the parking lot area, nor did anyone seem brave enough to step up to help her.

On a whim, the young Lebanese woman turned and looked Gary straight in his eyes from the short distance between them.

"Gary, could you tell him to let me go and leave me alone?"

It was a moment of truth and bravery that had come at short notice.

"Ah, don't get involved with that," Johnny warned him ner-vously. Gary was tall, but not that tall, and he didn't seem like much of a fighter. He was a pretty-boy American with a light beard. But once Gary reflected on the anger and helplessness of his past experiences, there was no way that he would turn her down. Besides, he was now trained for chaos.

"Hey, man, let her go."

"And what if I don't?" the man finally spoke in terse English.

Gary breathed deeply to remain calm. "Here we go," he told himself out loud. He imagined that Jonah could still hear him through his cell phone as he moved forward. But there was no more to be said. The big British man was asking for a fight.

"Hey, man, don't do it," Johnny said, reaching to pull Gary back. It was too late.

As the American approached him, the big Brit refused to budge. He was at least six foot five and two-hundred and fifty pounds. Nevertheless, Gary knew exactly how to handle him.

He asked the man one time, while standing less than three feet away from him, "Are you gonna let her go?"

He was in perfect distance to strike.

"No."

In a flash, Gary faked a right-hand punch, and when the big man moved to block it, Gary whipped him in the back of his leg with a kick that caught him off-guard. Before he could regain his balance, Gary cracked him with an overhand right to the jaw.

"Whoa!" Johnny cheered.

In less than five seconds, the British man was on his hands and knees, wondering what had happened.

Saeeda had scampered away to safety, but had turned around to see the rest of it. So did the gathering crowd who were all leaving the party for their cars.

Gary could have finished the big man off with another powerful kick while he was down, but he found no need to.

This guy has no chance of beating me, he convinced himself. Gary's years of personal military training with Jonah had prepared him to fight more skilled and dangerous men, and he could tell that his British foe was nothing more than big.

The man looked up from the ground and said, "I don't know what you just did, but you better run now."

It was Gary's turn not to budge. He stood there and allowed the man to climb back to his feet.

"I don't run so easily," Gary commented bravely.

The big man raised his arms and clenched his fists, but instead of throwing a punch, he charged at Gary with his head down, like a rhino. Expecting as much from an unskilled fighter, Gary countered him with a leaping knee while pulling the man's head down into it, creating a brutal collision that rattled the man's brains and knocked him flat on his face.

"Oh, shit!" someone yelled from the crowd.

The man hit dirt like a falling log with a pile of dust flying up into the air.

"Is he dead?"

Gary shook his head. "No, he'll live. He just has eggs for brains right now."

Saeeda laughed uncomfortably with the crowd. But deep down, she began to wonder how much trouble she had caused herself by getting him involved. The American stranger wouldn't be around her every day. And what if more men came after him? How many could he fight?

As the crowd continued to buzz about what they had witnessed out in the parking lot, the security guards rushed out to get involved.

"What's going on?"

Johnny frowned and said, "You guys are late."

"Yeah, you weren't here when I needed you," Saeeda complained.

The beefy security guards inspected the man, lying facedown in the dirt. Then they looked back at Gary, standing near him.

"Did you do this? What did you hit him with?"

They found it hard to believe the American could have knocked out such a big man. The Brit was even bigger than them.

"Ah, he just ran into my knee," Gary told them lightly.

"And he *deserved* it," Saeeda said. "He's always bothering me."

"Well, who is he?" Gary asked her. He didn't want to assume anything.

Saeeda became vague with a shrug. "He's just a friend of a friend."

That was Johnny's cue to get him out of there. "All right, man, we got places to go."

As the security guards woke the man up and helped him to his feet, the crowd began to disperse to their cars, including Johnny and Gary.

Saeeda ran them down.

"What are you doing? Where are you guys going?" she asked them.

"He's my *guest*. I'm showing him a good time," Johnny answered through the car door window. He didn't even bother to roll it down. He was noticeably upset.

"Are you still gonna call me?"

"Yeah, I'll call you later," he snapped and started the car.

Saeeda decided to wave to them. "Bye, Gary. Hope to see you later."

"Yeah, whatever," Johnny mumbled under his breath as he pulled off.

As soon as they were out of the parking lot and on the road again, he said, "Man, I didn't like that at all. What if you couldn't fight and you got your ass beat back there? It would have been all her fault. I'm never speaking to her again. She's bad for business."

Gary smiled at him and shook it off. "What did you expect her to do? She needed help, and no one wanted to help her."

"Yeah, because they all know that she's full of drama."

"And yet you wanted me to make movies with her."

"Because she's *drama*," Johnny repeated. Then he broke out and laughed. "You kicked that guy's ass back there, man. You know martial arts or something? You only hit him four times."

"Three times," Gary corrected him.

"So you *do* know martial arts?"

Gary flirted with not admitting anything, but it was too late for that.

"Maybe."

Johnny looked at him. "Maybe my ass. What are you, a trained fighter or something? You went into that guy like you knew you could beat him. I just thought you played baseball or something ... a pitcher."

Gary reflected on all of the sparring he had done over the past few years with his training team, and he shrugged. "I haven't done any rounds professionally. But I bet that guy hasn't either. He scares most people with his size. But the more dangerous men are usually smaller."

Johnny continued to watch him and listened in awe as he drove. "I don't know what to say, man," he commented. "You're over here all by yourself, and you wouldn't even give me your name. Is Gary your real name? No wonder you called yourself 'The Traveler.' I feel like you're over here on a secret mission or something."

Gary smiled and didn't comment.

"Are you? Are you on a secret mission that you can't tell anyone?"

"No," Gary said sternly. "Now let's get to the next party."

"Yeah, like you're gonna tell me anyway, right?" Johnny asked him sarcastically.

"Exactly," Gary countered.

They were back to a cat-and-mouse game.

"Well, this *sucks*. Now I don't know what to do with you. Are you even supposed to talk to women? I noticed how you turned them all down in there. And they all liked you too."

"What makes you so sure?"

Johnny frowned at him. "My friend, I work these clubs every night. Give me some credit. I just *know*." Then he grinned and added, "The girls at the restaurant liked you too. They called and told me already. So you have a lot of options over here if you wanted to use them."

Gary shook his head and grinned, thinking nothing of it. He understood through his past experiences that having a bunch of the wrong women could be dangerous for a guy.

"Like you said, women can be bad for business," he hinted.

"So you *are* here on business?"

"I didn't say that. But what if the rest of these women have big, jealous boyfriends like that one?"

Johnny thought about it and shook it off. "No, most of them are single. And the ones who do have boyfriends, they wouldn't have a chance against you. You'll take them out in two hits. I know these guys."

Gary chuckled. "You're not giving them enough credit. Every man can be beat."

"Yeah, like 'Iron' Mike Tyson, right?"

"Exactly. But let's stop talking about fighting and get back in the mood for meeting girls."

Johnny grinned. "Now you're talking my language. So how many do you want? Have you ever tried four at one time?"

Gary shook his head and grinned. *This guy is unbelievable,* he thought. *I don't think I was ever this bad.* Then he thought about Colombia again. *Or maybe I was for a minute.*

* * * * *

When Gary made it back to his hotel, he was exhausted. It

was three-thirty, which translated to only seven-thirty at night back home. But it sure didn't feel like it. He hit the bed like a sack of bricks. That's when Jonah called him back. At first he ignored the phone, until it rang louder.

"Hello?" he answered, disturbed.

"I'm not interrupting anything, am I?"

"You wouldn't know?"

"No, I wouldn't."

"Well, why are you calling so late?"

Jonah paused. "Oh yeah, it's in the middle of the night over there, isn't it?"

"I'm sure you know that already. So what do you want?"

"I just wanna to tell you to watch yourself. Don't try to be a hero over there."

Gary shook his head against the plush white pillows and began to laugh.

"Unbelievable," he stated. "I thought you told me you wouldn't intervene."

"I wouldn't, but that doesn't mean that I'm not concerned."

"Well, just so you know, I think I handled myself pretty good tonight."

Jonah responded with silence.

"Hello?" Gary called her.

"I'm here. And I guess there's no more to be said. So, how long are you planning on staying?"

"Why, you thinking I'm gonna be in five more fights?"

Jonah chuckled. "Maybe two more, but not five. Just be careful who you're picking. But saving a damsel in distress can't be too bad. Just don't try to save them all."

"Oh, believe me," Gary commented, "I don't plan to. The women over here have just as many issues as Americans."

"Hey, you watch your mouth," Jonah warned him.

"Oh yeah, I forgot ... you're one of them."

"You know what ... go on and go to bed."

"Thank you." And he hung up and crashed to sleep without another word.

Chapter 14

EARLY THAT MORNING IN the capital city of Abu Dhabi, Abdul held and kissed his eighteen-month-old son, Rafi Maalik, while Hamda stood by them, smiling regally in all white.

"He's a beautiful young prince," she noted.

Abdul agreed with her, cracking a broad smile of his own. "And I will teach him all about good business," he promised. He then handed the energetic boy back to his mother.

Dressed in a light-gray suit, white business shirt and a red silk tie, Abdul was ready to head off for work at his offices in downtown Dubai. It was slightly after six, and his young family was up bright and early with him.

"When are we going to meet with your uncle? He's been calling all this week, and I can tell that he is anxious to see you," Hamda said.

Abdul nodded. "I know. As you can imagine, with all that has gone on, I have been very busy this week. I planned for us to visit with my uncle at his house this weekend."

Hamda grimaced, surprised. "Are you just now telling me this? I need to prepare. What day are we visiting?"

"Tomorrow, so you can prepare today."

He would rather his wife remain at home and plan for their visit to his uncle, Sheikh Al Hassan, than for her to drop by again at his office. Hamda and her tendencies for outspokenness and attention could be very distracting to Abdul and his staff members. She was a very magnetic woman, which made him proud but also leery and overprotective.

"Thanks for telling me in advance," she said.

Abdul grinned. "You are welcome."

Hamda leaned forward to kiss her husband on the lips and finger his red silk tie as their young son pulled away in her arms to stop from being squashed between his parents.

"Have a good day at work," she told Abdul.

"I plan to."

He called for his driver and security team as he walked briskly through his elaborate seven-bedroom mansion. He planned to move into a larger one once he and his wife had added to the family. A gigantic foyer of white marble columns awaited him at the front door and emptied into a driveway outside, where his white Rolls Royce was parked with the security team in the Cadillac SUVs surrounding it.

"Good morning," Abdul told his men.

"Good morning."

He climbed inside the back of his car and immediately dialed a number on his cell phone to reach a private investigator for individual counsel. Abdul wanted to know more about the accident and other recent events at his construction sites before anyone else knew, so that he could later respond preemptively to inquiries. But before he spoke, he pushed a button that raised a soundproof window for privacy, separating his backseat from his driver.

"It's Abdul. What have you found out?" the *Emirati* businessman asked.

His counsel answered, "There were several men onsite that

day who had been on the job for less than a few weeks. They then quit immediately after the incident. But did they quit because of the dangers of the job, or because they had already served their short-lived purpose?"

It was a good question. "What are your thoughts?"

"If I may be frank," the counsel responded. He didn't want to insult the *Emirati* developer.

"Yes, please, be honest."

"Well, many of the men have complained about being driven hard at work, like camels, and they have not particularly liked your site managers. But others could have been placed there to create more discontent with the workers you already have."

Abdul had not even thought of that. "Do you think that someone would have them to do that?"

The counsel paused. "Abdul, how many adversaries do you think you may have in your development business? Do you think there are men who may not want you to be successful?"

Abdul began to think of the many older *Emirati* developers of tourism properties around Dubai. Of course, he had beaten out many of them on bids for new projects, and as a much younger man in business, some of his elders had pointed to his powerful uncle as his only key supporter. Nepotism was common around the world. Nevertheless, there were much bigger developers in the United Arab Emirates, and so many properties to build, that Abdul could not imagine anyone being that concerned about him getting some projects.

"Sure, some of my elders have felt that I had not properly earned my position, but that was years ago when I first began to develop properties. The International Suites hotel was one of my first big developments, and I am still very proud of it," he boasted. "But surely, my elders have gotten over that by now. They know that I am a qualified builder with vision and ambition, and my age no longer has anything to do with it."

The counsel paused again, then dug deeper.

"What about some of the men who have worked for you?"

Abdul had not thought of that idea either. "What about

them?" he asked.

"I don't know. Are there any past workers who may not have liked you?"

Abdul felt the question was beneath him. *"Past workers?* So what, they are *immigrants.* You think they could organize themselves enough to try and shut down *my* construction? What good would that do them? They only want the work. They cannot make any money for their wives and families back home without it."

The counsel fell silent. He did not want to create a dispute; he was only bringing up the facts of his investigation.

"You are paying me to present every option. That is my job. So if I cannot obtain the answers I need from the immigrant laborers, then I would next think about asking the management."

Abdul took a breath to calm himself. Manipulative management would be even more troubling for him to imagine.

"Thank you. That is enough for now." He was obviously still irritated. He wanted to gather as much of the information early to ponder during his day, yet he did not want to be upset by it. However, as soon as he hung up the call with his private investigator, he began to think of the many men that he had fired over the years for their inferior performances on the job.

He frowned and asked himself, *What honorable man would complain about his own lack of performance and then try to poison the minds of others who need the work?*

He felt the idea was sacrilege. There was no excuse for failing to complete tasks. Either you were driven to be successful or you were not.

You cannot blame anyone else for your own lack of accomplishment, he insisted to himself in the backseat of his car. So he felt nothing of it. Nevertheless, he was compelled to ask.

With a quick glance at his Rolex, it remained early, before seven. However, Abdul was adamant in handling his investigation queries promptly rather than later—that way he could return to focusing on the real work of his day without lingering questions. He dialed his phone again.

"Hakim, sorry to call you so early, but I must ask you, have you recognized any immigrant men on the job who have influenced the others negatively?"

"Yes, I *have* noticed. So has Khalid. But many of these men we do not even know."

"What do you mean you don't know them?"

Hakim hesitated to give his honest answer.

Abdul read his hesitation. "Hakim, you may be honest with me. I need to know."

"Okay," his overseer responded. "Over the past few months, to speed up the construction as you have ordered, we have hired far more men than we could ever learn the names of. And yes, some of them have not been professional or friendly. I have had a few run-ins with them myself. And the Egyptians are usually the worse."

"Egyptians?" Abdul asked.

"Yes, the Egyptians and Pakistanis act as if they are above the work that we give them. So if you must know, then I would say that they are a bad influence on the rest of the men."

Abdul paused before jumping to conclusions. *The Egyptians of Dubai surely have the egos of a historical people. It is normal for them to think above laboring and to become stereotypically unruly. And the Pakistanis are a militant people because of their own nation.* Abdul broke from his thoughts. "Is there anything else you have to tell me?" he asked Hakim.

"It has gotten much better over this past week," his overseer said. "Many of the rotten apples have left."

"You mean after the accident?"

"Yes. Remember the group of men I said who had walked off?" Hakim reminded him.

"The same day that it happened?" Abdul questioned.

"Yes."

"Well, how come you didn't tell me that then?"

"I *did* tell you."

Their conversation was growing more intense by the minute. But Abdul stopped and thought, *Maybe he did, and I was not thinking about it at the time.*

"Were there Egyptians and Pakistanis in that group of men?"

"Yes, and I believe Rasik knows them."

"Rasik?"

Abdul was not familiar with the name.

"He is an Indian—a Hindu. And he speaks several languages. He has helped me to keep peace with the workers whenever he's had to push them."

"Well, you ask him for the names of these other men."

"Yes, I will."

"And you call me back as soon as you have them. Are you at the site now?"

"I will be there in twenty minutes."

"Good."

As soon as Abdul hung up, another thought popped into his head. *Mohd Ahmed Nasir, a proud Egyptian soldier and engineer! And I fired him when he asked to return home to be with his sick wife, who later died.*

Abdul had forced himself to block the incident out of his mind. He had been too young and too stubborn to apologize. It was an early period in his development, where he was out to prove himself to the older *Emirati.*

"Is he still here in Dubai?" Abdul asked himself aloud. He remembered that Mohd lived in the residential district of Sharjah, before the Palm Islands were complete.

Abdul made a return call to his private counsel with the new information.

"I have a name for you: Mohd Ahmed Nasir. He was an Egyptian engineer who worked for me during the time of constructing the International Suites. His wife had needed an operation at the same time as the crucial months of finishing my first big development, so I forbade him from returning home, because I needed his expertise on the job. But I *did* give him the money he needed to send home to his wife and family for the operation. I told him then to place his wife's health in the hands of Allah. Nevertheless, she had complications and died later ... after I had fired him for leaving his post."

"Hmmph," his private counsel grunted. "Where did he live?"

"At the time, he lived in the residential district of Sharjah. But I don't know if he ever returned to the Emirates. It was a hasty decision that I wanted to forget. This was nearly ten years ago."

He paused and added, "I have tried to make amends from my earlier immaturities, but I guess I have not yet done enough."

"We have all been young with haste at one time," his private counsel stated, then said, "I will check into it."

When he hung up his phone again, Abdul dropped it beside him on the leather seat of his Rolls Royce and prayed, "Merciful Allah ..."

* * * * *

Hakim arrived at the dusty construction site amongst the hundreds of men on the early shift and sought out the amenable Indian man, Rasik. But Rasik was not to be found.

Spotting Khalid, who had hired the resourceful Indian and knew him well, Hakim asked, "Have you seen Rasik today?"

Khalid shook his head. "No, I have not. He would usually be here by now."

Hakim looked around and was ready to ask some of the other men.

Overhearing their conversation, a short Filipino man nervously offered them what he knew.

"Ah, Rasik, he, uh ... someone killed him last night in Deira."

The Filipino man had been disturbed by the murder, and he knew that someone would ask about Rasik sooner or later. So he was courageous enough to be the first one to tell them in honor of Rasik's humility and friendship. He had been a good man.

Hakim heard him and became excited. "What? He was killed in Deira? Last night? How?"

Rasik had been at work, happy and healthy the day before.

The Filipino spoke up with dignity and bravery as the other immigrant laborers began to listen. The man explained in slow and choppy English, "He was stabbed and robbed on the street."

"Near his apartment?" one of the other laborers asked.

Many of the men lived in different working-class areas in and around Dubai, but the Filipino man lived in the same gray cement building as Rasik, in Palm Deira.

"Yes, last night ... right around the corner from our building," he said. "I saw the ambulance and police take his body away."

As he continued to speak, other men from the Palm Deira district began to fill in the details of what they knew while Hakim listened and thought to himself in shock, *Merciful Allah! What is going on?*

Hakim could not imagine why anyone would want to murder or rob Rasik. He was a peaceful man who sent every dime back home to his wife and family. Everyone already knew that about him. He practically bragged about it.

But that was only the beginning of the news. The men then began to speak about two older laborers, who were found with their throats slashed in the same neighborhood of cement apartments in Deira. And when the men repeated their names, Hakim recognized them as old hands who had also worked for Abdul.

Hakim immediately broke away for privacy and could not wait to call Abdul back.

"Hello," Abdul answered quickly.

"Merciful Allah!" Hakim said. "Rasik was stabbed and killed in Palm Deira last night, and they found two older men in their apartment with their throats slashed—older men who had worked for you," Hakim added in nearly a whisper.

"Merciful Allah. Is there a conspiracy?" Abdul asked rhetorically.

Hakim answered him anyway, "I don't know. But this has to be more than just a coincidence."

Abdul could overhear the commotion from the men in the background. So he told his overseer tensely, "Hakim, you keep this all to yourself, settle down the men and get them all back to work. I already have someone working on it. That's why I asked you these questions this morning."

"Yes, I understand," Hakim responded. But as soon as he hung up the phone and turned to look into the eyes of the men, filled with panic and disbelief, he knew that it would be a very long day for all of them.

* * * * *

Back inside Abdul's car, the *Emirati* businessman took another deep breath and exhaled. He had arrived only a few blocks away from his downtown Dubai office. He then made another cell phone call to his private investigator and counsel.

"Yes, it's Abdul again," he stated glumly. "I have more news to report. And names."

Chapter 15

RAMIA FARAH AZIZ RECEIVED an unknown call on her cell phone. She was up early, watching old footage of herself from a month ago where she had logged hours of interviews and features on the people, places and things in and around Dubai. She had nothing more to do with her time that morning, and she did not want to read so early in the day.

She looked at the unknown number that popped up on her cell phone screen and hesitated. The call came in slightly after nine. "Who is this?"

She then thought of all the applications she had filled out for employment that week and snapped out of her apprehension.

Oh, wow, my first job call, she thought to herself, her eyes wide. "Hello."

"Yes, I'm calling for Ramia Farah Aziz," a subtle male voice said in clear English.

"Yes, this is she," Ramia responded.

"You applied for a job with the Dubai Safari Tours?"

"Yes, yes I did."

Her excitement jumped through the phone.

The gentle-voiced man even chuckled at her over the line. "I heard that your interviews went quite well. And you take a nice picture."

"Thank you."

"Are you able to come in by noon today for your first training session?"

"Yes! Yes!"

"I would advise you to wear long shorts or pants for the sand and good walking shoes. We will give you a safari hat and a shirt when you arrive at the office before noon."

"Okay. Thank you, thank you, thank you. I'll be there," she told him profusely.

"Your enthusiasm is good. It should rub off on our guests and make them feel very comfortable."

"Yes, thank you. I love to meet new people."

When she hung up, she jumped for joy and pumped her fist. "I have a *job*! And I love to have something to *do* and make money."

She was as giddy as a child.

"My dear cousin Basim was right," she admitted aloud to herself. "Allah has blessed me this morning. And *quickly*."

She immediately dialed her cousin's cell phone number to share the news with him.

Basim answered all of Ramia's phone calls as soon as he could, with a hint of nervousness in case there was some type of emergency, especially after the rash of vicious knife murders that had broken out in their neighborhood the night before.

"Guess what?" Ramia asked him.

Basim was not in the mood for charades. "What? What is it?" he questioned her solemnly.

"You were right! I was called today for a *job*, just a minute ago. Isn't Allah magnificent? I start training today at noon," she told her cousin.

"But I do not get off work with the car until late. How will you get over there?"

Ramia frowned. "I will take a cab. I still have some money."

"You shouldn't take a cab after those murders last night," her cousin said, overprotective. He had been thinking about the murders in their neighborhood ever since he left Ramia that morning to head off for work. He was even tempted to take her into work with him, like an intern.

"You should not be waiting outside for a cab," Basim insisted.

"Then I will call one to wait for me at the curb," Ramia countered. "What is wrong with you? People all around the world are murdered every day. But that should not stop us from living the life we all want to live."

"What time are you supposed to be there?" he asked her.

Ramia cut off his plans, saying, "You are *not* coming to get me. I will not allow it. You have a job to do and now *I* have a job. So I will call you when I leave and call you again when I arrive there ... and you can pick me up afterward."

Basim's younger cousin had it all mapped out. There was nothing left for him to say. But he thought something up anyway.

"You call me as soon as you step into the cab, and I'll talk to you until you get there. All right?"

He was trying his hardest to make a safe deal with her.

Ramia sighed deeply and thought it over. Her cousin had a way of wearing her down with his calm persistence. "Okay. I'll call you."

* * * * *

Gary rolled over in his king-sized bed at the Hilton downtown and stretched in a gray University of Louisville T-shirt. It was eleven o'clock, and he felt for a moment like a lazy college student sleeping in and skipping class.

"Urrrgghhh, that was a good sleep," he moaned, pushing out his arms and legs while kicking off the white sheets and thick quilt. "Here comes my first full day in Dubai."

He looked over at the clock on the nightstand and marveled

at his perfect symmetry. He had a tour appointment at two, giving him plenty of time to shower, get dressed and grab something to eat before leaving.

On cue, his phone rang. Gary picked it up and answered without looking to see who it was. What difference did it make? He was up and he could use the conversation.

"Hello."

"You were a big hit last night, man. They all want you back for more. What are you doing tonight?"

It was Johnny. Gary shook his head and grinned. The guy was a living dose of coffee.

"I didn't do anything but smile and talk to people. What could they possibly want more of?" Gary asked him.

"They want more of *you*, man, your presence and essence. You have the *it* factor. No one can explain it, it just *is*," Johnny told him. "You're like *me*, man. *I* have it. So me and you together make a great team."

Johnny continued, "I don't even have to charge you for this. You took my game up a level. I got numbers I never could have gotten before last night before meeting up with you. So I need to thank you for that. People were talking about the fight you had with the big bloke at The Beach last night in the parking lot too."

"Yeah, well, don't get too used to that. I need to avoid problems over here. So no more drama girls, all right?" Gary joked.

"Oh, I hear you, my friend. No more of Saeeda. But she did call me twice last night for you. *Twice.*"

"Well, thanks for not giving her my number."

"No way, man, she'd have to pay me for that. Nothing's on the house unless you make me money," he boasted. "So what are you doing today?"

"What are *you* doing?" Gary asked him back. The man sounded like he had a lot of free time on his hands.

"Oh, I've already been at the airport since eight this morning. I'm making my third trip back now. I got four-hundred *dirham* in my pocket already. I'm on my way to six before noon."

Outside of his obvious British accent, Johnny would fit right in with the movers and shakers of New York, Philly and Boston. He was fast paced and constantly buzzing.

"Do you ever sleep?" Gary asked him.

"Yeah, I'll sleep when I'm dead," he joked. "So what are you doing today?" he asked Gary again. "I wanted to give you a few more hours of sleep before I called to wake you up. You know it's only one o'clock in the morning American time. It's eight o'clock in Britain."

"Thanks for reminding me," Gary said. "But I'm going on a Dubai desert sand tour today."

"Oh, man, I love those tours. They're big fun, with the dune buggies, sand skis and camels. What time are you going?"

Gary hesitated. He had been around the guy enough for a while. He needed a ten-hour break, or maybe a day or two.

"You're not planning on going are ya?"

"Aw, heck no. It's Friday! I'm not leaving the airport until I make two thousand *dirham*. Then I'll go home and kick up my feet for an hour or two," Johnny said. "Those desert tour things take all day. They're just fun to do when you have the time for it, especially if you take a girl with you. You got her all day and night, and everything is already paid for. That's the best date ever."

Gary laughed. "You're something else, man. If I would have met you six years ago, we could have really had some fun. But I'm a little older now."

"You're only as old as you allow yourself to be, my friend. You remember I said that. But I gotta go now; I'm back at the airport. Time to get back to busy."

Just like that, Johnny was off the phone and back to his life-style.

Gary mumbled, "That guy probably has a heck of a life over here. But let me get my day started." He climbed out of bed and headed toward the bathroom for a shower.

* * * * *

The Dubai Safari Tours picked up three or four passengers in white Jeeps from various locations around the UAE and drove them all out to a desert tour ground. Once the tourists arrived in as many as twelve vehicles, the group formed a caravan to drive up, down and around the sand dunes in the desert. But before the drivers could start their fun in the sand, a tour guide asked them all to climb out of the vehicles for an official introduction and a chance for the tourists to meet each other.

A middle-aged British-Indian man addressed the group of thirty-six with an introduction in English while they all stood out in front of the white Jeeps.

"Hello, everyone. My name is Conrad Murymar, and I want to personally thank you all for signing up to enjoy the Dubai Safari Tours. In addition to the buggy rides through the sand dunes behind you, we have a fun-filled day planned for you all with sand skiing, camel back riding, belly dancing, flavored hookah pipes, a full-course meal, fireworks and plenty of photo opportunities to share with your friends and loved ones back home.

"But before we start our packed, fun-filled day, at this time we would like you all to greet each other, as we have participants from ten different nations," Conrad said. He wore a tan bucket sand hat with a matching Dubai Safari Tours T-shirt. The other drivers were all dressed identically, except for their different pants, long shorts and shoes.

Conrad then read from a printout, "According to my list of participants today, you all are from Australia, Japan, Brazil, the U.S., the UK, Italy, Germany, South Africa, Canada and France. So we definitely have a good mix of people."

Representing the U.S., along with a couple from Florida in their forties, Gary looked around and assumed that he was the only lone tourist in the large group. As they began to shake hands, greet each other and take pictures, the other tourists were mostly couples, families with children, or good friends on a vacation.

"Hi, I'm Gary, from the U.S."

"You came alone?" an Italian woman asked him. She was in her late thirties and had come with her slightly younger girlfriend.

"Ah, I'm afraid so," Gary answered sheepishly.

"Would you like to ride with us?" she asked him.

Wow! Gary thought. *They waste no time with that.*

He didn't even know their names.

One of the young tour guides overheard their forward invitation to him and beamed right into Gary's eyes. It was the understanding of awkwardness, and they shared an international moment of connection that needed no words.

"Ah, sure, I don't see why not," he answered. "What're your names again?"

The older Italian woman chuckled and reached out her hand. "I'm Sophie, and this is Anastasia."

Anastasia was not only younger but shorter, with light-brown hair that was in contrast to Sophie's jet black. But they both had the deep-tanned skin and robust bodies of proud, fit Italians.

"What part of Italy are you from?"

"Venice."

Gary angled toward the young tour guide to include her in the conversation. Tour guides were people too, so he didn't want to leave her out, especially with her striking hazel-colored eyes that dazzled like a rainbow in the sand.

"And what country are you from?" he asked the young Dubai Safari Tours woman. Her sand hat covered her hair.

"Jordan."

Gary reached out his hand to hers. "Are you a driver?"

She looked too young and fragile to drive, but she could have surprised him.

The young Jordanian giggled. "No, I'm actually in training. This is my first day."

"Oh, this is Maria. She came with us," Sophie interjected. "Isn't she gorgeous?"

The young woman smiled graciously and said, "*Ra*-mia," to correct her name.

Cat fight brewing, Gary thought.

"Oh, so *close*," Sophie commented with a snap of her fingers.

"*Ra*-mia."

The young woman nodded and continued to smile. "Yes."

Before they knew it, it was time to climb back into their vehicles and get started.

"Ramia, can you please take our picture," Sophie asked, practically jamming her camera into the young woman's hands.

"Sure."

Sophie grabbed Gary by the wrist. "If you don't mind," she said.

"Okay," Gary agreed.

Anastasia jumped in on the other side of him, creating a sandwich, while Sophie dictated her terms.

"Okay, now take a few long shots of us as well. Gary is very tall."

Ramia took at least eight different angles with the digital camera before returning it to the zestful Italian.

Sophie forwarded through the pictures on the view screen and nodded, while showing them to Anastasia and Gary.

"She's good, very good," she commented.

Ramia was all smiles. "Thank you."

The tour group all climbed back into the vehicles, with several couples swapping Jeeps as Gary moved in with the two Italians and Ramia, who sat up front with a male driver.

"Has everyone met each other back there? I'm David," the late-twenties driver introduced himself, mainly to Gary. He was as brown as Johnny. Maybe he was Sri Lankan as well.

"I'm Gary."

"All right, Gary, well buckle up your seatbelts back there, and get ready for a fun and rocky ride. That means you too, Ramia. We don't want to lose you to a concussion on your first day of training," he teased her.

Ramia smiled and said, "Okay."

The line of Jeeps faced the towering sand dunes as the drivers began to take air out of the tires. A flat wheel was much less likely to flip. In a few minutes, they were all blasting away through the sand.

"Oh, my goodness!" Sophie screamed as if on a rollercoaster ride. A few times she even grabbed Gary's thigh to balance herself inside the back, as their jeep cut in, out, up, down and around the sand dunes with the others.

All the while, Gary continued to connect to Ramia, who held a secret empathy for the American man. And with every look, grin or eye that she was able to give him from the front, they understood each other.

She really is beautiful, Gary admitted to himself. *She has a good spirit. But I wonder how young she is. I know she's older than a teenager, but she looks that young. I give her no more than twenty-two.*

The young Jordanian held his attention the entire time, even while the Italian flirted mercilessly. In fact, Gary couldn't wait to ask the young woman more questions later, if he was able to. Surely, a young and beautiful woman could relate to being cordial under fire.

After cruising the sand dunes, the Jeeps drove through an ostrich and camel farm before arriving at a campground in the middle of the desert, with tents, tables, food, drinks, a circular stage and a DJ for music. The drivers parked and let all of the tourists out to eat and enjoy themselves at the camp, including sand skiing down a nearby slope, camelback riding, snake and hawk petting, hookah smoking and plenty of pictures. But Gary didn't have many opportunities to speak to Ramia again. She was in training with the other tour guides, who continued to show her the ropes around the campgrounds. She also helped to prepare food and tables and collect the trash.

Gary could tell that she watched him. Her hazel eyes continued to glimmer, no matter the distance between them. Gary showed off his athleticism, hoping to impress the beautiful Jordanian as he skied down sand slopes. He also sparred with Middle Eastern swords, held the snakes and hawks and petted the guard dogs around the camp.

Ramia *was* impressed. The tall American continued to stand out—a lone, handsome and rugged Western man out in the desert. And as the sun began to set, with the DJ playing music for a team of Syrian belly dancers, Gary finally had his chance to get next to her again in the crowd.

"This is really a great tour. I'm enjoying myself," he told her casually.

She gushed. "I know. This is the greatest job in the *world*."

Gary was overtaken by her spunk and happiness. However, he was also leery of singling her out too much in the crowd. She was so young and exotic, but she was also an Arab woman in the Middle East. So he remained cautious not to offend anyone. With her sand hat off in the dim light, her auburn hair, just a shade darker than his own, along with her perfectly toned and flawless skin, she looked even more beautiful. She was a young goddess in the desert sand.

Now I see why they cover their women up, Gary joked to himself.

Ramia looked into his green eyes again and smiled, as if waiting for more of his conversation. That only made his desire to talk to her burn stronger inside of his heart.

Okay, I need to get away from her before I make a fool of myself out here, he mused. The urge made him feel very uncomfortable.

Finally, he said, "Okay, well ... enjoy your training."

"Thank you."

Only Gary was not able to force his legs to move away.

"Where are you from in the States?" she asked him.

"Louisville, in Kentucky."

She nodded. "Yes, the basketball team."

That surprised him. "You know about Louisville basketball?"

"Kentucky, my cousin likes to watch them online."

Gary smirked. "Oh yeah, it's a big state rivalry between Louisville and Kentucky."

Just as he had warmed up enough to think about asking her how old she was, Conrad Murymar called her away.

"Oh, excuse me," she said as she left.

Gary could feel a strange cloud of loneliness in her absence.

He hoped that she would return. And she did, but only for a second.

"Enjoy your stay in Dubai," she told him with a smile.

"Oh, you're leaving?"

She nodded. "Yes, I train again tomorrow or Sunday."

"Okay, well enjoy your Friday night," he said.

"I doubt it. I don't live in a fun neighborhood," she responded.

But before he could say anything else, she moved away to say her goodbyes to the other tourists, including the two Italian women. And as she walked toward the Jeeps in the dark, Gary took a deep breath.

Can't have everything, he thought.

"There you are, Gary. You disappeared for a while," Sophie said with a flirtatious glee, swaying her hips and grabbing his arm. "We wanted to get some more pictures of you in case we don't see you again. Where are you staying, by the way?"

Not even her sexy Italian accent could tempt him. He felt alone, staring in the dark at tourist tents lighted with fiery torches. His mind was definitely not with Sophie or any of the others on the tour.

"I don't even know the name of the place. I'm just over here on a whim. I've been hanging out all night anyway."

Sophie was ready, with her information written down on the back of a business card. "Well, in case you want to hang out again with us, here is the hotel and my phone number to contact me."

When he looked down at the card, it was the International Suites, *again.*

Chapter 16

ABDUL SENT HIS MAN Hakim to the Palm Deira district after work that evening to check in on the investigation of the recent murders. He wanted Hakim to find out whatever he could on his own and report back to him. Abdul desired all of the information that he could get and from as many different sources.

When Hakim arrived in Deira, he found the UAE police steadily combing through the area with random questions for some and detailed interrogations of others. With a mostly immigrant population who spoke several different languages, the police had their work cut out for them. And they were far behind what was already known by Abdul's construction site overseer, as well as his private counsel and investigator, Tariq Mohammed. Both of Abdul's men had an inside track on what to ask and who to look for.

A big Arab man with a neatly trimmed beard in casual street clothes, Tariq was an imposing and respected figure. He was also very sharp. He recognized Hakim, snooping around the crowd outside of the gray cement buildings, immediately. In his white garb, Hakim stood out amongst the uniformed workers like a sore thumb, but Tariq did not bother to speak to him.

As long as he doesn't get in my way, he told himself.

There were plenty of immigrant onlookers that night. They were all amazed by the three cold-blooded murders all in one treacherous night.

"This is impossible," a young Indian worker commented with his hands to his lips in prayer. "Three murders in the same night, all within two blocks of each other. What's going on?"

The crowds had gathered around a dozen police cars that encircled the area. UAE police officers and investigators were everywhere, with many of them attempting to control the crowds.

"Move back! This is police work!"

The crowd retreated reluctantly as Tariq flashed his special investigations badge on his way inside of the building. Hakim watched him from the crowd, while continuing to listen in on chatter from the streets and sidewalks.

"Why would someone want to kill two old men?" a bystander asked rhetorically.

Maybe they knew something they were not supposed to tell, Hakim thought, particularly considering the details of the murders. Two slit throats of wise old men was obvious, even to a construction worker. They knew too much.

As Tariq walked into the five-story building to investigate the scene for himself, he listened in on a few of the police interrogations inside of the hallways.

"You did not see any strange men enter the building last night?"

"Not any who looked unusual, no," a young laborer answered. He was still in tan uniform.

"What does 'unusual' mean?" the officers asked him.

The laborer shrugged. "Any man who would look ready to kill someone," he answered. "Most of the men who live here are peaceful workers and laborers."

"Where do most of them work?"

Tariq listened in as well. *How many of the immigrant men in Deira have worked for Abdul at one time?* he wondered.

"All over Dubai," the laborer answered the police. "It is much cheaper to live here in a small room that is close to where we work. We only have to cross the main bridge back into Dubai."

With the majority of the tenants working daytime shifts, the police had no choice but to ask the same questions of various residents as they began to arrive at home that evening. Not even a double murder inside of their building would stop them from getting up and heading to work. Work was the only reason for them to be there. Few immigrant laborers could afford to enjoy the luxuries of Dubai. The affluence of the United Arab Emirates only served as an opportunity to create a living for their families, many of whom lived far away in a dozen foreign countries.

Once Tariq had ascended the floor of the murders, he found more of the police asking questions of some of the few women who lived in the building.

"Did you hear any men fighting or screaming from inside your room last night?"

The young woman was a Somalian in her mid-twenties, with smooth brown skin and long braided hair.

"I was asleep," she answered. And she was now irritated that three separate teams of officers had knocked on her door to question her.

"Are you sure you did not hear anything?"

The murders had occurred right across the hallway from her door.

"Yes, I am sure," she snapped.

One of the officers began to peer into her apartment in curiosity. He asked her, "Who do you live with?"

"I live with my cousins, and they are all women. I told the police this earlier."

The officers all looked at each other, suspecting prostitution.

"And what work do you do?" one of them asked suspiciously. There were four of them, all local Arabs.

"I work at the mall," the woman answered. "I have today off."

"In what store do you work?"

By that time, Tariq had heard enough. The woman did not know anything, and harassing her would only make it harder for them.

"That is enough," the private counsel spoke up. "She does not know."

Three UAE officers turned to face Tariq and immediately paused in a show of respect. But that didn't mean they liked him butting in.

"We are only doing our jobs, as you do yours," the lead interrogator piped up. They were all familiar with Tariq Mohammed and his experienced work, and they envied him.

"And your job should never be to harass innocent women." Tariq liked to make strategic friends with any witnesses who could grow to like and trust him. It made his job as a private investigator and counsel a lot easier.

The Somalian woman took note of him and nodded. "Thank you."

He nodded back. "It is my honor. How often do guests take the stairs instead of the elevators?" he asked. "These elevators appear to be slow and overused."

The woman grinned. "They are slow. So we use the stairs a lot. It keeps you in shape."

Tariq looked to the exit staircase to his left and decided to take another look. He had already gathered plenty of information during the day, including a look inside of the apartment of the double murder. But he did not want to compete with so many hands and bodies from the police force that had arrived earlier. The evening shift of police was lighter and more manageable, but they were also less experienced.

"We have already checked the stairs several times now," the lead officer informed him.

"And now it is my turn," Tariq responded.

The officer shook his head and breathed deeply, disturbed by the nuisance of the hired hand. Nevertheless, Tariq had served

on the UAE police force for many years himself, as well as earned
a law degree, which helped him to solve many high-profile cases
in and around Dubai. So he had earned a great deal of respect
from the police chiefs at the headquarters. Realizing as much, the
officer stood down and allowed Tariq to perform his methodical
investigation.

The lead officer nodded to the other men. "Let him be."

"Thank you."

Tariq entered the barren cement stairway that was without
railings and studied the outside walls for fingerprints. More than
halfway to the bottom, he found a small grease smudge in the
middle of the outside wall. He leaned in and sniffed it before
pressing the smudge with his finger to get a better whiff and feel.

"Fish oil," he confirmed.

When he had visited the scene of the crime earlier, Tariq had
discussed the dried fish oil with higher-ranking officers, but he
had not yet studied the exit staircase. He wondered if the investigation team had found the small grease mark as well.

Tariq walked out of the building's fire escape exit, where the
police and bystanders remained abuzz out of the sidewalk and
street. As they all watched him, he looked right and then left,
imagining which way the assailants could have run. Then he
spotted a tall brown trash can to his left. It stood waist high and
toward the back of the sidewalk. As he walked over to investigate
it, the police officers and the crowd all watched.

"We checked the perimeter of the building already," one of
the officers commented.

Tariq looked inside the trash can, searching for more fish oil.

"What are you looking for?" the officer continued to question
him.

Tariq ignored him and found a plastic shopping bag with another grease stain on it. But as he searched for more evidence, he
could not find the additional items that he anticipated—a mask,
a knife or a pair of leather gloves.

"What is that?" the officer asked him.

Tariq shook his head and refused to reveal his thoughts or

evidence.

He dropped the grease-stained bag back into the trash can and answered, "Nothing."

One of the two men must have been ready to throw away the evidence and was told not to, he assumed. *So there was definitely a professional and an apprentice involved.*

Tariq knew more than the investigating officers. He then looked back out into the crowd of men.

Some of them know who did it, I am certain. But they are all silenced by fear, he mused.

As Tariq looked out into the crowd, Abdul's man, Hakim, continued to watch him while listening to the rumblings and speculation of bystanders.

"Who is he? And how long will they be here? Will there now be a constant police watch in Deira?"

Some of the men were concerned about their privacy. A heavy police presence in their neighborhood only drew attention.

As Hakim eavesdropped from the crowd and watched Tariq perform his work, Saleem, the militant Pakistani man, spotted Hakim amongst the mob of men, and he watched the construction overseer who watched the private investigator.

Not trusting Hakim's intentions, Saleem backed away from the crowd and thought of checking in on Mohd Ahmed Nasir in the building up the street. *Would Mohd feel comfortable with so many UAE police officers combing through the area, where his armed men carry deadly assault weapons?* Saleem imagined not. As soon as he arrived at Mohd's building, he had his answer.

Several men hustled the respected Egyptian leader into the back of a white moving van that had pulled quickly into the dark alley of the building. Saleem had arrived there with perfect timing to see it. But he was not the police, nor would he be a willing witness. In fact, he smiled and nodded to himself.

"The area is now too hot to handle," he mumbled. "Even for me."

He figured with Hakim snooping around, the police might have been swayed to interrogate him like they had done with many other laborers who lived in the area.

But where could I move to with no money? he pondered.

"Saleem," someone called him.

The Pakistani turned to his right, alarmed, and faced a stout Egyptian man who held a folded note in the shadows. Saleem immediately recognized him as one of Mohd's men from the night of the meeting.

"Yes," he answered calmly and stepped forward into the dark. It was an obvious conversation of privacy.

The man quickly handed him the folded note. "Mohd said to contact him there. And leave this area as soon as you can. It is not safe here."

Saleem frowned and breathed deeply, thinking about his lack of income after quitting the construction job. He could hardly buy himself a good meal to eat, let alone move to a new place to live. But before he could open his mouth to explain his situation, the Egyptian man handed him a thousand *dirham*.

"Use that to move your things tonight, and stay at a cheap hotel room downtown. And call the number first thing in the morning."

Saleem stuffed the money and the note into his pants pocket as the man walked away and disappeared into the night. The Pakistani militant liked the Egyptian leader even more now. However, he remained baffled.

"I wonder what they have planned," he muttered to himself. He knew that something was going on. There was too much unexplainable activity for there not to be a plan. A sound explanation was likely to be revealed in his phone call to Mohd that next morning. But at the moment, Saleem agreed with the urgency to vacate the area.

He took two steps out of the shadows toward his building to the north, and a big commotion broke out in the street from the crowd that was now a block away behind him.

Someone pushed, pointed and shouted, "You! I saw you speak to them on the street—two masked men from my window."

With a frantic push and a shove, the crowd of more than thirty turned to face a small Asian man from Laos. Hakim was close enough to the crowd to witness the panic that flashed across the man's face.

With all eyes on him, the Asian man shook his head and responded, "No, no, no me."

He raised his hands in innocence but lacked the fluent English to explain himself. And once the crowd began to advance aggressively toward him, the man could imagine the angry mob attempting to rip him limb from limb, so instinctively, he took off running before it could happen.

"Get him!" someone yelled.

In two seconds flat, the crowd of more than thirty men began to chase behind the delirious suspect, including the alerted UAE police.

"Get him! Get him!"

Saleem watched from the distance and felt sorry for the man. It looked like another chain reaction of planning. *The Art of War* says create confusion. He did not know what to expect from anyone. Every action was suspect, and the Asian man seemed to have been in the wrong place at the wrong time.

He then doubled back, away from the police, and fought his way through the crowd as he started to run in Saleem's direction.

Saleem's eyes grew wide with panic of his own.

"Shit!" he cursed.

He's bringing the crowd and the police straight to me!

He swiftly crossed the street, hoping that they would catch the man before they arrived near him, but it was wishful thinking. The man from Laos was running for his life, and not even several men could bring him down or stop him. He looked like a professional track star and kickboxer, outrunning those who could not keep up with him, while bashing the others who could with vicious kicks and fists. But that only made him look guilty as charged. So the police drew their guns, tired of the clumsy and frenetic street chase.

"Stop or we'll shoot!"

Saleem watched again as the poor man raised his hands high

to surrender. However, as soon as the first police officer reached him to secure him in handcuffs, he spun the officer around in a twist move and pushed him into the others. Then he took off running again.

Hakim and Tariq watched the entire scene in amusement from the opposite end of the street. Hakim had even studied the Asian man's face to see if he had worked for the company, but as far as he knew, he had not.

"Crazy," Tariq finally commented. He had gotten close enough to Hakim to no longer ignore him. "It looks like they've found the perfect man for a diversion."

Hakim smiled and chuckled. "I thought the same thing myself. That man had no idea what was going on. He only knew that they were accusing him of something and were ready to attack him."

In the short distance, once the man from Laos had made it around the corner to escape the angry mob, several UAE policemen had clear shots at him.

"Shoot him!" the chief commanded. Bullets flew.

That was all that Saleem needed to hear before he continued moving. There was no need to look back. There was only more trouble there. Maybe someone in the crowd would point him out as the next scapegoat to chase down and kill.

Something is definitely going on, he thought. *That's four deaths now in two nights ... and all for what?*

Hakim and Tariq were inquisitive themselves, standing a block behind him.

"Who was the first man who accused him?" Tariq asked. "Did you see him?"

Hakim shook his head. "I don't believe he wanted to be seen. It could have been anyone. You just heard someone shout before the pushing started. Then they took off and chased after him."

Tariq grinned, expecting as much. "This is all elaborate scheming." He then eyed Hakim and asked, "So, how much do you know about Mohd Ahmed Nasir?"

Hakim became reflective and thoughtful. "He was a very

proud and intelligent man," he answered.

Tariq listened thoughtfully himself, while bringing his hands to his lips in prayer. From what he knew about Mohd, he had indeed been a wise and peaceful man who had only helped people. Cold-blooded murder did not fit his MO.

"Would you say that he believed in violence?" Tariq asked Hakim.

Hakim was visibly perturbed by the question. "In my first thought of him, I would say no. But then again, any man can become violent when provoked."

Hakim had a guilty conscious, remembering all of the peaceful immigrant men who he had pushed around and bullied over the years to speed up construction.

As if reading his mind, Tariq placed a soft hand upon his shoulder.

"May Allah have mercy and forgive us all."

Hakim could not agree more. He nodded eagerly and added, "Allah is forgiving. Praise be only unto Him."

Chapter 17

ABDUL COULD NOT SLEEP that night. In his Abu Dhabi home and bedroom, he sat up in bed in his white silk bedclothes and continued to think about Mohd Ahmed Nasir and how he had wronged him years ago. Maybe the man's wife would have still died from her ailments, but at least Mohd could have seen her, held her, talked to her and kissed her during those final days and nights of her life. So Abdul continued to feel sick about it.

Merciful Allah! All because of the pressures of my first building, he told himself.

"What is wrong, Abdul?" Hamda, who was beside him, asked.

Abdul shook it off and said, "Nothing."

Hamda sat up with him in their large and elaborate king-sized bed. It had gold trimmings along the head and footboard as well as the sides.

"Abdul, I am your wife. I know when something is bothering you. Who would you rather tell than me? I know all of your most intimate secrets and will die with them. And no form of torture could ever break me."

Abdul eyed his wife and chuckled. "Hamda, you are so over-ly dramatic." Yet he loved her for it. He knew that she had the courage and devotion to back him on anything, even when she disagreed with his methods. But her use of the word "torture" alarmed him.

He asked her, "Why are you thinking about torture?"

"What are *you* thinking?" she asked him back. "I am only reading your restless energy. And something seems to be tortur-ing you right now. Is it work again? Is it the meeting tomorrow with your uncle and the council members?"

Abdul frowned and denied it all. "No, I am not concerned about that. I already know what they will ask me."

"Then what is it?" Hamda pressed him.

Abdul breathed deeply and contemplated. He had already revealed more to his young wife than he could ever feel comfort-able with other men knowing. So he smiled at her, soothingly.

"Most men would laugh at me if they knew how much I have told you and trust in you."

"And those men are *fools* who envy how much your wife loves you," Hamda insisted with intensity. She placed her soft hand on her husband's shoulder. "If I were a man, I would pray to Allah for a woman like me."

Abdul laughed hard enough to wake their son in his room down the hallway.

"Why do you laugh?" Hamda asked. She had concern on her face. She meant what she said and did not consider it a joke.

Abdul continued to smile and held his wife's chin.

"I laugh because I am so fortunate and blessed to have you." And he pecked her lips with his.

"You would patronize me so late at night, would you?"

Abdul smirked. "Of course not. A man always tells his wife the truth at night."

Hamda knew better than to believe his healthy sarcasm.

"That is blasphemous. A million women around the world

could only *wish* that it were true."

"And a million women could only *wish* to have *me*," he countered with another kiss.

Hamda continued to grin, but she was not distracted by his charm. "All of your flattery will not make me forget what I have asked you."

Abdul shook his head again. "You are a tough wife to crack."

"That is why so many suitors were not able to have me," she told him. "They all left my father's house disappointed, all except you."

Abdul felt good inside.

But then he asked himself, *And what if Allah were to take you away from me far too early?*

It was such a horrifying thought that he dared not to voice it. But his pause of thought was pounced on again by his wife.

Hamda persisted, "So tell me, what is still troubling you? There is nothing more that we can do about the Indian worker and his family," she alluded. "We have been very generous to them, but we cannot bring him back. Only Allah has the powers to heal them now."

Abdul nodded. "I know, but it has now become more than that. Investigator and private counsel, Tariq Mohammed, now believes that there is a vendetta against me. And three men have already been killed in the working-class district of Palm Deira."

Suddenly, Hamda became serious. She squinted and asked him, "When did this happen? And *who* would have a vendetta against you?"

She could not believe that any man would have the gall to go up against the celebrated young developer of the Emirates, especially not with violence and murder. Who would *dare* such a thing?

"Just last night. And they were all men who used to work for me ... two of them on my very first building, the International Suites. They were both older men, much closer to their retirement than their prime."

Her husband had her full attention now. In her lime-green

silk nighty, Hamda sat up taller in alert.

"So who is it? Who does Tariq believe?"

Abdul took another deep breath. Now his wife would not be able to sleep. But she had asked him for it and had pressed him to tell it.

"I told him a story today about Mohd Ahmed Nasir, an Egyptian engineer who I denied from seeing his wife during her operation and while on her deathbed back in Egypt. At the time, we were too close to finishing the hotel, and I did not want to chance my best engineer not being available to help us complete it. So I advised him to leave his wife's health in the hands of Allah until we could finish the work on the building. That was several years before I ever met you. And Mohd's wife died only weeks after her operation from complications in her healing process."

Abdul looked into his beautiful wife's passionate, dark eyes. "That is why I waited so late in life to be married. I was obviously shaken by it. And I tried to drown it all out with more work."

Hamda thought fast. "Abdul, you cannot punish yourself for the decisions of Allah. Only *He* chooses who lives or dies on this earth."

Abdul shook his head and grew incensed. He even climbed up out of bed to make his point more firmly.

"But it was *my* decision to forbid him not to go. I cannot absolve myself from that responsibility. And I *fired* the man when he disobeyed me and left anyway. But by that time it was too late. His wife died before he could make it back home to Egypt."

Realizing her husband's discomfort on the matter, Hamda climbed out of bed to join him. She walked over and placed a soft hand on his chest.

"Abdul, you were young. We all make mistakes in our youth."

"Yes, but I seem to have forgotten. And I have pressed on to build more buildings with the same insensitive temperament."

In agreement with his assessment, Hamda stood speechless. Abdul had continued to push forward in his work like a vigorous bull. She liked that about him. However, his bullish demeanor was indeed a bit much at times.

"We shall pray on it," she commented. "The Merciful Allah will forgive you. In the meantime, there is still much work to do. Imagine how many lives you have already saved by providing work and income for so many men with families to feed. Have you ever thought about that?"

"Of course I have. It is what we all say as businessmen: 'I am giving the people work.' But who do the new developments benefit more, me or them, their country or the Emirates? We must admit that they are only hired hands."

"There will always be workers and those who hire them," Hamda responded. "There is nothing you can do about that. But would you rather be the worker or the boss?" Hamda had heard enough of Abdul's self-deprecation, and she wanted him to see himself as a confident and productive *Emirati*. "You are who you are, and Abdul Khalif Hassan is royalty."

The young *Emirati* developer nodded and regained his poise.

"You are right. I am not a poor immigrant laborer, and I never will be. But now we have a problem."

He held his wife by her arms and looked into her eyes again. "If there is indeed a vendetta against me from Mohd or whoever, then I must have even more security around my wife and my son."

Hamda frowned. She did not like the security that was already around them. It was often a nuisance. And although she had gotten used to it as a necessary component of wealth and safety, she could not imagine more of it.

"Then I will remain at home with Rafi, at least until this is all over. And you can keep all of your guards outside of the house."

Abdul cracked a slight grin at his wife's obvious displeasure. Hamda was never one to hide her emotions or thoughts.

"I do not like it anymore than you. But it is a necessary precaution."

"And what of your trips to work and your long hours at the office in Dubai? Maybe you should stay at home with us and work from your study."

Abdul looked appalled. His entire face changed. He did not

hide his emotions well either.

"I will do no such thing. No vendetta will stop me from going to my office to work. That is what they would want me to do—cower and retreat. But I will not do it."

"Then you have still not learned your lesson," Hamda snapped.

"And what kind of lesson is that ... that I am to stop living and performing my work?"

He may have felt guilty about his past with Mohd, but that did not mean that he would allow himself to become paralyzed by it.

Hamda explained, "I would never ask you to stop living your life, only that you would be more thoughtful about *everything* you choose to do. So as I choose to remain at the house for safety, so should you."

Instantly, Abdul thought about all of the whispers he had heard concerning his wife's control over him and her speaking out beyond her place—and he snapped.

"That is ridiculous! You are my *wife*! You do not have to leave for work. But if I were to remain at home, hiding inside of my study, can you imagine what they would say and think of me then?"

"I do not *care* what they think," Hamda lied in their heated argument.

"Well, I *do*!" Abdul yelled. "If I did that, I would never be able to leave my *house* again. They already think of me as too liberal of a man. But I will *prove* to them that I am afraid of *no one* and *nothing*!"

"Well, then, meet Mohd and his men with yours and settle it," Hamda challenged her husband.

Abdul contained himself before he said another word or reacted too hastily. He paused and responded, "Maybe I will."

Hamda was stunned. She did not expect that answer from him, so she stood speechless. Then she heard their son crying from the commotion, and her motherly instincts kicked in.

"Now we've disturbed our son from his sleep."

As soon as Hamda opened their bedroom door to attend to their son in his room, Rafi ran and jumped onto her legs from out in the hallway.

She picked him up and cried, "Oh, I am so sorry, my son. Your father and I were too excited in our discussion."

Abdul spotted his son and smiled to camouflage the intensity of their argument.

"Yes, I am sorry," Abdul told them both. He reached out and rubbed his son's head as Hamda eyed him and smiled back.

"You are forgiven," she said.

Abdul leaned forward and kissed them both on the forehead. "It will not happen again," he said.

Nevertheless, he continued to insist, *But I will not agree to be a prisoner inside my own house.*

Chapter 18

RAMIA LOOKED OUT OF her cousin's Palm Deira apartment window for about the twentieth time in the past two hours, trying desperately to see what was going on out in the streets that night.

"You did hear those gunshots, right? You heard them?" she asked Basim, who stood behind her in the dark. He had turned off his lights because of Ramia's insistence upon looking out of the window at the gathered crowd of men, who were out in front of the crime scene building directly up the street from them. He did not want anyone to finger his young cousin as an eyewitness from the window. But there were plenty of people who stared down into the streets that night. It was only natural human curiosity.

"Yes, I heard them," Basim responded curtly. He would rather she not be so entranced by it all, but she was.

Ramia was more astounded than fearful, though. She couldn't believe that they were that close to chaos. But while positioned a block away and several stories up from the turmoil on the streets, she felt safe from it all. However, Basim did not feel the same way. He stood inside of his dark apartment behind her and was stone-faced.

"We have to move out of here *next week*," he promised. "I can no longer have you in this area. I will have to speak to my boss about the necessary move."

Ramia heard him but did not respond. She remained thrilled by the wonders of her day, including a fun new job, where she had met a very sexy American man staying at the Hilton downtown. She had secretly taken a peek at his drop-off point from the desert tour that evening.

"And where would we move to?" she asked her cousin.

Basim did not know yet. "Maybe the Palm Jumeirah Islands or the city of Sharjah. But I want to remain close to Dubai for work."

"Yes," Ramia agreed with an eager nod. She wanted to remain close to Dubai as well. She planned to do much more exploring on her own there. She had been inspired by a new fascination: an American tourist. She even thought of sneaking downtown to the Hilton Dubai Creek that weekend to see if she could accidentally bump into the man.

I know he had an interest in me. I could tell by how many times he looked and attempted to speak to me, she had told herself a dozen times after leaving her first day of work that evening.

Her youthful thoughts of infatuation with the American and all of the adventures of downtown Dubai became more compelling than the chaos outside of the window, so she broke away from her staring.

"Do you think I will receive a call from the International Suites to work there as well?" she asked Basim breathlessly. "We could both use the extra money."

Ramia also knew that the International Suites was not that far from the Hilton.

Knowing Ramia well, Basim read her excitement with a pause.

"They could call you, but I may not like you working a night shift there. I like the tourist position much better."

Basim realized that there were only so many hours in a day, and he considered the hotel positions more degrading for a young woman, particularly with the beauty and intelligence of his cousin. She could learn so much more about international life in her desert tour position, as well as have more to offer people in her daily interactions there.

"I would rather you work the night shifts at the convenience store behind me than at the hotels."

Ramia frowned and shook it off immediately. Whether they needed the money or not, the last place she wanted to work was behind her cousin at the gas station. So far, after asking his boss several times to hire her, he had not been able to get her a job. But Basim had no idea how nervous his boss would be at having such a young and beautiful woman to work in a store with him during the late hours. Ramia's stunning beauty could be more of a curse than a blessing in that way.

Nevertheless, she was a young woman, and she had a life to live. So she ignored her cousin's sarcastic offering and told him, "I want to go ask the hotel management if they would consider me in the early mornings for a part-time job until lunch hour then."

"What? And how will you get back home? I can take you there, but I have to work tomorrow. I won't have time to drive you back home and get back to work on time."

Ramia frowned again and barked, "Basim, I will catch a *cab*. I am not a *child*. Stop treating me like one."

Basim snapped, "No, you will *not* catch a cab!" He pointed back to his window and asked her, "Do you realize what is going on out there? People have been *murdered*. This is not a game *or* a place for a young woman to travel back and forth alone."

Ramia blurted, "The United Arab Emirates is one of the safest countries in the Middle East."

"Not in *this* area," Basim argued. "We are not the protected *tourists*."

Ramia countered, "Well, I see other women my age who live here every day. And they all do just fine."

Basim looked at his cousin and suddenly held his tongue. He considered her to be above the other young women who lived there in his district of Palm Deira. He did not honor the work that some of them had chosen to do, but he did not know how to say it without degrading them all.

"Well then, I can remain downtown in Dubai and look for jobs at the malls and shops until you are ready to pick me back up from work."

Her young and adventurous mind was working fast with counterarguments already prepared.

Basim took the bait and responded, "But you would be there alone for *hours*."

"Yes, in very public places that are even more crowded on the weekends. Or would you have me remain here in this apartment in Deira all day, where three men were killed last night and two in their own apartment."

The horrific news had quickly spread to everyone in the area.

Basim paused again, acknowledging his cousin's checkmate of an argument. She actually could be safer while job hunting in downtown Dubai, and since Basim was determined to move them out of the area in less than a week—Allah willing—he *did* feel more comfortable about her spending less time there.

Painstakingly, Basim exhaled and agreed to it with a contemplative nod. "But you are only to remain in the best areas. And you stay inside the malls more than on the streets."

Ramia grinned. "Of course."

Her plan had worked beautifully! Then she began to think about what she would wear downtown and to the malls—classy but daring, sexy but respectable, colorful but not loud.

As Basim watched his young cousin smiling away inside the dark room, he knew that he had been duped into something that she wanted very badly. But what could he do about it? He would feel nervous about her either way. However, Ramia was not nervous at all; she was cunning and resilient. Life was life, and people would find ways to live it however they wanted to.

* * * * *

Mohd found his way back to safety and away from Palm Deira. It was only a matter of time before he had worn out his welcome there, and his next location was already prepared and waiting for him.

After midnight, Mohd and seven of his armed men arrived at a warehouse near the industrial park of Jebel Ali on the far side of Dubai, and they pulled into a large garage. They waited inside the van for the garage door to close completely before climbing out.

The warehouse was filled with supply trucks and more than a dozen other armed men, who stood at alert as soon as Mohd appeared before them. They seemed awkward, as if they were confused and did not know what to say. Some of the men were in awe and had never met Mohd.

He nodded and greeted them in Arabic, "*Ahlan wa sahlan.*"

Those who spoke Arabic greeted him back, and those who did not nodded back to him.

Mohd looked around the large barren room and spotted a massive dark-green tarp in the far left corner.

As he eyed the tarp with curiosity, one of the men responded to him in English, "Yes, it is all here." He assumed Mohd wanted to see the supplies that they had gathered there for their mission. So he led the Egyptian leader over to the tarp, where several of the men pulled it back to reveal a collection of updated assault weapons and devices of technology, including several communications system jammers.

Mohd inspected the small black box of antennas in his hands. "Do they work?" he asked the men casually.

They nodded and responded eagerly, "Yes, they do."

Mohd pulled out a cell phone from his pocket and challenged them. "Let me see it."

As the wise old man dialed a number, one of the young men in the room worked the electronic jammer, immediately sending his phone into a constant roaming signal. Mohd attempted to dial a second and third number, but it was no use. The phone would not connect. Finally, he read a "no signal" message.

Impressed by it, he grinned, but only slightly. "Good," he commented with a slow nod. He seemed to be distracted by something else on his mind.

He looked around the large room again and toward an upstairs area that he assumed was for him.

"Yes, your bed and office is there," the same eager soldier informed him. He then led the wise Egyptian to it.

Before they reached the steps and railing to the room upstairs, Mohd looked around again, absentmindedly.

"Where is Heru?" he asked all of the men.

The room froze for a second, as if no one wanted to speak. Then the lead soldier answered him.

"He went to prepare the location."

Mohd remained there at the foot of the stairs.

"Will he be returning tonight?"

Again, there was a pause and a dead silence across the room.

The lead soldier took a deep breath, as if he was tortured by his own answer. "I don't believe so. He wanted to make sure on his own that nothing would go wrong."

Mohd took a deep breath too and nodded.

Then it is too late, he told himself. They walked up the stairs to the room in silence. There was a small desk there with two chairs and a computer. Behind the desk and chairs, against the far wall, was a small cot and a pillow to rest, the same as he had in Deira. It was how Mohd liked it—simple.

"Is there anything else you need?" the soldier asked him.

Mohd turned slowly to face him. "I need to be alone to pray."

"Yes," the soldier agreed with a nod. He then walked out of the room and shut the door behind him.

Mohd proceeded to take off his shoes before he sunk to the floor and crossed his legs with his hands down at his sides, not in the ways of a Muslim, but of Ancient Egypt, where he could meditate with discipline and focus to alleviate his mind and body from stress.

Chapter 19

AS ALL OF THE facts and new tips began to surface on the murder cases in Deira, Tariq spoke with the UAE police chief about what he knew, including the name of the respected Egyptian immigrant and engineer Mohd Ahmed Nasir.

Many of the police and investigators were still up after midnight, attempting to piece together the events of the evening, particularly after the police had shot and killed the poor laborer from Laos. That caused the heavy hitters to be called back onto the scene.

"Mohd? Did you say Mohd? The Egyptian last lived in this area," the UAE police chief commented factually. Ali Youssef was a gray-bearded man in his late sixties who looked forward to retiring soon, but only after a solid apprentice with enough wisdom and experience could take over. So he remained sharply dressed in business attire to appear younger and fresher in his tiresome work.

Tariq confirmed his tip. "Yes, but my most recent information was that he lived in Sharjah."

Ali shook it off. "No, he lives here now. My men thanked Mohd one night a few years ago when he settled another heated dispute in this area. That's how I know. But what about him? You think Mohd had something to do with these atrocities?"

The chief was doubtful. Mohd had been known as a man of peace.

Tariq grinned and did not want to say more around so many ill-equipped men. He did not want them all to know Abdul Khalif Hassan's personal business.

"I will tell you more about it in privacy. But if Mohd indeed lives in this area, then let's knock on his door and ask him what he knows."

The chief looked at his large gold watch. It was nearly one o'clock in the morning. "At this hour? There is such a thing called respect for your elders," the chief joked. The private investigator and counsel was more than a dozen years younger.

Tariq smiled back. "Well, if he helped you before, then why not apologize for your urgency. We can tell him that we meant to seek his advice on this matter much earlier, but that time got away from us. Nevertheless, this matter is still urgent, particularly to consult with a man of your respect and influence."

Ali laughed at his clever reasoning. He placed a kind hand on Tariq's shoulder and said, "When are you coming back to the force? We could always use you. You know I plan to retire soon."

Tariq chuckled. "I think I like to *choose* my work a lot more than I like it being assigned to me. I also prefer to work without the hassles of so many reports." He pointed to his head with his index finger and concluded, "I like to file what I know right here."

"You mean you like to be lazy while choosing to work for more money. I can't argue with that, my friend."

Tariq continued to counter him. "I don't consider sixteen straight hours on the job as lazy. But your point about choosing to make more money is a fact."

Ali reached out to touch Tariq's casual clothes and said, "Although I cannot tell from your style of dress. Maybe that's something else you don't want to do." The chief clapped his powerful hands. "Anyway, let's give Mohd a visit tonight and see what we can find out."

* * * * *

As soon as the chief and his men located Mohd Ahmed Nasir's building from their inquiries on the street, Tariq followed him and several UAE police officers into the gray cement apartment complex and up to the top floor in search of the Egyptian.

They all walked up to room 519 in unison and knocked on the door several times, with no answer.

"Hello. Mohd? *Hotep!*" the chief shouted through the locked door. He could be a loud and abrasive man, even after midnight.

He looked back at Tariq. "What do you think now? Should we break in the door? He simply may not be home."

Tariq shrugged. "He may have left earlier, at the same time that your men chased and killed the innocent laborer."

A few of the lower-ranking police officers fidgeted in embarrassment, but Tariq owed them no allegiances or kindness. They were men in need of more seasoning.

"It was a perfect diversion."

Before Ali could argue his point otherwise, someone cracked the door up the hallway. Tariq and Ali both looked and spotted a small Muslim woman inside the hall.

"He left," she whispered tersely in English. "He and his men." She then pointed at his door, shaking with fear.

Understanding the woman's bravery, Ali nodded and signaled for her to close her door back. She had said enough, and she did not need to make herself a target.

"*Shukran jazeelan,*" he thanked her in Arabic.

When the woman closed her door back, the chief went immediately into action.

"Okay, break it in," he told his men.

Three eager policemen prepared to smash down Mohd's apartment door with force before Tariq stopped them.

"What if there was an explosion behind the door?"

The men stopped in terror and looked toward Ali.

Ali took another look at the door wedge and assumed that everything was normal. Then he sniffed the door and smelled nothing peculiar.

Without another word to anyone, the police chief pulled out his pistol and kicked the door open, using his right foot with the force of a mule. His young policemen drew back, as if expecting a bomb to go off. But with no big boom of explosion, Ali aimed his gun inside the room before entering.

Tariq walked in behind his fearless veteran friend, followed by the shaken officers.

The apartment was empty with only scented candles on the floor. They were equally placed around the room. The chief continued to sniff around the premises, picking up the hovering aroma of hard steel and gunpowder. He knew the cold metal smell and ammunition of high-powered artillery without a need for dogs.

Even Tariq could smell it.

He nodded and stated the obvious. "They tried to cover up the scent with candles."

Ali placed his gun back inside of his hip holster. "I guess we have our man. But this looks like a lot more than just knives." He thought about it and stated his own obvious conclusion. "Something much bigger is being planned."

The police chief looked back at Tariq, expecting another big idea from him.

The private investigator and counsel concluded, "It's all about the workers. This entire area is filled with nothing but laborers. And those who were killed obviously knew too much."

Ali paused. "Well, now we need to find out who else knows and see what they're after," he commented, "and *quickly.*" He eyed Tariq and asked him, "How many hours of sleep do you need?"

At first Tariq hesitated. Then he answered, "None. Let's just keep working."

Chapter 20

TARIQ SAT INSIDE ALI'S unmarked police vehicle so he could tell him in private all that he knew about Mohd Ahmed Nasir and his vendetta against *Emirati* builder Abdul Khalif Hassan. He figured their dispute from years ago could now elevate into a much larger national concern.

Ali listened to it all while sitting in the driver's seat of his parked car, and he nodded. "Interesting. Indeed, I admit the *Emirati* practice of using so much cheap immigrant labor for construction has caused many issues with fair employment and wages. Even these man-made islands from the Nakheel Properties have been built from nearly *all* immigrant hands and have created new real estate and tourism for mostly foreigners."

"Precisely. And how much of this is enough?" Tariq questioned. "How much of the population of Dubai is even local to the Middle East?"

Tariq's own family was from the neighboring Muslim nation of Oman.

Ali shrugged and asked, "So what do you think Mohd and his followers are up to? You think he wants a workers' revolt or an uprising against Abdul and his properties? How many men do you believe Mohd has?"

Tariq thought about it and answered, "A few dozen men with assault weapons would be more than enough."

Both of them understood the strict gun and firearms laws of the United Arab Emirates, but where there was a will there was a way. Desperate men found ways to break laws all over the world.

Ali asked, "You think he has that many men?"

"He could very easily," Tariq answered. "If he has a dozen men here in Deira, a dozen in Sharjah and a dozen somewhere else, they could easily reach fifty."

"With weapons? And then what? Shut down Abdul's new construction sites?"

"Apparently, they have already begun to shut down Abdul's sites. Many of the men have quit since last week. But the guns now confuse me. That would lead me to believe that it is more serious than that," Tariq commented.

Ali paused before asking the unthinkable. "You don't believe Mohd and his men would try anything to harm Abdul's wife or his family, do you?"

A wife-for-a-wife proposition was not out of the question. However, Tariq shook his head immediately, doubting that extreme.

"That would be highly unlikely," he answered. "And I am sure that Abdul has already prepared for it. His wife and child are both very young."

"And his wife, from what I have heard, is also very outspoken," the police chief added.

Tariq grinned and thought of his own wife and young daughter. "They will all be that way very soon. It is the natural influence of the world. Women are regarded much more highly than they used to be. But where do we start now—in Sharjah? We need to go find him."

Tariq wanted to return to the business at hand with Mohd,

but Ali looked very weary behind his wheel. He exhaled and was ready to rest for the evening.

"Since you are now able to pick and choose when and what you work on, you can also choose when you would like to rest. But I do not have that choice, and I have already been called out of bed tonight. So if you are determined to drive out to Sharjah this evening, I can have some of my men go with you there, and I will have more the first thing in the morning when I arrive. But as of right now ..."

Ali looked at his watch again. It was closing in on two o'clock in the morning.

"I pray to Allah that they don't try anything tonight. But I seriously doubt they will. And we will have a few full days to figure out everything starting tomorrow."

Tariq considered the time as well. He had been working on sheer adrenaline all day long, but maybe it was best to rest up and think things through for the next day.

"I hope you are right. And we'll both go to bed then and start things off fresh tomorrow."

"That would be best," Ali assured him. "We can only do so much in a day."

The two men shook hands as Tariq climbed out of the chief's car and walked across the street in the night to his own, a black Saab. Once he sat inside behind the wheel, Tariq called his wife.

"Yes, it's me. I'm on my way home now."

His wife told him to drive safely, and Tariq started up his engine.

* * * * *

As the early morning sunlight began to rise that Saturday, airplanes landed and took off from the airport, trucks and cars made their way in out and around Dubai, and the early shift workers began to arrive at work, while the night shift left, particularly at the countless hotel buildings.

Trucks with fresh food, new sheets and towels and boxes of

cleaning utilities with bathroom supplies would pull up early and often. Supply trucks in downtown Dubai were perfectly normal. So no one became alarmed when the two trucks from the warehouse in Jebel Ali drove into the loading areas at the back of the International Suites. However, instead of a driver or two to unload supplies, the trucks were full of armed men. They backed into the loading gate, where the security guards and storage workers had been tied up and locked into a small bathroom from the early morning and the night before. The hotel's surveillance room, filled with dozens of security camera monitors, was the first thing they had sabotaged. That allowed Heru's men to watch everything going on in and around the hotel, including the movements of the United Arab Emirates police force.

"Hurry up and move into place," the men were told in several languages as they filed out of the two trucks, all dressed in hotel staff and technician uniforms. Several different groups of men split up and hurried to the hotel stairs to enter the building. Another group of men entered the electronics room to disable the phones, Internet and satellite communications systems, all when ready.

Back at the loading gate, the same soldier from the warehouse the evening before had a private conversation with the lead organizer.

"Heru, your father asked us where you were last night, and he did not seem so eager to move forward with our plans."

Heru was taller and younger, with a slight beard, and he was much more rugged than his father. Now in his early thirties, Heru's fierce brown eyes hinted that he was more capable of intense violence as well. He had already shown his lethal combat skills and speed with his knife the night before in Deira.

"That's because my father is still a man of reason. He is completely broken from his tragedy, yet he remains peaceful. As for me, I have not been blessed with the gene of peace. And I assume that my father asked for a private moment to pray."

The soldier smiled and confirmed it with a nod. "You know your father well."

"Of course I do. And my father also knows me. That is why he began to pray. He knows that there is no turning back from this. And we will make our presence felt today."

* * * * *

At the warehouse near the foot of Jebel Ali's industrial park, Mohd awaited a call on his cell phone. A half a dozen men were still there to protect him, while Mohd remained upstairs in his small office, running out of valuable time. Time was of the essence.

"May Allah choose to be merciful," he mumbled to himself.

I fear we may need a miracle to stop my son from his misguided madness, he thought.

* * * * *

Back at the Hilton downtown, Gary began to stir from his sleep. His cell phone was buzzing louder and louder from the nightstand to wake him, but he tried his best to ignore it.

Gary rolled over and slapped it with his hand to shut it off, as if it was an old-school alarm clock. But the cell phone continued to buzz.

"What the hell?" he muttered.

He grabbed the phone to view the call. It was Jonah. Gary checked the local time before he decided to answer. He had no choice. "Okay, what time is it over there, eleven o'clock at night?"

"Wow, you're good. Are you looking at the time translations off your phone?" she asked him.

"No, I'm guessing. But it's only seven in the morning over here, and I'm dead *tired.* So what is it?" he snapped.

"Actually, I just wanted to call and make sure you still had your phone on you."

"Didn't you hear my snoring?" he joked.

"Actually, no. From what I've been able to hear, you're a pretty quiet sleeper."

Gary shook his head and still couldn't believe that he was being tracked like an animal, even halfway across the world.

"Do other people know about phones like these?"

"Those who need to know."

"Yeah, so I guess I get to be one of the first guinea pigs."

"Actually, your father just wanted me to check back in on you, and I told him that I would."

"Oh, it's him again. I guess you told him I'm in Dubai."

"Of course I did. I can't lie to him. But he considers Dubai to be pretty safe. He's been there himself a few times. He believes you'll get into less trouble with the women there."

Gary thought about that and grinned. Had he still been a wreckless dating man, there was plenty of trouble he could get into with the foreign women of Dubai.

Jonah laughed at the idea herself. She said, "I know, right. I still don't think your father understands how incredibly *hot* you are to the young women out here, even when you're not trying to be."

"Yeah, I bet the old man had his ways with women too," Gary said. "After all, he did score with my mom."

"Ahhh, I'm not gonna touch that," Jonah commented.

"So when am I gonna meet him ? *Ever*?"

Jonah sighed, noticeably. "You dad decides when the time is right. I have no control over that."

"You're right. It's too early in the morning for this anyway. So just tell the old man that I'm fine. If he wants to know anything more, you tell him to ask me himself."

For all Gary knew, his father could have been around him countless times at ball games and events without making himself known, perhaps even at Gary's graduation from Louisville. Nevertheless, the cat-and-mouse game between them continued.

Jonah admitted, "You have a lot more patience than I would have. If my father were still alive, I would have pressed the issue five years ago."

Gary heard her out and paused to think.

"Ah, let me not put any ideas in your head," Jonah responded, backtracking.

"Yeah, it's too late for that. You tell the old man I need to see him as soon as I get back from Dubai. You're right. I should have nipped this in the bud a long time ago. And I'm assuming that you're tired of it now too."

"That didn't come out of my mouth," Jonah told him.

"Actually, it did. But don't worry, I won't tell him you said anything. You just let him know that our little game of charades is over. I need to see who he is."

Jonah paused again to compose herself as a show of serious-ness. "I'll be sure to tell him that you said that," she promised.

"Thank you. Now let me get back to sleep."

The problem was that Gary had left his blinds open while staring out at Dubai's skyline the night before, so the sunshine was already blasting through the windows that morning. On top of that, with a sudden growl of his stomach, he was hungry. And the combination of sunlight and hunger forced him to stare up at the ceiling, wide awake.

"I guess it's time for room service," he commented. And he climbed out of bed.

Chapter 21

RAMIA WAS OVERJOYED THAT morning. She had a lot on her mind and was already ironing her clothes to perfection—a lime-green, orange, yellow and brown floral sundress to wear with brown leather sandals. She even had a matching brown leather purse.

Basim opened his eyes in bed and wondered what was going on with her, moving around so early. It was barely after seven in the morning. They would not be leaving out for more than another hour. He had never seen her prepare so early.

"What are you doing?"

"What do you mean, what am I doing? I'm getting my clothes ready to get dressed."

"This early? It's only seven o'clock."

"Yes, and you still have to drop me off at the hotel before you make it to work on time."

"But why are you so consumed by your dress? Are you meeting someone?"

It was the right question, but Ramia planned to dodge it.

"No, I just want to look my best and to look for a second job at the mall. They want nice girls working at the malls," she gushed.

"I thought you wanted the job at the hotel."

"Yes, I do, but if I don't get it, I have to look my best for the jobs at the mall."

Basim stretched his arms and legs and climbed out of his bed to begin getting ready himself. His young cousin had been a constant issue of concern, yet her enthusiasm for life energized him. He wanted to do better in his own life because of her. Ramia made him think of experiencing more and setting higher aspirations for himself. Maybe he could go to the university and learn a profession as well. Why should he settle for store shopwork if he could do more?

Basim's young and wired cousin made him consider options that he had not thought about before. Several new considerations crossed his mind as he walked into his tiny bathroom to shower that morning.

Ramia will make someone a great wife if they could ever manage to keep up with her, Basim mused.

But the young man had no wife of his own, afraid that he could not afford to offer a woman a home.

What kind of life is this for any man? he thought. *We spend all of our days and nights in this place to provide a playground for the wealthy of the world, and what do we get out of it? A few hundred dirham a week to spend on ourselves or to send home to our families. Then what?*

While taking his shower, Basim's mood swung from optimism to gloom in a matter of minutes. Higher aspirations could do that to a man—make him feel how far away he was from achieving them. Sometimes it was easier to think of nothing.

When Basim was dressed and ready to leave for work in his uniform of a yellow shirt and tan khaki pants, his mood had turned completely sour, but he was not willing to reveal it. He was determined to show his cousin nothing short of complete faith in Allah. But all humans had their doubts. Why should one man feel blessed over another? Was it all by design? Basim began to question everything.

In near silence, he led the way out of the building and into the guarded streets of Deira. Ramia followed closely behind him as they reached his modest blue sedan to head downtown and to work, as he had done for the past two years. Before he owned a car, he had caught the bus to work. And although it was not much to brag about, at least he now owned his own means of transportation.

Noticing his cold silence, Ramia asked, "What's wrong?"

Basim shook it off as he opened the passenger side door for her.

"It's nothing. I'm just trying not to be worried about you."

Ramia grinned and slapped his shoulder. "That is something. Stop being so worried. I'll be fine."

She climbed into the car and strapped on her seatbelt.

Basim nodded and walked around the car to climb behind the driver's seat without arguing. That struck Ramia as peculiar as well.

"Is it really bothering you that much that I want to walk around downtown?"

Basim smiled and attempted to make light of it.

"Maybe if you had a chaperone I would feel better about it."

You mean like a handsome American named Gary? Ramia kept that to herself. She didn't want to give her cousin a heart attack. But he was asking for it.

"Don't joke to me if you don't want me to joke back to you," she warned him. She then thought about his own dating possibilities. She had not seen her cousin with a lady friend since she arrived there months ago, and he had not introduced her to any.

"Basim, do you like any girls here?" Ramia asked her cousin tentatively.

With that, she got his undivided attention. Basim grilled her from behind the wheel and said, "Of course I like girls or *women*. What kind of question is that?"

Ramia smiled at his alarm. She said, "I just wanted to ask,

because you have not introduced me to anyone or been out on a date since I've been here."

"And nor have *you*," he snapped at her absentmindedly. He said it mostly out of defensive irritation. But then he caught himself. "If I were to even allow it."

Ramia frowned and said, "If you were to *allow it*? *Really*?"She was more amused than upset by his comment. Basim was showing her a strong hint of his social immaturity. She did not believe that her cousin knew how to act with a woman or at least not with any confidence. He seemed to be a workaholic who would marry late in life if at all.

"What do you think of the foreign women who enter your store to buy things? Are you attracted to any of them? What kind of girls do you like?"

Ramia quickly became fascinated by the subject, and she knew that it would irk him.

"I do not even *think* of such things. I like Muslim women, and I will marry when I am able to provide for a wife."

"*A wife*? You have not even dated anyone."

Basim continued to frown. "Dating is not as important as preparation. You can date a woman all you want, but if you are not prepared to offer her a home, a family and safety, then what is the point?"

"Love, romance, surprise," Ramia answered in order. She had been preparing herself for a relationship conversation with her cousin for *weeks*. She believed that she needed to express it to him sooner or later, because she was not a virgin and she did not plan to allow him to treat her as such.

Basim shook his head and mocked her. "You have been following too much of Western society. And with your concept of love, romance and surprises, without proper discipline and preparation under the laws of Allah, you are sure to have cheating, heartbreak and then divorce."

He continued, "Have you followed those trends from Western society?" Basim knew the divorce numbers well. He had studied them to convince himself that the Muslim way of courtship and marriage was correct and much more stable.

"Well, at least it would be more unpredictable and fun," Ramia countered.

"Unpredictably bad," her cousin argued. "And then the fun would run out."

Despite their difference in age of seven years, Basim's average stature, his studious looks and his clean baby face made him look not much older than she did. Ramia suspected many women could easily view her cousin as too young to take seriously.

"Do you get overlooked by women?" she asked him, almost teasingly. She was not bothered by his traditional Muslim views at all, she just knew that she felt differently.

Basim faced his cousin. "Why are you so curious about my social life? What *is* this?"

"You are my cousin, and I am only concerned about you. I love you, and I do not want to see you so lonely and overworked."

Basim held his composure and took a deep breath at the wheel. They were nearing the downtown area and the International Suites, and he was anxious to drop her off. "Why, do you have someone in mind you would like for me to meet?" he finally challenged her.

That stunned Ramia, but she was up for the challenge.

"I could find one for you, *easily*. But she may not be Muslim. She could be Taiwanese." She had just the woman in mind who was very attractive and pleasant enough to date an inexperienced man, and Ramia was almost certain that Basim had not had much experience with women. He was far too rigid to let himself go.

Basim nodded and pulled into the loading and valet area at the front of the International Suites. It was a twenty-seven floor building of brown-tinted glass, and he was suddenly happy to get rid of his probing cousin.

"Now make sure to call me whenever you head to a new destination."

"You mean like, when I leave the mall to have a dinner with a hot German man?" Ramia teased him.

Her cousin was stunned and speechless. He looked as if he would turn into stone any second.

Ramia felt sorry for him. She smacked his arm. "I was only joking." But Basim remained frozen.

"Are you trying to ruin my day at work?"

By the time Ramia climbed out of her cousin's car, she was more irritated than sympathetic. Her cousin was being overbearing, and it was no longer sweet. However, her teasing him had not helped the matter.

I will not allow him to make me feel guilty about becoming a woman, she told herself as she marched toward the rotating doors.

Inside the car, Basim continued to watch her, hypnotized, as if wondering if he should allow her to walk alone, until finally, he acquiesced.

"I must leave her safety in the hands of Allah and wish her well today," he mumbled to himself. Nevertheless, when he drove off, he thought to himself, *She better call me!*

Chapter 22

RAMIA WALKED INTO THE International Suites, past the eyes of the United Arab Emirates police at the front of the lobby, and headed over to the information desk.

"What times does management review applications today?"

The Indian woman wearing an all-black hotel-staff uniform paused. She sat behind the counter of the information desk in peace, but Ramia's question stumped her.

"Review applications?"

"Yes, I handed in an application earlier this week to work here, and I wanted to see if I could get an interview." She was being very polite but was also assertive in her desire to get a job.

"I see," the Indian woman responded. "Let me check with management."

The middle-aged woman was secretly impressed, and she saw no reason why the hotel management would not hire such a beautiful young woman.

"Yes, I have ..." She looked up at Ramia to get her name.

"Ramia Farah Aziz," she added with a radiant smile. The Indian woman repeated her name and made her own pitch, "... and she is very prepared for an interview."

Then she listened while Ramia waited.

"Okay ... Okay ... Okay ..."

As soon as she tells me something good or bad, I can get ready to head over to the Hilton, Ramia told herself. She remained excited about the prospect of meeting the handsome American man again, if she could be that lucky.

Finally, the woman smiled and nodded. She hung up the phone and said, "The manager pulled your application and said he can speak to you later on today if you are still available around one o'clock."

Ramia couldn't believe it. She was using her job quest that morning as an alibi to see if she could find the sexy American. But she had hit pay dirt, or at least a face-to-face to score another job.

"Oh my, thank you. Thank you," she repeated. Her excitement was genuine.

The older woman asked her, "What position are you applying for?"

Ramia pointed and answered, "Registration."

"Yes, that's what I thought."

As the two excited women made small talk at the information desk, a security guard for the next shift, who was dressed in a black security uniform, walked briskly past them on his way to the basement camera room. The Arab man was right on time for work and walked with a happy bounce in his step. He reached the heavy exit door to the basement and entered the stairwell with no idea what he was walking into.

As soon as he stepped out of the stairwell and turned right toward the camera room, the butt of an assault weapon crashed down on the back of his head.

The security man stumbled forward and fell face down to the floor, knocked out cold.

"That was a good hit, Akil," one of the invading soldiers told the other. They had both been stationed strategically behind the door, waiting for the security guard.

The two men grabbed up the fallen guard and quickly carried him away to tie him up and lock him with the other security men and hotel staff.

Inside the surveillance room, the assailants continued to watch everything inside the hotel, including Ramia at the information desk.

"She is a beautiful girl," one of the eager men commented.

"Yes, I wish Heru would allow us to lock up all the doors now instead of later."

The men laughed, all impressed with the attractive, young Jordanian.

"Nooo, she's leaving," the first man whined.

"Habib, I'm sure there will be other attractive women inside the hotel, including Americans and Australians."

"Americans and Australians?" the man named Habib protested distastefully. "I am much more interested in Spanish and Brazilians."

"Ah, yes, yes," another one of the men agreed with him. They continued to watch the many cameras inside the room as their militia of men continued to make it to their stations around the hotel.

But as the men continued to tease and joke about the many foreign guests inside the International Suites, none of them noticed that their leader had appeared inside the room with them.

"Do you all believe this is a joke?" Heru asked his men sternly.

They turned and were startled by his sudden presence.

"No, no," Habib answered nervously for them all.

They eyed Heru's lethal blade in the holder at his side and understood how dangerous he was, even while they all held guns.

"In a few more hours you will see how serious we are."

The men did not deny it. They had all signed up to help carry out the plans, and they knew that some of them might lose their lives for it. But it was the chance they all took to make a historic stand in the tourist haven of Dubai.

Heru monitored the surveillance system to check particularly for the UAE police who guarded the front door and lobby area. He had no idea that his men were already inside the hotel.

Any minute now, and we will make our move, he told himself. *And the police have no idea that we are right under their noses.*

* * * * *

Across town in the area of Jebel Ali, Mohd finally received the call on his cell phone that he been waiting for all morning. But he did not recognize the number on his screen.

"Hello," he answered tentatively. He remained upstairs at the warehouse in his private office.

"I'm calling for Mohd Ahmed Nasir," the gruff voice of Saleem thundered from the line.

"Saleem," Mohd responded, "this is Mohd."

"I was told to call you," Saleem said, cutting to the chase.

"And I am glad you have. Have you settled in downtown with the money you were given?"

"Yes, I have. And thank you."

"Good, good. Well, I have a very important mission for you. I know you are an excellent military man and highly intelligent. And I need for you to follow your longing for justice."

There was a silent pause over the line.

"Are you there?"

"Yes, I am here," Saleem answered.

"I am making sure, because there is not a lot of time," Mohd commented. "In a life of justice, one must execute swiftly, even against our own when what we choose to do is wrong. Do you understand me?"

"Who is it who has chosen wrong?" Saleem asked.

The question forced a pause from Mohd. He admitted, "It is my only son, Ra-Heru Nasir. He has chosen a mission that has severely troubled me. And I am now too old and too deficient of zeal to deny him. But I cannot deny the pain that he felt in losing his mother when I could not be there for them."

Mohd told Saleem all about the struggle he had years ago with the young *Emirati* developer Abdul Khalif Hassan and how it had caused an unforgiving vendetta, not so much from the father, but from the son.

"Initially, Heru's pain was misdirected, causing him to stray into negligence and anti-social behavior. Then he began to blame me for what he considered a lack of vengeance, until finally, he was able to inspire a following of like-minded men on a mission here in Dubai."

"May I ask what it is?" Saleem questioned him respectfully.

"Yes, you *must* ask. You and several other men are my only allies. And it is the International Suites hotel downtown. They are now in position to take hostages. How far are you away from it?"

"I am not far from it at all."

"Good. Now I must tell you. My son is one of the best in paramilitary combat training. He has learned from instructors in Egypt, Britain and Russia. So he is a very dangerous man, and I would not hold it against you if you were to decide to walk away. But as I now reach out to those who I believe can foil his plans, we must all have courage in times of need to overcome the greatest of our fears."

There was another long pause over the phone as Mohd waited patiently for a response.

Finally, Saleem answered, "I know what it means to lose loved ones in the constant war of life. But to bring that war against innocent people in our individual designs for vengeance is cowardice. Forgive me for my honesty."

Mohd nodded with the phone to his ear. "You are forgiven." Then he added, "It is also cowardice to love your son more than you hate his injustice."

"Well then," Saleem responded, "there are a billion cowards all around the world. A father's love for an only son is natural. But yet, you have now allowed yourself an option to correct the deficiencies of the heart."

"Indeed, I have," Mohd uttered. "May Allah be with you today."

As Mohd ended the call, one of the several men who remained at the warehouse to protect him quickly turned away from the top of the stairs to the office. It was as if he was confused about coming or going.

Mohd caught him and immediately suspected that the man had eavesdropped. But he was not concerned. He had one of his best protectors there with him. And when the time was right, they planned to dispose of the other man.

* * * * *

When Saleem hung up his cell phone at an inexpensive downtown hotel, he had all of his answers.

So the Egyptian son has used the father to rally sympathy and support from groups of angry and impressionable immigrants, who now seek revenge against the Emirati developer, he told himself. *This same Egyptian son was a professional murderer, killing several men in Dubai an evening ago. And now his plan is to take over the International Suites hotel of Abdul Khalif Hassan.*

Saleem had to contemplate it all as he paced through his hotel room while looking out at the downtown skyline. It was a view that he had never been able to afford. And since he despised the practices of the *Emirati* developers, he was conflicted. Although he would never go as far as to take a hotel full of foreign tourists and families hostage to make his point, he acknowledged that the tactic was indeed a radical one.

"If he pulls this off, he will go down in history as one of the biggest terrorists in the world," he mumbled to himself. But it seemed almost inhumane to terrorize a tourist hotel in Dubai, a city of peace and grandeur.

"But grandeur for *who,* only the rich?" Saleem grumbled. *The poor can only stare at it,* he told himself.

Nevertheless, he considered it an atrocity to involve innocent tourists in the gripes of immigrant workers with the *Emirati* developers.

"There has to be another way to settle this." He stopped and spoke toward the window. "But first I must stop Mohd's son from his insanity."

He took a deep breath and thought about his preparations.

They will have guns and access to all of the surveillance cameras, I am sure. But most of the men will not be as good with their weapons or with combat as Heru, so I can pick them off one by one. However, the cameras will expose me. So I will need to take the cameras out as I go along. I can buy a box of dark trash bags and tape to do just the trick.

But his real challenge was Heru himself.

Saleem started to pace the room again, imagining their battle, and it excited him.

What if I were to wear Mohd's son's blood around me like cologne when I greet him again? How would he be able to take that? Then again, what if Heru was to wear my blood? I guess now we will see.

Chapter 23

BY THE TIME GARY had showered and gotten himself ready for breakfast that morning, he was far too energized and curious to stay put for room service. Why travel halfway around the world just to eat inside of a small hotel room? So he decided to get dressed for the dining room buffet that was being served downstairs.

I'm in Dubai. Socialize, he told himself as he left out of his room. Gary rode the elevator down into the lobby with the other guests, wearing a tan button-up, short-sleeved shirt, while the tourists all discussed where they were from, how long they had been there, and what they had all experienced so far. And there were fewer children at the Hilton than he imagined; it had more business travelers and older couples.

At the buffet downstairs, the food options were plentiful, including the normal serving of scrambled eggs, bacon, sausage, pancakes, potatoes, Belgian waffles, French toast, yogurt, bagels, fruit and pastries that any American would be used to, including orange juice, cranberry juice, apple juice, low-fat milk, tea and coffee. On the side, they had chefs cooking personal omelets.

Wow, this is just like home, Gary thought as he grabbed a large white plate to collect what he knew. He hadn't eaten yet at the breakfast buffet since he arrived in Dubai on Thursday, but on a Saturday it looked like the thing to do. Everyone was there to eat, the lines long. He found a lone, small table in the corner of the room to people watch.

Different cultures of people but the same ritual of humans eating, meeting and greeting at breakfast, Gary told himself in his chair, watching.

He took the opportunity to relax and reflect on his life and his trip for a minute. It felt good to be able to travel again for leisure. He had been locked into focusing on finishing school, getting trained in marketing and business, before committing himself to years of military survival skills training under the watchful eye of Jonah. And he had quickly lost track of time. Five years had flown by him in a blink.

With no family, job or major responsibilities, Gary saw no reason not to travel more. He wanted to see the world, to visit its most exotic corners, to understand its various cultures, to experience its foods, smells, sounds and people. There was only one major obstacle: a new girlfriend.

Maybe it won't be a good idea to settle down with Karla. Would she allow me to travel wherever I want without her? Or would I take her with me sometimes?

He still had a lot of thinking to do, but first he owed her a catch-up phone call.

By this late afternoon, she should be up, he mused. *Maybe I'll call her around six, which would be around ten in the morning DC time.*

As he thought about making the call, his cell phone rang and startled him again. He looked down at the screen and read Johnny Napur's local number. He hesitated.

"Do I really feel like hanging out with this guy again?" he mumbled out loud. He had a long day of sightseeing ahead of him, and outside of another tour, who would know Dubai better than Johnny?

"Hello," Gary answered.

"Hey, man, good morning. I'm back in business at the airport, and I've made over five-hundred *dirham* already. What are you doing, up eating breakfast?"

Gary looked down at several plates of mostly finished food. The cold eggs and potatoes had fared the worst and were still there.

"Yeah, you're late. I had breakfast already, but I'm still sitting here."

"Well, after around three or four, I can take you out to the Dubai malls today. They're packed on the weekends. But I have to make some more money out here first. Unless you could pay me a tour fee," he added.

Gary thought about it and didn't have a problem with Johnny as a tour guide, especially since they had gotten away from the recreational women and drugs talk. Johnny was just a fun-loving, fast-talking normal guy.

"All right. I'll pay you ... I don't know, a thousand *dirham* for the day."

That was roughly three hundred dollars. Johnny jumped at it.

"Okay, that's a deal."

"But don't pick me up until after two. I might go and hang out at the pool today, or take a walk along the waterfront or something."

"Go do it. Enjoy yourself. I can make another four-hundred *dirham* by then."

"Knock yourself out."

Gary hung up the phone and exhaled. *Another day with Johnny. What did I just get myself into?*

* * * * *

Ramia walked into the revolving doors of the Hilton Dubai

Creek with anticipation and excitement.

What if I actually see him? she asked herself of the hand-some, green-eyed American. *And what if he's with a woman?*

She thought about it quickly and concluded, *I'll just walk on by then.*

After nine in the morning, the breakfast room was the obvious place to look. After that, she planned to check the swimming pool.

* * * * *

As soon as Gary stood up from his chair to leave the dining room, he spotted the same young Jordanian woman with the magnificent hazel eyes from the desert tour.

"Oh, shit!" he responded, but he couldn't remember her name.

She stopped her walk halfway through the dining room and noticed him as well. They stared at each other for a few seconds as if both hypnotized.

"Hey, aren't you from the ah—"

"Yes, Dubai Safari Tours. Ramia," she told him, grinning.

"I'm Gary," he responded.

She nodded and said, "I remember." *If only he knew just how much I remember him,* she thought.

"So, what are you doing here?" Gary asked. "You have a room here?"

She chuckled. "No, I applied for a job."

"Another one?"

She continued to smile. Even at thirty-one, with his five years of military focus, Gary's boyish charm was apparent.

"Yes," she said. "I want money to go back to school."

Gary had heard that before. It seemed that many foreign women were trying to pay for school. But Ramia was indeed working at it.

"Okay. The American University of Dubai?"

"Yes. How did you know?"

"I guessed," he lied. There was no benefit in telling her the truth, that other women in Dubai had expressed the same thing to him.

"So, how do you like it here?" she asked.

"What's there not to like?"

Their comments could have meant many things, so Ramia smiled and looked away, bashfully. She was thinking much faster than he was. Then there was an awkward pause between them.

"So, did they hire you?"

It was sarcasm intended for a laugh. He could tell now that she liked him, and there was no urgency for her to leave.

"Not yet. But I filled out an application also at the International Suites not far from here."

"But you like this one better, right?"

"Of course. It's the Hilton," she told him.

"Well, are you in here to eat?" he finally asked her.

"No, I was actually just taking another look around the hotel."

"Oh."

Awkward silence again.

"Well, you want me to walk with you? I was just about to head out to the waterfront."

Ramia grinned. "Yes, the waterfront would be a good walk."

"So, you'll show it to me?"

She paused to calm her eagerness. "Yes, but I have to be back at the International Suites for an interview."

"What time?"

"Before one."

"Well, we better get to walking then," he told her. "That's a good three hours. And I'll treat you to lunch."

"Really?" she asked with sincerity.

He shrugged. "Yeah, why not?"

* * * * *

In Abu Dhabi, Hamda Sharifa Hassan prepared herself and her son, Rafi, for a big visit at their honorable uncle Sheikh Al Hassan's home. Abdul had already gotten dressed and ready

that morning while on his cell phone with his investigator and
counsel, Tariq Mohammed. Abdul was downstairs, dressed in
the traditional all-white Muslim garb topped by a checkered red
turban.

"So you have not found him yet?" he asked as he paced the
room.

"We will find him soon enough," Tariq said.

"And you have no clues where he and his men may strike?"

There was silence over the phone. Tariq answered, "We
were certain you would be well prepared for any uprising in
Abu Dhabi, but we do not know where else he may strike at this
moment. However, we are now convinced that he has an expert
killer amongst the group. There seems to be a lead enforcer here
among the amateurish men."

Abdul stopped his pacing to think. "So you believe that he
may have someone else to execute his plans?"

"From what I have discussed with the chief of police and
other witnesses in Deira, Mohd continues to be a riddle—a wise
man of peace surrounded by younger men with guns. So I am not
certain of anything at this moment, but there does seem to be a
more passionate motive here than what Mohd seems capable of.
Although he does have a tremendous amount of respect from the
immigrant workers in the area," Tariq added.

Abdul began to pace the room, in thought again as his wife
and son appeared at the top of the staircase.

Hamda smiled and said, "You are going to wear out your
shoes, Abdul. Walking back and forth in circles will not help to
solve anything. You are only showing more of the tiger spirit in
you."

Abdul smiled back and was impressed with the beauty of his
wife and son. She had adorned herself and Rafi with dark beads
and gold jewelry.

"You look *fabulous*, both of you," he expressed in contrast to
their bitter argument from the night before.

Hamda continued to grin until she witnessed the large group
of armed security men outside of her home. They were stationed

at practically every window and door. But at least they were not inside the house.

The security is a bit much, she told herself. But she did not want to discuss it around her impressionable son. *I will discuss this with Abdul when we have a minute of privacy later. I feel like a prisoner.*

Seeing that his family was now ready to leave, Abdul ended his phone call.

"Please update me on this matter throughout the day with texts or e-mail," he informed Tariq. Cells phones were indeed a priceless asset all around the world.

Hamda overheard her husband and shook her head. When he was done with his call, she told him, "You are to give the honorable Sheikh your undivided attention, or else you set a bad example for your son."

Abdul looked at his son and did not imagine that he would be in the same room with the elders when they spoke in private. Surely there would be a small council of sheikhs there to speak to Abdul about the recent events of his construction, and Rafi would definitely not be included in the room to hear them. So Abdul took it as another lapse in his wife's judgment to be so outspoken in front of their son. Hamda was far too eager to express her opinions, no matter the cost.

She is such a smart and beautiful woman, but she needs so much more training in good manners, he told himself.

They walked outside and into the center of armed men.

"Let's go," Abdul repeated to them all.

Half of the two dozen armed men headed for the Cadillac SUVs that surrounded the family Rolls Royce. The other dozen continued to guard the house.

Abdul climbed into the car with his son placed between himself and his wife. *It's better to be safe than unfortunate.*

At the same time, Hamda frowned and thought, *Will I ever learn to get used to this?*

Chapter 24

AS TIME TICKED AWAY on Saturday morning inside the warehouse in Jebel Ali, the plan to act became urgent.

Mohd looked down at the clock on his cell phone and saw that it was after ten. He then told himself, *The time is now!*

He quickly walked out of his second floor office room and stood at the top of the stairs to signal to his loyal protector. The tall Arab man below had been waiting for the signal all morning, with his assault weapon in hand. A nine-millimeter pistol and a seven-inch army blade were both in holsters at his side. The man was fully loaded.

Recognizing the signal, he immediately fired his assault weapon into the unsuspecting bodies of the relaxed men who surrounded him inside the room.

Three of the seven other men were hit, while the remaining four ran for cover behind the trucks and various obstacles inside of the warehouse.

"Bakar, what are you doing?" one of the men shouted at him

OMAR TYREE 179

from behind a cargo truck.

But there was no reason to answer. Bakar meant to kill them all, or they would likely kill him and imprison Mohd. So he moved into a better position to shoot and to protect himself, while Mohd ducked back into his office upstairs and found a pistol of his own.

The heavy artillery continued to splatter throughout the warehouse.

"Bakar has lost his mind!" the men continued to yell as they took cover.

More bullets were released from three directions. Another man was hit and killed instantly when Bakar's shot cut through his neck. With three men remaining, Mohd took aim from the top of the staircase with his pistol and a clean shot that Bakar did not have.

In an instant, Mohd decreased their number down to two.

"What is going on?" the remaining Arab men shouted. "Mohd, why are you doing this?"

Mohd listened and breathed deeply before he answered, "Because I do not believe this is the correct way to make our point. In fact, I should not have allowed it to go this far."

The remaining men heard his reasoning and were close enough to eye each other. They had no problem with surrendering.

"We can put our guns down, Mohd. You do not have to kill us."

Mohd paused as Bakar looked up at him to await his response.

"Yes, Mohd. We were not included with the rest of the men for a reason. Many of the men do not agree as well. But your son, Heru, he is very convincing."

"Yes. You either agree with him or you die."

Bakar continued to await Mohd's response. He knew exactly how intimidating Ra-Heru had been with the men, and he would not have even *dreamed* of attacking him. Heru was that impassioned and lethal. Despite his average frame of five foot ten, they all considered him to be invincible in his skills of combat and assassination.

As Mohd continued to contemplate the fate of the two men, he admitted to himself that he had allowed his son to advance in his plans because he secretly wanted to feel the energy of vengeance for his wife and family himself. Abdul Khalif Hassan, with his selfish determination to build at all cost, had brought great pain to the Nasir family and to the families of many other immigrant men who had toiled for him far below their value. So it was Heru's idea to wound the young *Emirati* developer where it would hurt and embarrass him the most—at his cherished hotel of international tourism.

Abdul Khalif Hassan would not only lose the honor of his family and his name, but he would lose the faith of the *Emirati* council and live for the rest of his life at the center of international bloodshed. With Mohd's immense understanding of the angry, disrespected and underpaid immigrant workers, their uprising at the hotel would also serve as a statement to all of the *Emirati* rulers that their policies for cheap foreign labor would no longer be tolerated.

However, as they neared the execution of their plans, Mohd's reservations increased until he could no longer agree. He then devised his own plans of a counterattack from the inside to thwart his son Heru and his loyalists.

After deep thought, Mohd nodded, agreeing to spare the men their lives.

"Put down your guns and walk forward with your hands up and in front of you."

The remaining two men placed their assault weapons on the ground and walked out from their barricaded positions in the room as Bakar covered them.

* * * * *

Outside the warehouse in Jebel Ali, several shipment workers overheard the volley of heavy gunshots and immediately called to alert their superiors on their cell phones.

"Yes, we just heard many gunshots coming from a warehouse we passed."

"Where? Where are you?"

"It was a few minutes before we reached the entrance to the docks, on a back road."

The shipment authorities on the other line hung up and immediately called the police.

"Yes, a couple of my workers just heard gunshots coming from a warehouse right outside the docks in Jebel Ali."

"They heard gunshots in Jebel Ali?" the police dispatch repeated.

"Yes, on a back road outside the docks."

The shipment supervisor named several roads in the area of Jebel Ali where some of the men would usually drive.

"Thank you."

The UAE police dispatch called Chief Ali Youssef as instructed. The chief had been on standby for any breaking news that morning, and he had directed all of the dispatch officers to be on keen alert for any and all incoming calls.

At the time of the call, the chief had just pulled up to join his force of police officers and investigator Tariq Mohammed in Sharjah.

"Yes, Chief Youssef," he answered through his squad car radio.

"There was a report of gunshots a few minutes ago at a warehouse right outside the shipment docks in Jebel Ali."

"Send ten squad cars there, and tell them to alert us immediately."

"Yes."

"And you continue to call me directly on anything else."

Tariq read the urgency in the chief's voice and body language as he climbed back out of the car.

"Did they find something?"

"Gunshots at a warehouse outside Jebel Ali."

Tariq's face lit up on a strong hunch. "That's it. A warehouse is large enough for many men with guns and supplies for an uprising."

Ali's response was more measured. "I thought of that myself, of course. But something tells me that is far too easy. So we let my men check there first, and if it is indeed what you believe, we will send our whole force there. But if it is not, we do not want to be fooled again into another distraction. They could be simply pulling us away from something much bigger."

Tariq nodded and understood the chief's point. He had an entire force of men to lead and his reputation to uphold. He was not allowed to jump to fast conclusions. However, they had found nothing there in Sharjah that morning after hours of searching, and Jebel Ali was just the place to hide a large group of men who could remain out of sight for weeks. There were large enough warehouses there to play a full game of soccer, so surely many men could remain there comfortably.

So Tariq wasted no time in heading to his car to drive there quickly.

"Where are you going?" the chief asked him.

"To Jebel Ali. You cannot make that decision, but *I* can."

Several of the surrounding police officers cleared a path so he could reach his car and back out of his parking space. The chief followed after him.

"If they are so organized and discreet in their plans to strike out, then what would be the purpose of shooting off their guns inside of a warehouse? It makes no sense."

"That is exactly why I'm going there to find out. There may be more clues there."

The chief nodded while admitting to himself that he did not have the energy of Tariq.

"You call me if you find something," he told him. He was actually pleased that his friend was heading to the warehouse. He knew that Tariq would be more thorough in his approach than his men would be.

"I will," Tariq promised.

As the private investigator and counsel drove off in his car, Ali continued to stare and think about him. *You really need to be the next chief of police, my friend. And I am fortunate to be working with you again.*

* * * * *

While Tariq drove hastily to the area of Jebel Ali in the southwest, he thought about the proximity to Abu Dhabi, farther south.

But they would be insane to go into Abu Dhabi, he assumed. *Not even Chief Youssef has mentioned the idea.*

Nevertheless, Tariq called Abdul to discuss the most recent information with him. But his first call went unanswered. Tariq was never one to leave messages. His work was too confidential.

"Hmmph," Tariq grunted.

I believe he has a family meeting this morning, he thought. *Maybe he'll call back when he gets a moment.*

* * * * *

Abdul quickly eyed his cell phone inside the car but did not answer it. He could feel his wife's eyes burning through his skin without even looking at her. After her earlier conversation with him, Hamda was practically daring her husband to answer his phone.

I need to know what Tariq has found out, but not right now, he told himself. *I will call once we arrive.*

But once they arrived at his uncle's, the Sheikh met him and his caravan of cars out in front of the house at the roundabout driveway, and he was disturbed that so many security men had come with him.

"What is all this?" the Sheikh asked.

Abdul was embarrassed by it himself. "After some recent events, the police and my advisors asked me to be careful," he answered.

"Be careful of what?"

The Sheikh did not understand the extra security, and he had not been informed about the details from his nephew.

"I will explain it shortly," he promised.

He did not want to address the details in front of his son and his men.

Sheikh Al Hassan exhaled wearily and decided to hear his nephew's explanation over their meal. He then greeted Hamda and Rafi with hugs and gentle kisses on the cheeks as they entered his massive and remarkable home of earth-tone stone and columns and domes inside of acres of gated land.

Abdul, Hamda and Rafi were greeted warmly by aunts, cousins and servants in Arabic.

"Ahlan wa sahlan. Sabaah al-khayr."

The men were then free to separate from the women and children, where Sheikh Al Hassan led his nephew Abdul into a large meeting room to the right. Hamda, Rafi, and the other women, children and servants headed to the left and their own private area.

Before walking in, the elder Sheikh Al Hassan stopped his nephew at the door to speak in a hushed tone. "Allow Sheikh Al Rashid to make his points without disturbance. It will be much better for you to hold your tongue and allow the rest of us to handle him. Do I make myself understood?"

Abdul nodded. He already knew what he was in for. Sheikh Al Rashid could be a very temperamental man. "Thank you."

Inside the room of men was a large oval table that was filled with fruit, salad, bread, food, wine, water, plates, napkins and silverware. Ten royal chairs with red cushions and high golden frames surrounded the table, where the elder, Sheikh Al Rashid, sat at one end and Al Hassan at the other. They were joined by Sheikh Al Naseem and the young Sheikh Al Falah, who was in his early thirties and of royal lineage.

Abdul greeted them all with individual hugs.

"As-salam alaykum."

He then took a seat next to Sheikh Al Naseem. After a short prayer from the elder to bless their meal, the men began to eat and discuss Abdul's recent events immediately, starting with the elder.

Sheikh Al Rashid asked, "Abdul, how do you feel about the mess you have made with your most recent construction?"

The elder planned to pull no punches. He had invited Sheikh Al Falah to their important meeting that morning for him to learn more about the pitfalls of development. Al Falah planned to enter the business of construction and development as well.

Abdul cleared his throat and held his composure. He knew that the young Sheikh had been invited there to learn from him, so he answered, "There is always the unexpected with any construction."

"But many of these problems have been caused by *you* and your rush to finish by any means. Is that not true?" the elder asked him.

Abdul's uncle Sheikh Al Hassan was helpless to defend his nephew until the elder had asked all of his questions. It had already been agreed upon. Abdul would have to stand his own ground, and respectfully.

He nodded and said, "Indeed. Some of it has been."

The other council members began to fill their plates with food as Abdul continued to answer. The young Sheikh Al Falah paid strict attention.

The elder commented, "And now you have instigated a commotion with many of your immigrant workers. Is that also correct?"

Abdul briefly looked to Al Falah before he nodded. "Yes."

He had no appetite at the moment and did not move to fill his plate, as he felt put on the spot by the elder. The Sheikhs of the United Arab Emirates were briefed on many concerns involving their nation, particularly those surrounding the tourist city of Dubai. The city represented a great leap into the business of the Western world. Yet Dubai also caused great concern for many of the elders of the ruling class, who feared too much Western influence in their rich, young nation.

The elder continued with his interrogation after a bite of watermelon. "Now tell us about your personal history with the Egyptian Mohd Ahmed Nasir. I believe he was one of your first building engineers."

Abdul's eyes grew large as he was shocked by the Sheikh's inside information. He immediately thought of his private counsel, Tariq Mohammed.

Why would he tell them? he asked himself.

The elder read the young man's surprise and addressed it with authority, as he had planned to do that morning.

"Abdul, do you realize that your rash executions with construction have now caused a national alert? You cannot withhold such pertinent information. These buildings are not yours alone. They belong to all of the Emirates in the sense that we have *allowed* them to exist," the elder reminded him.

"There are no buildings that can be erected in this nation without the Exalted One's agreement and the confirmation from the council."

Abdul realized as much, nevertheless, he had rarely been forced to deal with the ruler of the United Arab Emirates or the council of elders on even a *monthly* basis. There were far too many developments going on in and around Dubai and the UAE for that much personal attention. But while he was on the hot seat, Abdul realized that the safety of their nation depended on transparency of information on any grave danger.

The elder was relentless to make his point. "Now you have hired an army of men to protect you and your family. But who will you hire to protect everyone else?"

Sheikh Al Rashid allowed the young developer to sit and take his medicine all in one dose. He wanted to make it perfectly clear that his immaturity and reckless business practices would no longer be tolerated.

"This has come down from the Prime Minister himself, the Honorable Sheikh Al Maktoum. So tell us, what is your past relationship with the Egyptian?"

Abdul realized that the Sheikh already knew some of the story. However, he was being forced to tell the rest of it in his own words for more clarity and questions. And although he would bring up the revelation of his story to his hired man Tariq, he realized that his private counsel had a responsibility to reveal any and all information that would serve to endanger a number of people in the United Arab Emirates who were far more important than Abdul's privacy and business practices.

So Abdul took another deep breath, and as his uncle nodded to him to come clean, he began to tell them all his personal story.

"Mohd Ahmed Nasir was an excellent engineer on my very first development ...."

Chapter 25

MOHD ORDERED THAT THE two surrendering men be
tied up in the back of the white van with him as Bakar backed
the small service vehicle out of the warehouse to head to Dubai.
Mohd had been tipped off through his sources that the investigating police were in search of him the night before in Deira,
followed by a search that morning in Sharjah. So he dared not to
sit up front in the van with Bakar. The wise Egyptian needed to
remain in hiding. And after their desperate shootout inside the
warehouse, there was no longer time to deliberate his plans. It
was now or never.

Just as the white van pulled out of the warehouse, a phone
call went out from a spy who was planted outside the building.

"Just as you expected, your father has escaped and they are
now headed in your direction."

"Thank you. I was prepared for it." And that's all that was
spoken.

As Bakar turned the white vehicle onto the main road, he

had noticeably changed into a light-blue uniform of a shipment worker, and he convinced himself to drive casually as instructed. Mohd did not want him to bring any attention to himself with any nervousness or haste at the wheel. And it was a good thing that Bakar had listened. Three police squad cars shot past him, headed in the opposite direction toward the warehouse.

Mohd heard the sirens and remained calm inside the back of the van as the sirens passed. But his two prisoners panicked with wide eyes. Both young radicals from Syria, they did not believe the UAE officers would be a blessing and save them. Instead, they would be served a crueler form of justice in the young but intolerant Arab nation. They imagined themselves being tortured, shot and hung there, but they would rather die fighting with their hands on their guns.

"What if they find the blood of the slain men inside the warehouse?" one of the prisoners questioned.

He was curious to see if he could bring a sense of alarm to the elder. So far, Mohd did not seem the least bit concerned about anything. He had forced the young Syrians to remove the bodies of the deceased and place them in a storage room that they locked at the warehouse, but they did not have enough time to clean up all of the bloodshed, only most of it.

Mohd answered, "Until they bring the dogs to sniff out the warehouse and find the bodies, we will have enough time to make it to Dubai and the hotel."

The second imprisoned man eyed the wise Egyptian and asked, "As a man of peace, how do you now feel with fresh blood on your hands?"

It was an incriminating question of guilt, but Mohd handled it well.

"I was a soldier myself as a young man in the Egyptian Army. That is where I learned my trade of engineering. So I have killed men before. But as you see me now as a man of peace, I can only tell you that the greater good in the eyes of Allah is much stronger than our necessary evils."

The first prisoner grinned and responded, "Even peaceful

men have been known to twist the intentions of Allah to serve their own reasons."

Mohd countered, "And some of the most peaceful men have been called upon throughout history, in times of human need, to become fearless warriors, driven by the passion of divine intervention. And only Allah gives us this power."

The Syrians stopped their argument and looked at each other. They could not disagree with the man's logic. They believed in divine purpose and intervention themselves. Unable to match Mohd's intellect and reserve, they chose to remain silent. To debate with the wise Egyptian would be useless. But when they heard another whine of police sirens outside of the van, they panicked with wide eyes again. It sounded as if the new sirens were right there behind them, and they were. However, the second group of police cars that were headed from the right just missed an intersection with the van as Bakar continued to drive forward.

With two close calls at the wheel, Bakar remained nervous, but he was remarkable at holding himself together. He felt for sure that the UAE police would stop him in their white van and force him to open fire on them with the assault weapon. He had placed it on the floor below the passenger seat, and he knew at no time was he to stop their vehicle without firing bullets to back the officers away and protect his elder. But so far it had not happened, and when their white van reached the busy streets that were closer to Dubai and away from the industrial area of Jebel Ali, Bakar was able to breathe normally again.

Praise be to Allah! he told himself. *Maybe we'll have a chance to arrive at the hotel and help save the day.*

* * * * *

When Tariq Mohammed arrived on the scene at the empty warehouse in Jebel Ali, he joined more than a dozen UAE police officers and began to reimagine what had happened there. The officers also brought a police dog to sniff out any evidence that would go unseen by humans. In no time, the dog led them to several areas around the room where there had been gunpowder and bullet shells, before finally taking them to a locked storage room.

"What's behind there?" one of the men asked rhetorically. The dog had gained all of their attention.

Tariq looked on as well, while inspecting the rest of the room.

After breaking open the storage room door, the officers responded instantly to the sight of five murdered men with bullet wounds.

Tariq moved in to investigate the slain men. He carefully studied the angle of bullet entries into their bodies. The men hadn't been dead that long either; their blood remained fresh.

Tariq then looked to the upstairs area and what appeared to be an office on the second level.

He nodded to himself and was convinced of his conclusion. "Mohd was here, and he has decided to take matters into his own hands."

He searched around the massive room again and came back to the empty spaces near the warehouse's rolling doors, where several vehicles had enough room to park.

"Did any of you pass a truck or two on the way here?"

The officers searched each other for a response.

One of the officers commented snidely, "This is Jebel Ali. We passed plenty of trucks, and I saw none of them that appeared to be anything but normal."

The officer had a point. Jebel Ali was the nation's primary shipment area. There were plenty of trucks driving in and out at every hour of the day.

"Perfect," Tariq responded. The insurgents had indeed picked an ideal place to remain undiscovered.

Tariq took a deep breath and thought, *This may be much harder than I thought. And where are the other men that a place this large could hold?*

He immediately pulled his cell phone from his hip to call the chief of police back in Sharjah.

"Mohd was here, and he left only recently," Tariq informed his old friend. "But there now seems to be some infighting. Maybe he did not agree with the direction of his men."

"Which would mean that he is no longer in charge," the chief commented. "Interesting. So, what all did you find there?"

"There are five dead bodies here and plenty of space for at least a hundred men and supplies."

The chief paused momentarily. "I seriously doubt if they have that many. But no matter how many they have, they will turn up sooner or later. Hopefully, we will find them before they are able to do anything disastrous."

"Indeed," Tariq agreed with the chief.

He hung up his phone and continued to think. *What would be the most likely target for an angry group of immigrant workers to make their disagreements with the Emirati rulers of the United Arab Emirates known?*

Tariq reflected again on the history of the dispute between Mohd Ahmed Nasir and Abdul Khalif Hassan, and he froze. Suddenly the private investigator's eyes widened as he considered the most obvious target. "The International Suites," he commented out loud.

The officers looked on and were dumbfounded. They had no clue about the history.

Tariq reminded himself, *That is where it all began, to finish his first hotel years ago.*

Without an explanation or another word to the men, Tariq hurried to return to his car while redialing the chief on his cell phone.

"Yes, Tariq, what is it now?" the chief answered urgently.

"The International Suites hotel. What if that is the target?"

The chief said, "I thought of that idea as well, right after you told me Abdul's story. Even the Sheikh suggested that we send men there."

Tariq reached his car outside the warehouse and repeated, "The Sheikh? You told them about this?"

"Of course. This is now a national security concern, and it is much bigger than Abdul and his ego. So we sent men to all of his buildings, including his offices downtown."

The chief continued, "Abdul is only one man, but thousands of other people work, sleep, eat and are in and around his buildings every day. And that makes this vendetta important to us all."

Tariq nodded and was quickly reminded of how much responsibility his friend had. He was actually impressed with the amount of command Ali was exerting as the chief of police. In the meantime, as a private investigator and counsel, Tariq was forced to drive around to all of the locations himself, starting with Abdul's first hotel.

"Well, I will go and join them at the hotel then," Tariq informed his friend.

"You do that. And you tell me what you find there as well."

Tariq hung up his phone and started his engine with a new concern: his employer's policy on privacy. But there was nothing he could do about a national security alert. Abdul would need to understand the level of importance his case had taken on for the nation and face up to the music. Abdul's personal story was at the center of it all, and there was nothing he could do to change it.

* * * * *

After a second phone call and conversation with Tariq, Ali made a check-up call of his own down to his men at the International Suites in Dubai.

"Anything to report there at the hotel?"

"No, nothing. We've been here all morning and everything is fine," the officer told him.

Ali paused to think, then said, "Have you and your men checked the back loading area for trucks and shipments?"

The officer paused himself. That was a bad sign for the chief.

He answered, "The trucks and shipments have been fine as well."

"What about the hotel security? Are they where they are supposed to be?"

"Yes, we saw the daytime shift security walk in earlier, more than an hour ago."

"What about last night's shift? Did he walk out?"

"Good question. I don't know. He could have changed out of his clothes where we wouldn't notice him."

Ali continued to probe for more answers. "Did you check in on their surveillance system inside the camera room?"

The officer paused again. "No, we have not. Do you want me to send someone?"

"No, I want *you* to go and find out for yourself, then report back to me immediately," the chief told him sternly.

"Yes, I will."

As soon as he ended his call, Ali felt fortunate again to have Tariq on his way over to check the hotel out.

"We can never have enough good men," he told himself. He realized that it was going to be a long day.

* * * * *

Inside the surveillance room of the International Suites, Heru's men had been watching every move of the UAE police officers in and around the hotel that morning. So when the lead officer gathered up six of his men inside the lobby and headed toward the security entrance door for their basement location, the men called for a red alert on their high-tech walkie-talkies.

"Yes," Heru answered them instantly.

"The police are finally headed toward us in the basement."

Heru was calm and deliberate in his response. "It is time then. And we are all in position. So do what you must do."

The surveillance team watched all of the men move in position in and around the hotel, all dressed in the serviceable clothes of hotel staff and technicians, with their weapons hidden inside the oversized laundry and clean-up bins.

"Habib, tell the technicians to shut down the communications system. And I will handle the policeman."

Akil grabbed his assault weapon and headed out of the room

to meet the policeman as soon as he appeared in the basement hallway.

With no clue of what he was walking into, the UAE police officer opened the door from the basement staircase and stepped into three close-range shots to his unprotected chest. The man had no chance of surviving and was likely dead before his body hit the floor.

Nearly in unison, a dozen armed men appeared in the hotel lobby with assault weapons and shot down the other police officers while locking down the hotel's front doors and exits.

"Back away from the door!" the men yelled at the international guests.

That's when the screaming, crying and panic started, followed by shots into the high ceiling of the lobby.

"If everyone remains calm, then no one will be hurt!"

Scores of international tourists grabbed their loved ones tightly and panicked all over the building—inside the lobby, the restaurants, the workout rooms, the swimming pools, the hallways and the individual guest rooms of the twenty-seven-floor hotel. With a flick of a switch, all communication was disabled— televisions, telephones, Internet, radio, *everything*. And not only did Heru's men secure every exit and high-traffic area of the hotel, but another half-dozen men secured the roof of the building.

However, Heru remained in hiding, allowing his men to make all of the explanations and demands instead of him.

"You all have the *Emirati* developer Abdul Khalif Hassan to blame for this. And we demand to see him and his wife, Hamda, before anyone is allowed to leave. We do not intend to harm you, but we will not allow you to escape, nor will we allow any of you to harm us. Do I make myself clear?"

Front and center inside the lobby was the same American family that Gary had met on the airplane ride in from Atlanta. They were headed out the building for another fun-filled day in Dubai, with plans to go skiing inside the famous Mall of the Emirates. But they were just a minute too late.

"Daddy, are we gonna live?" the blond-haired boy with big

brown eyes asked his father.

The father squeezed his son, wife and daughter tightly as if attempting to squeeze out the fear itself.

"Yes, we will," he answered. "We will survive it."

Chapter 26

SALEEM, THE RUGGED AND fearless Pakistani, made it into the hotel building right before the group of armed immigrant workers took it over. It was perfect timing for him, but it would have been more perfect had he been able to make it out of the lobby and into the hotel hallways. Instead, Saleem was caught in the middle of everything while carrying a plastic grocery bag filled with two boxes of dark green trash bags and tape for the surveillance cameras.

As he surveyed the posturing men around the room, he could tell from the unsteady movement of their eyes that most of them were amateurs. Some of the armed immigrant men were as terrified as the foreign hostages that they had threatened. However, there were others in the group who held the steely glare of assassins, including their lead speaker.

"If you remain calm, then none of you will get hurt."

As the large and daring man repeated his words to inspire

confidence and poise in the hostages and families, a muscular German attempted to play hero and lounged at one of the gunmen. He was successful in grabbing the gun, but he was not fast enough to aim it and use it before being shot down by the lead speaker.

The German met his death quickly as the hostages yelled again in terror.

The awkward incident and fast death forced the lead assailant to repeat his words: "As I have told you, if you remain *calm*, you will not be hurt. But if you do *not,* then you will suffer the consequences of your own actions."

Saleem assessed that the lead speaker would be a handful to deal with. He was unnerved by any attack and was unafraid of the reality of death. He was also quick to pull his trigger. That made him a qualified solider. But he was not Ra-Heru. He looked nothing like Mohd, and he was too far out in the open to lead their mission. He made himself far too easy to kill. However, with his confidence and reserve, he may have been a second or third in command.

Saleem reflected on his own size and skills as well as the contents of his bag. He felt that it would be unwise for him to continue standing. He did not want to intimidate any of their men or attack too quickly, especially with so many cameras in the front lobby. So he decided that it was much safer for him to stoop, sit or get on his knees, like many of the terrified tourists around him. He also remained aware of the dark, round eyeballs of the cameras that were up above him. So he had no choice but to remain calm and wait for the best opportunity to make his first move.

This may be more challenging than I thought, he told himself. *And hopefully, Mohd has other men from the group that are on his side.*

* * * * *

Outside of the hotel, the remaining police were in a bind.

They had witnessed their fellow officers gunned down inside the lobby, but the doors were locked and flanked by a dozen armed men before they could react fast enough to counter the attack. And with hostages spread throughout the hotel's entrance and reception area, there was nothing they could do without putting innocent people and themselves at harm. There were no clear shots without snipers, but the men inside had clear shots at them. So the remaining police were forced to scatter behind their squad cars.

"Aaal-laahhhh!" a few of the Muslim officers screamed in distress. It all happened so suddenly, it seemed surreal. Did a group of armed men really take over the International Suites in broad daylight, killing several officers in the process? They had also witnessed a valiant tourist who was shot in a bold move to defend himself. But his actions were in vain.

"Call Chief Ali!" the men yelled amongst themselves. "Call him!"

* * * * *

As soon as Ali received the urgent call in Sharjah from his men in downtown Dubai, he took a deep breath and nodded. He told himself and his men calmly, "So the worst has now happened. Let's call in the National Guard. They have taken over the International Suites hotel downtown."

His men in Sharjah were as shocked as those who were at the scene.

"Merciful Allah! They are *insane*," one of the officers commented, unable to contain himself. He could not fathom an immigrant insurgency taking over a popular tourist hotel in downtown Dubai. It was suicide.

"Apparently, they are," the chief told him. He then called his friend Tariq, who was already headed toward the scene.

When Tariq answered his phone, the chief told him, "You won't believe what you are now driving into."

Tariq surprised him when he said, "I do believe it. I am only upset that I did not think of it earlier. So the men are there at the hotel?" he asked to make certain.

"Yes, they are," the chief answered. "They have disabled all of the communications systems and killed six of my men and one hostage."

"They are serious," Tariq said.

"Yes, so I am now ready to call in the Union Defence Force and inform the Emirates, the Prime Minister and the President. This is far bigger than Abdul," the chief added. He understood his friend's loyalty to his clients, but they also had a young nation to protect.

Tariq told him, "Indeed it is much bigger. So if they have taken over the hotel with hostages, then what have they asked for?"

Ali took another breath and paused. "They have asked for Abdul and his wife, Hamda."

"You are kidding me," Tariq responded.

"When have you known me to tell a lie in our business?" Ali quipped. "This vendetta between Mohd and Abdul is real. And they now want an eye for an eye and the destruction of the Hassan family in Dubai.

"And my friend, I tell you all this in advance so you can figure out what to do," Ali added. "But I must prepare now to go to war. Let me know what you figure out when you arrive."

By the time the chief was off the call with Tariq, his men had the UAE authorities on the line.

"Chief Ali, the Defence Force is ready to speak to you."

Ali inhaled and prepared himself for the conversation. He then sighed and nodded before taking the call.

"This is Police Chief Ali Youssef." He listened intently to the higher chain of command on the line, who asked him a series of questions. "Yes, at the International Suites in downtown Dubai. It was confirmed by my men a minute ago, and I am on my way there now."

He listened again before he answered more questions. "We do not know how many there are yet, but if they have taken over the

entire hotel, then we suspect as many as a hundred ... or more."
He would rather err on the side of safety than to shortchange
their number. And he felt that he had already underestimated
the men and their mission the night before.

Then the chief answered the final question. "Apparently,
there was an old vendetta between a highly skilled Egyptian engineer, Mohd Ahmed Nasir, and the young *Emirati* developer
Abdul Khalif Hassan, and this old vendetta has finally showed
its ugly face, while intertwining the innocent tourists in its path."

When the chief hung up from the call, there was no more
time to waste. Most of his men had already left, with the dispatch
office calling as many cars to the scene as were available.

Ali told the rest of his men, *"Yalla!"* in Arabic to head off to
the hotel. Then he climbed into his unmarked car to leave.

* * * * *

As he sped into downtown Dubai, Tariq was far too much
in a hurry to obey the changing stoplight, and he charged
through the busy intersection before the crossing cars could
move forward.

He was also on the cell phone as he drove in haste, trying
again in vain to reach Abdul, who would not answer.

In the meantime, a traffic police officer caught the tail end
of Tariq's unmarked car as it ran through the light, forcing the
dutiful officer to switch on his siren and take off after him.

As Tariq shook his head at another unanswered phone call,
he heard the police siren behind him and looked up in his rear-
view mirror at the squad car that was fast approaching.

"We have no *time* for this," he told himself angrily as he continued to drive. He was only blocks away from the hotel and
could see it up ahead. Helicopters were already circling the roof.

"Did they not inform this officer of what is going on?" Tariq
blasted as he approached another changing stoplight at the
corner. However, he was not close enough in his car to make
a second light before it changed. So when his car came to a full

stop, the officer jumped out from behind him and pulled his gun, racing to his driver's side window to arrest him.

The officer pulled his gun at an angle behind the passenger side door and yelled in English, "Out of the car!"

The officer was young enough to be Tariq's son, so the old veteran prayed for him.

He is a good young man, he thought. *But he has chosen the wrong day and time to look like an idiot.*

Tariq let down his window and showed his investigations badge.

"I am Tariq Mohammed, and I am heading to the International Suites to help Police Chief Ali Youssef and the National Guard. Have you not heard what is going on?"

The young Arab officer paused and looked up at several helicopters that flew over the downtown hotels ... right before gunshots rang out from the roof and struck one of them.

"Al-laah!" he yelled.

The helicopter spun around in circles, wildly, and headed for the Gulf before crashing down into the water.

As the people in their cars and on the streets of downtown Dubai began to panic, Tariq took the opportunity to jet off in his car again toward the hotel building. But it was much harder to navigate through the traffic once the drivers ahead of them began to stop and marvel at the uncharacteristic scene.

"No, no, noooo!" Tariq yelled as he crashed into the back of a car that suddenly stopped in front of him. Undeterred, the private counsel and investigator jumped out of his car with his pistol in hand and began to run toward the scene.

"Excuse me! *Awfan!*" he shouted in English and Arabic as he hurried past the many local citizens and tourists on the sidewalk. It was an amazing scene to Tariq as well. There had not been much terrorism in the United Arab Emirates. The people there understood that it was a Middle Eastern haven established with a vision to connect to the technology, entertainment, individualism and capitalism of the Western world, yet they also knew the complications of bitter human disagreements were liable to escalate in any country. So now they all rushed to figure out how to stop a massive rebellion from occurring. But maybe it was already too late.

Chapter 27

FIVE MINUTES EARLIER, GARY had walked and talked along the waterfront of the Persian Gulf with the beautiful, young Jordanian Ramia Farah Aziz at his side. A small section of the Persian Gulf was not far from his downtown hotel at the Hilton, which was not far from the International Suites.

The two of them had been enjoying each other's company for the past few hours that morning. They compared and contrasted their opposing Christian and Muslim cultures, while locked in an obvious, yet measured, fascination with each other. Ramia was young and naïve, but she was also adventurous and eager, whereas Gary was older now and more jaded. Nevertheless, Ramia's audacity and spirit enlivened him. She had been raised as an obedient Muslim woman who was now in transition to something more ... *individualistic*. And he had been raised as a young Christian who didn't know *what* he was transitioning to. He just knew that it would be more *global*. So they continued to discuss their perspectives on life.

"I really love my freedom here in Dubai," Ramia told him with her arms swaying to prove it. "And my cousin Basim is sometimes overly protective of me, but he is such a good man. I really love and appreciate him, even though he thinks I do not."

Gary smiled for the twentieth time while in her presence. The young woman held nothing back, and he was not used to that. For as *free* as the world may have believed Americans were, Gary understood that many of them had been forced to keep their guards up, including him. So he continued to withhold certain information from her, as he had learned to do with everyone else. Only Jonah knew his full story, or *most* of it. But Ramia was the opposite. She was very talkative and forthcoming.

"I think he believes I'm still a virgin," she said, to Gary's surprise.

He was so shocked by her revelation that he began to look around them to see if anyone else had heard her. But they were presently separated from bystanders.

Oh, my God! Is she supposed to say that?

He had heard and read about the strict Middle Eastern codes on sexuality. Even Johnny had advised him on a few things not to do there while out in public. So Gary was uncertain about how to respond to her. Such brutal honesty would have been shocking as well in America, particularly on a first walk together. It was not even an official date.

"So, what about you?" Ramia asked. "What do you plan to do in your life?"

Thank *God*, she was letting him off the hook with more basic questions. Gary had already told her that he was unmarried with no children. And Ramia did not ask him more about his dating status. He was single, and so he was still available. That was all she wanted to know about it. In the Middle East, the concept of a long-term boyfriend or girlfriend was frivolous. Either you were getting married, or you had not found *the one* yet. So unless he was engaged, in Ramia's eyes, Gary Stevens had not found the one.

"Sometimes I just feel like traveling around the world for the rest of my life," Gary said in a modest tone.

Ramia's colorful hazel eyes lit up even brighter in the sunlight.

"Oh, that would be such a *dream*," she responded. "Paris, Shanghai and Russia. Brazil, South Africa and Australia. Antarctica, Switzerland and Tokyo. The Philippines, India, Mexico."

She named the cities and countries as if she were reading them from a world atlas.

Gary chuckled at her exuberance and her display of world knowledge.

"Yeah, that's how I think about it. There are so many places out there, you know."

Ramia felt, for that brief moment in time, that she had not only broken away from her home in Jordan to experience the spontaneity and wonder of life in the United Arab Emirates, but that she could break away from the *world* and travel *everywhere*.

Would this American man be willing to take me with him after only just meeting me? she pondered. *Could I love him strongly enough in bed to make him want to keep me? Would Basim and my family back home in Jordan disown me if I left with this American?*

The questions all dampened her fantasy. Suddenly Ramia began to feel foolish. She thought, *Is this gorgeous American man pulling my leg? Is he a con man on an international scheme? Is he really married with a wife and children back at home, while attempting to sell a young and innocent Muslim girl the world?*

So she paused to consider Gary's information and answers the way Basim would have asked her to view it. It was all too good to be true, yet the possibilities all crossed her mind. Ramia was as human and opportunistic as any other woman could be.

As she stood there in a brief silence along the waterfront and considered it all, Gary began to look up at a group of four helicopters that seemed to appear out of nowhere. They hovered in military formation over the nearby hotels.

Gary winced and wondered what was going on. Ramia read the deep concern in his eyes and turned to look at the helicopters as well. Then they heard gunshots ring out.

Ramia ducked and cringed, surprised. But she remained amazingly calm, not screaming or panicking.

Gary instinctively secured her hand in his for protection.

"Something's going on," he told her. He began to lead them back in the direction of the hotels. But as they jogged forward, one of the helicopters was hit before spinning wildly in their direction near the waterfront.

"What in the world?!" Gary exclaimed as he began to duck and run them both for cover under the tall palm trees that stood to their right.

The spinning helicopter careened out of control right above their heads and crashed into the Gulf waters less than a hundred yards in front him.

"*Whoa!* That was *close!*" Ramia said. She was more amazed than terrified. She had witnessed military battles as a kid near her home in Jordan. There was always a violent dispute going on in the Middle East, so helicopters being shot down did not unnerve her. Nevertheless, the falling helicopter in Dubai was closer than she had ever been to one.

"It looks like they're circling the hotels," Gary said, pointing.

"Which one?" Ramia asked.

"Let's go find out," Gary responded.

They quickly climbed back to their feet, brushed themselves off and began to run for the downtown hotels. There were at least three major hotels in that same area, including the Hilton, the International Suites and the Executive on the backside around the corner. But as they jogged closer to the area, they could clearly see the helicopters, UAE police officers and military troops that were just arriving in armored trucks. And they were all focused on the International Suites.

Ramia raised her hands to her face and was filled with anxiety. "Oh, my God! I could have been in there." Fortunately, it was not yet noon, and she was not due back for her impromptu interview with the hotel's management until one.

She immediately thought of calling her cousin on his cell

phone to let him know that she was all right and that she was not inside. The scene was so loud and filled with commotion that she decided not to call her cousin, knowing he would worry about her safety. As for Gary, as he ran forward his heart began to pump faster as his mind raced through a collage of memories and emotions. He reflected on all of the military lessons he had learned over the past three years of group training in Northern Virginia. He felt flashes of the pain, despair and helplessness of losing his mother and his best friend to separate acts of murderous terrorism five years ago.

Even though the old incidents in Kentucky and in Colombia, South America, were disconnected from the present, in Gary's mind they *were* connected. The moment of tragedy and urgency in Dubai connected *everything* for him.

Several men inside the helicopter had just died or were on their way to dying. Gary was sure of it from their violent crash into the Gulf, a crash that made him think back to his mother and her carjacking wreck while trying to escape two criminals near their home in Louisville. And every gunshot reminded Gary of his best friend begging for his life in Medellín, Colombia, before one gunshot splattered his brains all over Gary's head and back, while Gary was tied to his friend back-to-back on a hard, cold floor of a dirty Colombian warehouse.

Since he had not been around another urgent tragedy in recent years, he had been able to contain himself and suppress his emotions. All that Gary could think about was running to save his mother and his friend from being murdered. He didn't even respond to his cell phone that was ringing loudly from the holder on his hip.

"Your phone is ringing," Ramia said. It was the loudest phone she had ever heard.

Gary looked down at the screen and saw that it was Jonah calling again, likely to calm him down and make certain that he avoided trouble.

I don't have time for her right now, he thought. *I'll call her back later.*

Once he and Ramia arrived at the scene, the news traveled to them quickly from the gathering crowd. Most of the men were already talking, groups of immigrant taxi drivers who had pulled over and had jumped out of their cars in the middle of the street.

"Some men took over the hotel and are holding everyone hostage!" someone yelled.

"What do they want?"

"I don't know. They are just mad at the Emirates."

"Someone said they are immigrant workers who want fair treatment for their work," another man informed the crowd.

"So they respond by doing *this*? This is *insane*! They will all be put to *death*, and nothing will come of it but stricter rules for the rest of us who work here."

When Gary heard the word "hostages," he began to think immediately about all of the tourists and innocent families involved. He didn't care about anything else that was going on. Who could ever understand the disputes of the Middle East anyway? Desperate men seemed to always do desperate things, even the criminals and mad men in America shooting up innocent people in movie theaters and children and teachers in grade schools. And no nation or people were exempt from the psychosis of terrorism.

Whether they were individuals or groups, it was *all* insane and someone had to do *something* to stop it. Gary stood there in the crowd and thought about it all, with Ramia still clenching his hand.

Ramia felt Gary sweating and thought *Maybe the American isn't so brave after all.* She was not sweating. War, death and tragedy happened all the time in Jordan. It was disturbing, but it was perfectly normal. Gary felt like a race car engine that was revving up at the starting line before blasting forward. He felt like a bull in a holding gate in Spain, before charging out at the people who ran through the streets. Then he thought about the American family who traveled into Dubai on the same Delta airplane with him from Atlanta, and the cute blond-haired boy who sat next to him to with excitement and questions. Gary was ready to *explode*. He was now trained to *do* something about it, but so far he had not budged. The police were holding everyone back anyway.

Ramia finally pulled her clammy hand from him and stretched her eyes wide. She then clasped her hands together in prayer. "Oh, my God! Aren't those two Italian women in there—Sophie and Anastasia, who rode with us yesterday?" She shook her head. "It's such a shame. I pray that everything works out for them."

That was it! Gary's racing heart, along with his civilian hesitation and his feelings of continued helplessness, finally flatlined. He reflected on the philosophy of combat and military training that he had been given by Special Command Officer Cummings in the hills of Northern Virginia:

"In life or death combat, every move is the *right* move, so you must complete it with authority. You cannot hesitate or rethink it and expect to survive. Every move must be fierce, fast and done with the intention to win. And if it is not, then hope and pray that your opponent will hesitate on *his* part. Otherwise, you can expect to lose—and possibly die."

With that Gary, wiped his sweaty hands across his chest to dry them, and as his phone began to ring a second time, he told Ramia, "Pray for me too," before he took off running toward the hotel entrance.

Ramia watched him in confusion. *What is he doing?* Then she ran behind him to see.

From the right side of the crowd, Johnny saw Gary and Ramia running, and he yelled out to his American friend to get his attention, "Hey, Gary!"

Johnny had just called him on his cell phone, with no answer. He wanted to ask if Gary knew what was going on near the Hilton. But obviously, the American traveler was already out and about, accompanied by a beautiful Arab woman to boot.

"GARY!" he yelled again, louder.

His loud and pressing shouts through the crowd had unexpectedly distracted the police officers, enabling Gary to find a crease between them and make his way toward the entrance of the hotel. Without stopping, the crazy tourist ran right past the Union Defence Force of Arab soldiers, while they began to yell at him, "STOP! STOP! STOP!"

The crazy tourist was running, unprotected, right into the range of bullets from the men who waited inside the lobby of the hotel with their assault weapons.

As soon as they saw him running out from the left, three of the men inside began to fire in the man's direction through the thick hotel glass windows, which deflected their bullets away from the target while shattering the glass.

Expecting as much, Gary dove forward into a perfect summersault, rolling over and popping right back up on his feet. He was untouched by a single bullet as he continued on his reckless and sudden path toward the basement driveway to the right of the hotel entrance. It was where the valet staff would park exotic cars. As an experienced striker in the American game of lacrosse, Gary had performed the same forward rolling move ever since he was eight years old, albeit on grass instead of concrete. Nevertheless, his execution of the move was the same—an astounding success.

The UAE military and police looked around at each other in shocked silence until the commanding military officer spoke up.

"What was that? Who is he?"

The police had no idea. "We don't know. We were trying to stop him," they said excitedly.

The commanding officer sensed an opportunity. Gary had acted as a decoy. "He just showed us another way in," the commanding officer shouted. "Establish a formation to follow him."

Even the immigrant men inside the hotel were astounded by what they saw: one man charging the terrorists, dodging bullets and unscathed.

"You idiots!" the lead man shouted at his three fast triggermen. They had shot down their own protection of glass.

"He came out from nowhere. We were surprised," they yelled in their defense.

"Call surveillance and see if they caught him on camera," the leader told his men.

The brief distraction was just what the Pakistani, Saleem, needed to slip into the nearby bathroom unnoticed.

Meanwhile, Ramia and Johnny watched Gary's amazing feat with the rest of the crowd outside of the front entrance. They stood far behind the military and police but were still able to see it all.

"Did you see that?" members of the crowd asked.

"That was *amazing!*"

"Yes, but what will he do now with no gun? He will get himself *killed*," someone else called out.

Johnny reached Ramia in the crowd. "What is he doing?"As far as he could tell, the American traveler looked like a maniac who had gotten lucky.

Ramia shrugged her shoulders and answered, "I don't know. He just took off running and told me to pray for him."

Johnny shook his head and thought about it. All of the mysteries of Gary Stevens were beginning to add up. He even began to question if the American man's name was really "Gary Stevens." He first called himself "The Traveler," as if he didn't want to reveal his identity.

Johnny leaned into Ramia and whispered in her ear, "I think he may be a secret agent."

Before Ramia overreacted, she faced him and asked, "Who are you?"

"I'm Johnny Napur, his tour guide in Dubai for the past three days. I picked him up from the airport when he first arrived here. And I saw him kick a man's ass the other night who was *twice* as big as him."

That made Ramia rethink everything. Maybe Gary's sweaty palms meant the opposite of what she thought. "He was in a fight?" she asked the excitable British hustler.

Although he was obviously Sri Lankan, from his exotic brown skin and thick black hair, Johnny's British accent was very strong. He said, "Man, was he *ever*. He knocked this huge guy on his ass with just *three* moves. It was *amazing*, just like that one!"

And the women also love him! Johnny kept to himself. *He's gotten me plenty of status these past two nights!* He planned to take the American out again for more status. But now he was unsure if he would even survive.

"Man, I hope he makes it back out of there. I had big plans for him tonight."

That got Ramia thinking about her big plans for the American, with desperation of her own.

She thought, *Okay, so how can I get him back out of there?* She began to look for another crack in the police force or a way around the back of the building. But the police and the UAE military were scouting around the back as well, where the armed immigrant men were barricaded against them.

Nevertheless, Ramia looked back at Johnny. "Would you help me to find another way in?"

Johnny looked at her as if she were a screaming lunatic. "What? You want to go in there?"

Ramia shook her head at his foolishness and began to walk away without a response. She wanted to think of another route in and had no time for him.

Johnny watched the beautiful Arab woman walk away in an obvious fit. *Is she serious?* he wondered. He was curious to see if she was, so he decided to follow her. "Hey, wait up. I'll help you."

Ramia stopped and turned. "Really?" She had no patience for games. This American mystery man had her majorly intrigued now. She was out of her senses.

"What's your name?" Johnny asked her.

"Ramia," she answered hesitantly. She hoped that he wasn't trying to use the opportunity to hit on her, because she was *not* interested.

But Johnny didn't plan to do that. He realized that the American had left her seriously love-struck.

"Okay, let's go this way," he said, as if he were suddenly in charge.

Ramia shook her head at his fake swagger and followed him

through the crowd, reluctantly.

Johnny thought, *She's crazy! But let me at least see how far she's willing to take this.*

Chapter 28

TARIQ FINALLY MADE HIS way to the edge of the crowd in downtown Dubai. Cars and trucks were stopped all over the street due to the disturbance at the International Suites. No longer the young man that he used to be, Tariq huffed and gasped to catch a breather.

While leaning over, he spotted an unmarked white van only twenty yards in front of him. There was nothing peculiar about the van, and it was too small to load anything more than a dozen men. But then Tariq watched as an imposing driver looked around him before he quickly opened up the back doors. Had Tariq still been standing, the man might have spotted him. But in his stooped position, he was able to witness the prime prize of the day: Mohd Ahmed Nasir, who calmly jumped out of the back with two other men as they all followed behind the driver to the sidewalk and around the nearest corner.

"The Honorable Allah," Tariq said to himself. He happened to be in the right place at the right time. So he followed after Mohd and his men while keeping a safe distance from them.

He rounded the corner and caught the four men just as they stepped into a building. To camouflage his move, Tariq continued walking across the street like an average citizen. Once he was out of eyesight from the building, he made an immediate phone call to his friend.

"Yes, Police Chief Ali Youssef."

"I found him—Mohd Ahmed Nasir," Tariq responded. "He is with three men inside of a building in downtown Dubai. And they are not heavily armed. They could have maybe four to six pistols on them, unless they have more inside."

"Give me the address, and I will send my men to obey your command," Ali said. "We cannot even make it to the hotel through the traffic, and the Union Defence Force is already there. So capturing Mohd would be even more important to us at this time."

"Exactly," Tariq agreed. "I will stand guard and await your backup. But *please* tell your men in *advance* that we must capture him *alive*. So it would be wise to send me your best and most experienced officers."

"Indeed," the chief said. "I agree one hundred percent. I will send only the best."

After Tariq hung up, he thought again about calling Abdul, but he was still uncertain if the *Emirati* developer was free to answer.

"Don't worry, my friend," he mumbled to himself. "I will help you get to the bottom of this. I give you my word."

* * * * *

Back at Sheikh Al Hassan's home in Abu Dhabi, word of the immigrant takeover at the International Suites in downtown Dubai had gotten back to their distinguished group, where

Abdul was forced to sit and listen to the much wiser and older men while he steamed and got agitated over their conclusions.

The elder Sheikh Al Rashid insisted with an angry balled fist upon the brunch table, "You and your wife will go nowhere *near* Dubai for a *week*! And we will allow the *army* and the proper authorities to handle this absolute *embarrassment* to the United Arab Emirates. I will advise the building commissioner myself that your license should be suspended for at least ten years! But I will strongly recommend *twenty*!"

Each dramatic point was made with a hammering fist to the table, as the food, plates and wine glasses shook from the force. All the while, Abdul took his medicine like a man, with measured breathing and incredible poise. To lose his building license for ten to twenty years would be torture. But under the present circumstances, there was no argument he could make in his favor. His inflammatory business practices and inhumane treatment of the immigrant labor force had put the young and celebrated nation under an extreme weight.

Nevertheless, Abdul eyed his loving uncle Sheikh Al Hassan to speak up on his behalf.

Sheikh Al Hassan cleared his throat. "If I may, I will remind you that *all* of Dubai's developers use the same immigrant workforce—"

"And yet none of them have caused an *atrocity* like this one," Sheikh Al Rashid responded, cutting him off. "If it were up to *me*, he would not be able to build a children's playground in Dubai."

Abdul was beyond humiliation in a multitude of ways. But if he were to react, like he would do with almost anyone else, he knew that he would only make it worse. His uncle had advised him to allow the elder Sheikh to blow off his steam, and that's what Abdul continued to do. But it was much easier said than done.

Finally, the young Sheikh Al Naseem tried to lighten the mood. With a plop of a purple grape into his mouth, he said, "Brother, please, be merciful. Even Allah recognizes mistakes. And surely he would allow Abdul to build a playground."

Abdul understood his fate. He would be made an example for the line of young and ambitious developers behind him. The young Sheikh Al Falah was right there at the table with them to learn his lesson of respect for his elders and for the work of development in the UAE. And Abdul realized that it was best to accept a hard reprimand from Sheikh Al Rashid, who knew him and his uncle well, than to accept a much colder denunciation from the Prime Minister and the President, who would surely be involved afterward.

Outside of their closed room, Abdul's wife eavesdropped. Hamda understood that Abdul was in a grave situation that needed serious discussions, so he had wisely given her his cell phone. That way he would not be tempted to even look at it during their talks.

"Sister, please, come back to the sitting room," she was told by one of the elder wives.

Startled by being caught, Hamda could only apologize for her worry.

"*Ana aasifa*," she stated in Arabic. "I'm just so concerned," she admitted.

"It's okay, just come back to the room," the elder wife told her graciously. "Let the men talk and work it out."

The wives already knew that Hamda was particularly independent, and some of them secretly admired her for it. Nevertheless, there were still times to reel the young wife back into the hold of tradition before she caused herself and her husband more difficulties.

Hamda was told as much when she arrived back in the sitting room with the rest of the wives and young children.

Her aunt and head wife of the Hassan household, Maryam Abdullah, was blunt. "A restless foot will stub its toe on many closed doors, believing that they are open. And some toes will not learn their lessons until they are all broken and cannot be fixed."

Not only did Hamda get the message loud and clear, but so did the other wives inside the room, who may have been overly inspired by her audacity. So Hamda retook her seat in a tall comfortable chair and could not *wait* until their visit was over. Every visit with the elder wives seemed to last much longer than she could stand. But like her husband in the room with the elder men, Hamda was forced to swallow her pride and hold back her tongue for as long as she was in their presence, unless she agreed to respect *all* of their feminine customs.

* * * * *

While Abdul and Hamda received their reprimands at the house of Hassan in Abu Dhabi, in downtown Dubai a tactical war was now fully engaged on a hotel roof, in the loading docks, at all the exits and at the entrance and lobby.

"We are forced to be extra careful with so many hostages here," the commanding army officer noted to his men and the police. Their advanced weapons and trained soldiers were at the mercy of the immigrants to refrain from using the hostages as human shields. But whenever the soldiers had strategic and technological advantages, the immigrant rebels would use exactly what the UAE feared: human shields while firing many rounds of their ammunition. They were not even able to follow the crazy tourist into the valet parking area, creating a need for immense patience.

So far, seventeen of their men had been killed and several injured, including those who had gone down in the helicopter. Only eight of the immigrants had been killed, and mostly on the roof, where there were no hostages. There was still no count of exactly how many there were. But they seemed to be all over the hotel.

"What next—do we use the snipers and tear gas?" the second in command asked the commander in chief out front.

From the front entrance, there were many obstructions that took away many of the clear sight lines, and the immigrants made sure to stay out of range of clear shots. So the lead commander shook it off.

"Not yet. Let's see what reports we have from the roof and the other exits."

* * * * *

After losing one helicopter, security forces continued in their efforts to overtake the hotel roof without landing and killed several of the terrorists with a barrage of machine gunfire. Amid the gunfire, one of the immigrant workers shot three of his colleagues in the back.

"Did you see that?" one helicopter pilot radioed to another. "He shot down his own men."

The roof was riddled with bullet holes, bodies and blood. The Union Defence Force, wearing SWAT team gear, awaited orders to descend down their rope ladders to the roof to enter the hotel. But landing there was still too risky. That's was how they lost the first helicopter. The pilots relayed the progressive report to their commander on the ground.

"We are in position now to drop off several of the men on the roof," they told him. "And some of the immigrants are now helping us. But it is still too dangerous too land. So we will use the ladders."

"Excellent. Commence. We are at a standstill here," the commander told them. "Report back to me when the men make it inside."

"Yes."

* * * * *

Inside the surveillance room in the basement of the hotel, Habib and Akil watched the tourist break into the door from the valet parking lot.

"Akil, I told you, he's making his way in. The American."

"How do you know he's an American?" Akil asked.

"He *looks* like an American. His hair, his clothes, his skin. I've seen enough American movies to know. He even *moves* like an American football player."

Akil frowned at his friend's unfounded assumptions and asked him, "What did he use to get in?" The parking area door had been locked.

"I don't know. But go kill him. We're not making an American movie here."

Akil grabbed his assault weapon. "These cameras are going to your head, my friend." And he left the room to do his work.

A moment later, one of the other surveillance men caught an act of treason happening on the roof.

"Did you see that? He shot three of our own men."

Habib watched the replay of the tape from the roof and smiled. "Heru expected this. Some of the men are still loyal to his father and will try to sabotage our mission. I will tell Heru immediately."

* * * * *

Ra-Heru was already near the twenty-seventh floor when he was hailed on his walkie-talkie. "Hello," he answered.

"We've found the first traitor on the roof."

Heru nodded and readied his assault rifle. "I'm there."

He hung up the call and made his way up the final staircase to the roof as several UAE soldiers made it down their ladders from the helicopters.

The traitor ran back into the building, acting overwhelmed by it. He spotted Heru heading fast in his direction up the stairs and yelled, "Heru, they have taken over the roof! It was too many of them!"

Without seeming to respond, Heru took out his blade with his left hand, while still carrying his rifle in his right, and he curved his blade quickly around the traitor's neck in one swift motion, cutting him open like a pig.

"Thanks to you, we have one less man on their side now," Heru said, and he allowed the traitor to fall to his death down the steps without the alarming noise of gunshots … so when the men on the roof approached the door, they had no warning of what they were up against.

Heru waited patiently for their position, and instead of allowing them to open the door and charge in on him, he charged them instead, using a similar forward roll that the American had used earlier. However, Heru carried a fully loaded assault weapon with him, and he let loose with it.

Before the men could react properly to counter him, Heru killed four of them, with seven more who scrambled for cover.

Two more of the men were shot as the leftover soldiers from the helicopter took aim at Heru's rapidly changing position. He was as lightning quick on his feet as a deadly Ninja, and when the shooters missed, Heru did not.

Three of the men in the helicopter were shot, falling to their deaths. The pilot was protected behind bulletproof glass, so Heru took aim at the propellers instead.

Struck perfectly, the helicopter began to spin out of control and hit the roof, killing more troops.

* * * * *

Back at ground level, the commander in chief was puzzled while hearing all of the gunshots from the roof and seeing the helicopter crash into it. He was still awaiting a new report of a successful entry into the top of the building.

"What is going on up there?" he asked the reporting pilot.

The pilot was shaken, stammering as he spoke. "We, we, we had several men in place on the roof, then one man came out and shot down everything."

"*One* man?" the commander repeated doubtfully.

"Yes, one man. And they could not hit him. He even took down a second helicopter by himself."

"Well, where is he now?"

"He went back inside."

"Well, get in there and *get him*!" the commander barked.

"We don't have enough men now," the pilot complained. "He

just killed a dozen trained soldiers by himself."

The commander looked up to the roof and saw the remaining two helicopters retreating from the scene like dogs with their tails caught behind their hind legs. But the commander was unnerved by their small defeat.

"Call for four more helicopters and men," he told his second in command. "We must secure the roof. It's our best way in." Then he paused. "And get the snipers and tear gas positions."

"Yes!" the second in command answered gleefully. He would have gone Rambo much earlier and not allowed the rebellion to pick up any confidence. But he was not in charge to make the call.

* * * * *

Back inside the basement surveillance room, Heru told his man Habib on his walkie-talkie, "Send more men to the roof. They will return with backup shortly."

"Yes," Habib responded. He completed the call just in time to witness, on the monitors, his comrade Akil lose a decisive battle to the American.

"What the ... Play that back again," he told the other men who saw it as well in the room.

They all watched again as Akil approached the American, who slid beneath him and grabbed his assault gun before head-butting him and bashing Akil in his head with his own weapon.

"Did you see that? That looked like something Heru would have done," one of the men commented.

Habib continued to look on in shock as the American made his way up the stairs toward the lobby with the gun in hand.

"Yes, but Heru would have *killed* him," he concluded. Habib then called their lieutenant inside the lobby on his walkie-talkie.

"The American man is headed your way with a gun."

Their imposing lieutenant in the lobby was not pleased. "Who? An *American*?"

"Yes, the man who ran past the entrance is an American, I'm

sure of it."

"Where did he get a gun?" the lieutenant asked.

Habib was embarrassed to even say it, but he was forced to.

"He beat Akil in the basement hallway. But he knocked him unconscious and took the gun instead of killing him. So I believe that he is *soft.*"

"I see," the lieutenant responded. "Well, we will be prepared for him."

Chapter 29

TARIQ WATCHED AS SEVERAL UAE squad cars full of police officers pulled up through all of the chaotic traffic downtown to help him capture Mohd and his men from inside of a three-story brown-brick building.

He pointed to the building. "That's the one they went into right there. So guard the back exit doors, and I need several men on the adjacent roofs to surround them."

There were about twenty police officers in all, and most of them were experienced.

"So, you want *all* of them alive," the lead officer asked for clarity.

"No," Tariq answered definitively. In case they didn't know what the Egyptian looked like, he showed them all a photograph of Mohd on his cell phone that he had downloaded earlier. "Only him," he stated. "The others are disposable."

The officers all looked and nodded. "Thank you. Let's get to work then," the lead officer spoke for them all.

The men split up and went in their separate directions to make the crucial arrest.

* * * * *

Inside the downtown office building, Mohd took a deep breath and contemplated his fate. He was unable to reach the International Suites in time to make much of a difference there, and now he was hiding out in a business center restroom with three men that he had no use for. There was no amount of protection that Bakar could provide for him now. His son Ra-Heru had begun a war that could cost both of them their lives. Therefore, Mohd thought only of telling the United Arab Emirates authorities their story, so that the world might know the truth.

"So, what are we to do?" Bakar asked him. They had all locked themselves inside of the bathroom to think.

First, Mohd considered the two men who had been loyal to his son, and he saw no reason for them to follow him.

"You two may go your own way," he said. "And I pray that Allah may guide you in the rest of your days. But if there are men here who would still connect you to the rest of the group, then I would no longer remain in Dubai. I would leave here as quickly as possible."

The two men glanced at each other and looked back at Mohd as if waiting for more.

"But we have no money to leave," one of the men commented. "We have nothing but the clothes on our backs."

Mohd looked at Bakar and nodded. Bakar dug into his clothes and gave them several hundred *dirham*. "That is all that I can offer you. Now go."

"Thank you, thank you," they both spoke and nodded.

When they were gone, Mohd addressed Bakar in private. "You take the rest of the money and leave here yourself. I will no longer be needing you."

But Bakar was insistently loyal. "What do you mean? I have sworn my allegiance to protect you until my *death*. You have

helped me to provide for my family back home, and you have
been very gracious and giving to me for years."

Bakar took more of the *dirham* from his pockets in his left
hand and said, "This means *nothing* to me." Then he put his right
fist over his heart. "But this means *everything*."

Mohd took a deep breath and was moved by Bakar's loyalty,
yet he would not change his mind. "You have an allegiance to
protect a man who is still *alive*. But I am a dead man now."

"You are *not* dead," Bakar argued. "So I will continue to protect you."

Mohd shook his head and eyed the pistol that Bakar still held
at his waistline. "You can no longer protect me with that. You
would be better off to throw it away."

Bakar took the gun from his waistline and tossed it into a
trash can. Mohd then looked down at the man's leg, forcing his
bodyguard to do the same with the knife that he held inside the
holder at his ankle.

"So I now protect you with my heart and my spirit alone,"
Bakar told him.

Mohd nodded. "And are you ready to suffer the consequences
of torture?"

Bakar paused and nodded slowly. "So we will turn ourselves
in?"

"There is no other way for me," Mohd confessed. "I must tell
my son's story. It is the way he wanted it to end."

Bakar agreed with him. "Then that is what we will do then."

* * * * *

Outside of the building, Tariq had no idea what Mohd's plans
would be. So he advised the officers to flush the men out from
the back door and into the front as they began to clear the street
and the sidewalks of pedestrians. To his surprise, two of the men
walked out of the front door unprovoked, as if attempting to
appear as normal citizens. Had Tariq not spotted them earlier,
they might have gotten away with it. But as they made their way

safely out of the building and quickly walked toward the corner, Tariq gave the signal from his position across the street for the UAE police officers to arrest or kill them.

"Stop!" the officers yelled with their guns out.

Understanding that their arrest would mean death, both men took off running and were willing to take their chances. However, with several sharpshooters already on the roofs, and the streets cleared of people, the two men were easy targets.

Bullets slashed the air.

Mohd and Bakar heard the gunshots outside and stopped momentarily as they approached the front door. The building was an open office of several businesses with a front lobby. With three floors of different offices, no one was particularly concerned about who walked in or out, until they realized that two of the four men who had entered the building earlier were obviously dangerous fugitives. They then looked at Mohd and Bakar, who had walked in with the others, and they panicked.

"We mean you no harm," Mohd told them in the front lobby. He raised his arms high in surrender even before they reached the door, and he had Bakar do the same.

Back outside the building, Tariq could see Mohd and his security detail walking toward the entrance with their hands raised high, and he realized that his quest was over—or at least a part of it. He now would have to find out pertinent information about the hotel and the men.

"Do not shoot! He is surrendering!" Tariq reinformed the men. "Do not shoot!"

He even walked out from his position across the street from the building to show his own confidence in Mohd's surrender. Mohd recognized his graciousness and nodded to him as he kneeled with Bakar in expectation of their arrest.

As the UAE police quickly handcuffed the surrendering men, Tariq said, "You have a lot of explaining to do, Mohd."

Mohd looked up at him and grinned slightly, with his arms and hands cuffed behind his back. "And you have a lot of listening to do."

Tariq nodded and was very satisfied to make his phone call.

"Yes, Tariq, what have you found?" Ali asked him immediately. "I have just now arrived at the hotel."

Tariq told him the remarkable news. "We have Mohd now in custody. And we will bring him to the scene to discuss everything."

"Praise be to Allah," the chief said. "Bring him then. Bring him here *immediately*! The Union Defence Force has told me they have an expert man who leads the immigrants. He has killed nearly twenty men by himself. And I am certain that Mohd knows who he is."

The chief was so loud over the phone that Mohd was able to overhear him. And he grinned again, realizing that his son would surely make a name for himself. Right or wrong, Ra-Heru would be known throughout the Middle East.

* * * * *

Back at the International Suites, Gary was preparing to go into real warfare. Throughout his three years of training, he had never killed anyone and rarely aimed to do so with his targets.

So what am I gonna do now, shoot at all of their legs? he asked himself inside the staircase. *And what if they're holding hostages? I could get a bunch of people killed, including myself.*

He looked down at his cell phone and saw that he had cracked the screen in his forward roll move from earlier. And his phone would no longer work inside the building.

Maybe this phone isn't foolproof after all, he mused. But while fiddling with it, he remembered Jonah's fateful words of advice: "Gary, I know you may feel a little uncomfortable about shooting a gun to kill, but in a real-life situation, a man or a woman who is still alive ... can still kill you."

Gary reflected on her words and took another deep breath before he could launch himself through the door.

"Well, here I go," he mumbled. "And if I die, at least I get to join my mother and Taylor in Heaven."

* * * * *

Inside the surveillance room in the basement, Habib watched and waited for the American to show his hand. In the meantime, his men were able to collect Akil from the hallway and bring him back to the room. Akil watched the monitors in a daze as well, while clearing his aching and injured head.

"We will now see how good this American is with a gun," Habib commented.

"What are they waiting for?" Akil grumbled. He was angry that he had lost so swiftly to the American. "Tell them to shoot him through the door."

"No," Habib argued. "That would only give the American a warning that they are waiting for him."

"So what? Send the men down in the stairway to get him. Or I will go finish him off myself." Akil even grabbed another assault weapon before falling sideways into the wall.

"Akil, you need to clear your head before you can do anything," Habib said.

The other men inside the room had to stop themselves from laughing. Akil had a pretty violent temper. In the distraction, one of the cameras in the bathroom lobby disappeared.

"Did you see that one? That's the bathroom near the lobby."

Habib looked. "It may be another traitor. I will tell the lieutenant. But Heru said not to bother him with anything below the twelfth floor of the building."

* * * * *

Right as the lieutenant answered his walkie-talkie in the hotel lobby, where his men were ready with their guns and plenty of hostages, Gary slammed open the basement door, expecting an ambush, and he tossed his tan button-up shirt fifteen feet into the air, like a parachute. The immigrant gunmen immediately responded to that with a hail of bullets.

The floating shirt was just enough of a distraction to divert their eyes and allow Gary to launch himself low on the floor with his assault weapon aimed and ready in his white tank top undershirt. And there was no hesitation in his rolling floor moves.

Gary shot at their toes, where it was easy to distinguish workman boots and dirty shoes from the sandals and bright, new tennis sneakers that the average tourist wore. And it worked. Gary was able to hobble six men inside the room.

In unison, the snipers from outside with the UAE Defence Force began to fire and pick off more immigrant men inside the lobby. They had used the distracted attack from inside as a signal of their own.

The hostages and their families were terrified, screaming in agony as the bullets flew back and forth all around them.

* * * * *

"It's the crazy tourist! He's inside with a gun now!" one of the UAE snipers commented outside to the commanding officer.

Again, the commanding officer was baffled. "Who is this man?"

Ali, who had just arrived at the scene, saw the opportunity for their men to overwhelm the immigrants immediately. "Now is the time!" he advised. "We should charge them!"

But the commander was not as certain, nor did he like the police chief telling him what to do. So he eyed him down before deciding to give his men his own signal.

"Move forward."

* * * * *

Inside the lobby, Saleem made his move from the bathroom and instantly secured a gun from an overmatched immigrant. Realizing that the American tourist was not shooting to kill, Saleem picked off more of the men. All around them, the hostages continued to scream and run for their lives.

Gary even spotted the American family right there in front

of him.

"Move! Run! Out of the building! I'll cover you!" he shouted
to the families.

A flood of terrified foreigners began to run free and out of the
front entrance of the hotel amidst the chaos.

"Hold your fire! Hold your fire!" the commanding officer
yelled to his snipers.

And the people ran free.

* * * *

Watching the scene from the surveillance room, Habib was
shocked by it all and decided to call back Heru on his walkie-
talkie.

"They are attacking the front entrance with snipers and an
American tourist who snuck in!" he informed their leader. Habib
had not mentioned the American to Heru before because he did
not think that the man would survive.

"An American?" Heru asked him, concerned. "A military
man?"

"He must be. He moves as fast as you, but he is not trying to
kill. However, there's another traitor with him who is. I noticed
him from the meetings with your father, Mohd, in Deira. And the
soldiers are headed in with their snipers, while the hostages in
the lobby are running free. It's time for phase two," he suggested
nearly in one breath. The man was full of nervous tension.

"Then do it!" Heru barked at him. "What are you waiting
for?"

From the crowd of gathered citizens in back of the UAE
soldiers and police, another group of a dozen immigrant men
attacked with smaller assault weapons that they pulled from
workbags. They began to immediately fire through the crowd at
the snipers, the police and Defence Force soldiers.

The commanding officer and Ali ducked behind the cars and
the armored trucks as several more of their men were killed by
unexpected bullets from behind.

"Ambush!" the commanding officer screamed. "We need more backup, *now*! How many of them are there?"

With the second wave of immigrant attackers mixed in with the crowd, it was nearly impossible to counter them without striking innocent people.

In the middle of the attack, Ali made a call on his cell phone.

"Tariq! Ask Mohd how many men there are!" he screamed into his phone. "It is not safe here! We are being ambushed from the crowd behind us!"

* * * * *

On the backside of the hotel, Ramia and Johnny found another way in as the UAE soldiers formed an aggressive wall to penetrate the building at a weak point. They pushed back the immigrant gunmen and were able to enter the back left hallway. With more police officers in position to stop bystanders from getting too close when the ambush occurred at the front entrance, an opportunity was created for Johnny and Ramia to slip inside while the police were called to the front for backup.

"Come on. Hurry!" Ramia told Johnny as she jogged forward.

Johnny was still amazed that she was that serious. *She's crazy!* he continued to tell himself. Yet he followed her into the embattled building anyway.

Once inside, they made their way to the second floor and headed back toward the interior of the building, passing countless rooms of terrified guests. "Is it over?" a Filipino mother in her thirties asked Ramia. She was peeking out from her cracked room door with her three small kids right behind her.

Ramia stopped and thought about it. The woman's family could easily make it down the stairs and out the back exit. So Ramia took a chance.

"Come on. Hurry," she told the woman and children.

Johnny looked up the hallway to make sure the coast was clear. And when the family made it down the stairs and out of the building to safety, Ramia felt like a hero herself.

"We could help more people to escape," she told Johnny.

Johnny was more apprehensive. He wondered why there were no men there to secure the exit. "I don't know about that," he commented. "I don't want to get anyone killed." *Including me,* he thought.

But Ramia was inspired. "We can do it," she said. "We can help a lot of people." And she started knocking on hotel doors. "Hurry, you can all make it out."

* * * * *

Down in the surveillance room, Habib and Akil watched their plans to hold an international hotel full of hostages falling apart.

"We are losing too many hostages, and the soldiers are now inside the building."

Akil disputed him. "We have plenty more hostages on more than twenty floors."

"Not if the soldiers continue to kill off our men."

Akil watched the monitors as the UAE soldiers quickly worked their way up each floor, shooting down the inexperienced immigrants inside the stairwells and hallways.

"Tell Heru the soldiers are headed straight toward him," Akil stated.

Habib picked up the walkie-talkie and relayed the message. "Heru, the soldiers are coming for you on the left side of the building and killing plenty of the men."

After the report from the roof and the loss of the second helicopter, the mission was to take out the lead man and to find out who he was. But Heru had no worries.

"Let them come," he told his men.

* * * * *

Meanwhile, Heru's lieutenant, with reinforcements, continued to hold his own against the UAE soldiers and the American at the front entrance.

"Shoot to kill, not to maim!" the Pakistani Saleem yelled at the American. He could have made their task a lot easier with his great aim. And Saleem was growing tired of finishing off his leftovers.

Gary understood his alarm, but he had allowed the Pakistani and the UAE soldiers to do the killing for him, and it had all worked out fine. But as more immigrant men forced new hostages into the lobby from the cafeteria, the workout room and the swimming pool, it was obvious that they planned to hold down the lobby at all costs. And there were too many of them to remain there.

"You came in from the basement?" Saleem asked the American. They ended up side-by-side while running behind the reception desks. It was the best place for them to avoid so much firepower.

"Yes," Gary answered.

"Did you see a surveillance camera room there?"

Gary shook his head. "I didn't look for one."

"That is how they know our positions. This hotel is filled with security cameras," Saleem told him. "We need to go there and take them out."

Gary looked around the lobby and asked, "What about the hostages?" He saw that they had the two Italian women from the sand tour, Sophie and Anastasia, in their group.

"We will have to come back for them," Saleem insisted. "But we must take out their cameras to stop their preparations."

Gary didn't like the idea of leaving the hostages, but he had no choice. They were greatly outnumbered.

"So, how do we get back to the staircase?" Gary asked.

"We have to cover each other. I will go first."

Saleem still did not trust the American to shoot to kill, so he decided to make them a path himself.

Gary nodded and agreed. "Okay. You go first, and I'll cover you."

Saleem nodded and wasted no time. He ran low from behind the reception desk and cleared a path to the basement door with a round of bullets.

With the men concentrating on the Pakistani, the American came right behind him, firing as they had planned.

When they made it into the basement staircase successfully, Habib, Akil and the rest of the men inside the surveillance room grabbed their assault weapons and prepared to hold their positions.

"They are coming now for us," Habib stated nervously. Both the Pakistani traitor and the American were very good with their guns and their movements, and Habib had little confidence that they would survive an attack from the two men.

"I must tell Heru that the American and the traitor are coming for us."

Akil nodded and did not dispute that they were in danger. His head continued to hurt from the American's first attack on him inside the basement hallways.

"Yes, tell Heru now."

Akil hoped that Heru would arrive in time in the basement to save them, but he realized that that would be unlikely. So he prepared to fight for his life.

Chapter 30

AFTER RECEIVING THE URGENT call from Chief Ali Youssef of the dangers at the hotel, Tariq asked the UAE police officers to pull their squad car over less than a mile away from the hostage scene. They were so close to the hotel that they could practically smell the gunpowder of warfare from their cars.

Ali had strongly suggested that it was no longer safe to bring the Egyptian there to the hotel amidst the violent insurgence.

Nevertheless, Mohd expected to talk to them *all* and more than just one, so that his story would not be lost on the ears of only one man. He had prepared himself for a climactic performance, and did not plan to speak to the lower-ranking officers alone. So when Tariq climbed into the back of the squad car with him, Mohd was determined to avoid saying too much.

Tariq began, "I have already heard of your story, and I am sorry for the loss of your wife. But to take the International Suites hostage, endangering *hundreds* of tourists and families, is barbaric. And I would not expect that from a man of peace."

Mohd nodded patiently and was not offended. He planned to keep his poise. "Indeed, you may know some of *my* story, but you know *nothing* of my son and the love that he had for his mother."

Tariq was noticeably surprised. With Mohd in his mid-sixties, his son could easily be a grown man in his thirties, and more than capable of leading a group of rebels.

"So your son has served in the Egyptian military as well?" Tariq asked. With Mohd having military training himself, it was easy to imagine that his son would have followed in his footsteps.

But Mohd had no more to say about it, at least not to him. "I will reveal more to the proper authorities at the hotel."

"I *am* an authority," Tariq snapped. "You can tell the rest to me. It is not safe at the hotel."

"And it will not *be* safe unless you know *all* that you need to know," Mohd hinted.

Tariq became alarmed. *What if they are planting a bomb at the hotel?* he thought. *They surely have enough warehouse space, trucks and plenty of men to do it.*

Instead of wasting more time with an older man who had no reason to bend, Tariq nodded and made his swift decision. "Then we will take you there."

He stepped back out of the squad car and closed the door to inform the officers: "To the hotel."

"But I thought Chief Ali said not to."

"The plans have changed, and we have no time to argue," Tariq answered calmly. "My good friend Ali Youssef will understand when we arrive. In the meantime, call the Union Defence Force and have their intelligence division do a full search on the sons of Egyptian Army engineer Mohd Ahmed Nasir."

The lead officer was surprised by the new information as well. "So his *son* is leading them. How obvious."

Tariq nodded. "We would have found out eventually. This has all been very sudden. But I can only imagine how long they've been planning it. So call the Defence Force intelligence while I speak to the chief."

* * * * *

Up on the top floors of the hotel, Ra-Heru continued to prepare, with his men, a counterattack on the UAE soldiers. He had
gotten word from the basement that his surveillance force was
under attack.

"They are coming up the staircase to the left, so be prepared
for them," he told four of his armed immigrants on the seven-
teenth floor. On each level of the higher floors, at least six men
guarded the hallways at each exit and the elevators to make sure
that no families escaped. But on the lower floors, up to level
five, the soldiers had infiltrated the building, and hostages were
rapidly escaping to safety.

"Do you need any help, Heru?" one of the men asked the
tactful and energized leader.

Heru paused, reflecting on the men who had been most loyal
to his father. And he was still looking for traitors to dispose of.

"Yes," he answered. "I could use you. Come with me."

The man quickly followed him into the staircase to the left,
where the UAE soldiers were heard shooting their way up.

Heru aimed his assault weapon down into the staircase for
his man to attack. But the man looked surprised and confused
by it.

"You want me to go right into them?"

Heru was already skeptical of him. Then he came up with
an idea.

"I have a plan." He pulled out a thick rubber rope from the
carry bag on his back that he planned to use later. He also had a
belt of hooks to attach it to. "Put this on," he told his man.

The immigrant put on the belt reluctantly. "What is this?"
he asked.

"It is a way that you can help," Heru said. "They will not be
expecting this."

* * * * *

Back down in the basement, Habib, Akil and the other men

inside of the surveillance room were expecting a fierce battle with the American and the Pakistani.

Then the cameras began to disappear in the basement, one by one.

"He's covering the cameras with bags," one of the men stated.

"Let's go," Habib told the others. It was time for them to defend themselves.

"You go first," one of the men responded nervously.

Unafraid of the challenge, Akil decided to go, firing first into the basement hallway at ghosts.

They all waited for a response and heard nothing. Akil then stooped down and began to work his way up the hallway. The other men followed him, standing tall, with Habib in the back. Only one of them was left inside the camera room.

With only the sound of whipping wind, a seven-inch hunting knife spun through the air and landed in the neck of the first man behind Akil.

"ULLKK!" the man responded with the knife poking through the back of his neck. His death was certain.

Akil immediately fired up the hallway again, while Habib nearly lost his lunch. He could only imagine how much blood would squirt out of his man's neck if he ever attempted to remove the blade.

Before they knew it, a second man was struck in the chest from a single bullet.

The immigrant man looked down at his chest in shock at the bullet hole that had sliced through his shirt. He slowly dropped his gun to the ground and fell to his knees, knowing that he would die.

Akil and Habib watched it all as if it was in slow motion, before their man fell sideways into the wall.

Incensed, Akil shouted, "We must not die like *pigs*, but like *men!*" and he charged forward like a maniac, shooting his way up the hallway. Habib breathed deeply and followed him, but the two remaining men looked at each other and ran the other way, deciding to escape through the parking lot exit in the back.

Through his recklessness, Akil was able to make it up the hallway, only to be tripped by the same American that he had lost in combat to earlier. But this time he was more prepared, kicking the American with a right foot that sent him crashing hard into the wall and losing his gun.

Habib took aim at the American with his assault weapon, but he was too slow to pull the trigger before being struck by bullets from the Pakistani.

As Habib fell backward, shaking dreadfully in response to his fate, he still fired his gun in the direction of the American.

Gary ducked the bullets just in time, but only to take an elbow to the jaw from the fierce fighting of Akil. The two men were too close for Akil to effectively aim his gun, so he prepared to fight the American in close combat with it. But the American grabbed the handle of the gun again. Remembering the headbutt from their earlier fight, Akil released the gun from the American and shoved him into the wall with it.

Akil followed up with a jumping right knee to the American's ribs. He then grabbed back onto the long assault gun and headbutted the American back.

In amusement, Saleem watched the two grapple. It was a one-on-one fight, and he wanted to see how well the American could handle himself in combat.

The American stomped on the Arab's toes and kneed him in the chest. He followed up with a right elbow to Akil's jaw that sent him crashing to the floor. And before he could recover, Gary kicked him in the face with his heel.

Saleem was impressed. He nodded. "Good. Now finish him."

He then moved forward with their mission to overtake the surveillance room. He was sure that there were more men inside, so he led with his gun and was very cautious. But when he arrived at the desired camera room, there was no one there.

Saleem grinned to himself and mumbled, "To live another day as a coward is far more important to some men than to die in valor."

He then viewed the dozens of small monitors that filled the

room, in search of one man: Ra-Heru.

As he continued to eye the many screens in search of Heru, Saleem could see where the UAE soldiers were finally overtaking the building and allowing the hostages to escape from the lower levels. He also viewed a beautiful and uncovered Arab woman with an immigrant man who helped her to guide tourists and families to the exits.

As expected, the American man walked in and joined him there inside the surveillance room. He had obviously won his second battle over the tough immigrant.

Saleem looked back at him and grinned. "How did it feel to finally kill a man?"

Gary paused. "If I didn't kill him, I would be dead. I had no choice," Gary said somberly.

Saleem turned away and had his doubts. But at the moment, he had other urgent matters on his mind. He pointed to a monitor from the top floors of the hotel and said, "Here. Once we manage to kill him, this nightmare will be over."

Gary looked at the monitor and saw an average-sized Middle Eastern man helping another to attach a rope to his belt.

Saleem became excited. "That is Ra-Heru, the Egyptian leader of this insane revolt. And he knows that he will die today. Nevertheless, the immigrant laborers of Dubai have already made their point. We will never be ignored in Dubai again."

Gary thought about what Saleem meant when he said, "We will never be ignored." *Could Saleem be part of the revolt? But why would he kill the other immigrants? Why would he work with me?*

Gary thought he must have heard Saleem incorrectly in all of the excitement, then he scanned the monitors and focused on one screen. He spotted Ramia and Johnny in the middle of rescue missions inside the hallways.

"What are they doing? The police allowed them in here?"

Saleem looked back at him and asked, "You know them? I thought they looked out of place myself. But they are doing a good service for the tourists. They are showing extreme bravery.

You must admire that."

Gary made a note of what floor they were on to get them out of there and back to safety outside. He saw no reason for them to be there. He felt the police and the soldiers should have been more involved. But they had their hands full in the lobby.

"That lobby entrance will be their last stand," Gary said.

Heru's imposing lieutenant was still holding down the fort there, and with more hostages and more men, he showed no signs of breaking his reserve.

Saleem asked the American, "Do you think you can handle him?"

Gary sized the man up and nodded confidently. "Yeah. But the hostages are the problem."

"Indeed they are," the Pakistani agreed. "And Heru is my problem."

They watched again as the rebellion leader prepared a daring tactic inside of the left staircase, more than halfway up the building.

* * * * *

Back inside the high staircase up the building, Heru attached his immigrant follower to the thick rubber rope at his waist. He then looked down the staircase to measure how many flights down the soldiers were.

"I still don't understand what you're doing," the immigrant gunman said apprehensively.

Still loyal to Mohd, he felt that his initial ideas of catching the determined son Heru off-guard and attacking him were getting further away from reality.

But Saleem the immigrant traitor did not want to die at the hands of the soldiers without at least taking a shot at Heru, as Mohd would have inspired him to. Nevertheless, the thoughts of a sneak attack were growing slimmer. Heru checked the position of the men below them a final time. He then turned his man to face his toward the staircase window.

"I love my father and can forgive him for his treason against me, but I do not love you."

In one ferocious move, Heru ran his man toward the window and shot out the glass before tossing the armed immigrant through it and down the side of the building, while the man screamed in shock, "NOOOO!"

As the man careened down the side of the building like a bungee jumper, the UAE soldiers were momentarily distracted by the screaming man falling, seemingly to his death. In that instant, Heru made his way down the stairs and began shooting down the soldiers like bowling pins.

By the time the remaining soldiers realized his successful ploy, Heru's end of the rubber rope yanked him back up the steps, where he was able to fly back up in the air while firing his gun down on more of them.

With no training of how to defend themselves against such insane tactics, a dozen more of the soldiers were shot and killed as more of them retreated back into hallways of the building. Heru then cut himself from the rubber rope, sending the hanging immigrant gunman to his death below.

* * * * *

Inside the surveillance room in the basement, Gary asked the Pakistani in confusion, "Why would he kill his own man? Is he sacrificing him?"

Saleem grinned sheepishly and said, "No." He was utterly amazed at the American's naivete. "There are men amongst him who have been planted by his father, Mohd, to stop him. Obviously, he knows."

Gary had no idea how layered the situation was. There were subgroups within the immigrant revolutionaries sabotaging the terrorist attack. Immigrant fighters and the United Arab Emirates soldiers were being killed like pawns on a chessboard. Father was battling son, police were battling immigrants from the crowd outside, and innocent tourists were the ultimate victims in a class-warfare dispute that had nothing to do with them.

All Gary knew was that a group of terrorists had taken over the International Suites that was filled with unsuspecting, innocent people. So he chose to act.

Saleem took a deep breath and secured his assault weapon in his right arm. "Wish me luck," he said to the American. "Heru is mine and will die at my hands." As he turned to walk out of the room, Saleem came face-to-face with Akil, who was severely injured but still alive. Akil stood in the doorway and aimed his gun.

But before he could shoot, Gary grabbed Saleem's gun and pushed them both to the floor while shooting the immigrant adversary multiple times in the chest and avoiding his return of bullets.

As Akil fell out of the doorway to his death, the Pakistani gave the American a serious eye from the floor where they both landed out of harm.

"Let that be your final warning," Saleem told the American. "This is not an occupation of compassion." He then climbed to his feet and brushed himself off. He took the gun back from the dazed American and added, "If your intention is to save lives in warfare, then you must overcome your avoidance of death."

He then stepped out in the hallway, over Akil's dead body, and pulled his knife from the neck of the man that he had killed earlier. He wiped off the blood of his blade on the man's clothing. Then he headed for the staircase to find Heru.

Gary exhaled as he remained inside the surveillance room alone. He was only inches away from death, and the realization of his fatality had finally caught up to him. He gave the man that he had shot and killed a good, long look. Gary had to accept the fact that he had truly killed someone now. He felt numb and emotionless, like the dead bodies of the men that now flooded the hallways.

Chapter 31

IN THE MIDDLE OF the madness outside the hotel, Tariq hustled Mohd into the Union Defence Force's armored truck headquarters. Chief Ali and the UDF's commanding officer awaited them while viewing a screen pulled up with information about Mohd's first son, Talib Aquil Nasir, or better known as "Ra-Heru" and "Heru" for short. And there were few pleasantries exchanged when the Egyptian father entered their truck.

Ali eyed him sternly. "The last time we met, you were on the side of peace and justice. But this time you are on the side of war and treachery."

They sat the Egyptian down in a chair with handcuffs before they released them so that he could talk freely with use of his hands.

Mohd ignored the chief officer's slight and looked past him in the armored truck to view the computer screen that was pulled up on Heru.

"I see that you've now done your research on my son," Mohd

said.

The commander of the Union Defence Force nodded with deep respect. "Your son's military record is impressive. Trained in the Egyptian Special Operations unit, he has served in *eleven* tours of anti-terrorism, including Afghanistan, Iraq, Jordan and Lebanon. So it is *blasphemous* that he has now reduced himself to his own acts of terrorism here in Dubai."

Mohd continued to ignore their slights. He knew that he was there for them to listen. They had no choice. As the prime suspect and architect of the terrorist rebellion at the hotel, the police and the military were commissioned to report all information and findings to the Prime Minister and the President of the United Arab Emirates so that they might prevent another incident of an immigrant laborer revolt in the future.

Realizing his level of importance in their case, Mohd was able to take his time with them. He even asked them for something to drink.

To move the process along quickly, Tariq granted him his wish with a fast bottle of water, while the other men showed their obvious disdain with much slower movements.

"Thank you," Mohd said to Tariq. "You have been very kind to me."

Ali impatiently scowled at the Egyptian again. "This is not a *game*. You are only here to tell us what we need to know." He stopped just short of reminding the Egyptian that he would surely be put to death when the dust settled, and that they would be ordered to torture him if needed. But Mohd already knew as much, and he did not plan to stall them any longer. He understood how valuable his story would be for the future of immigrant laborers in Dubai, for his nation of Egypt and as a lesson for the wealthy Arabs of the Middle East.

"Do any of you know the Egyptian legend of Osiris?" Mohd asked.

Including the UDFs second in command and the intelligence officials, Mohd had an audience of seven men. A few of them knew the story of Osiris vaguely, but they were not willing to admit to it to the extent that the wise, old Egyptian would know it. So they remained silent and let the man continue his revelations.

"In the ancient Egyptian legend, Osiris was a god and the king of Egypt, who was murdered by his jealous brother, Set, to capture his throne. Set chopped Osiris up into many pieces and spread his body all throughout Egypt. Then Isis, Osiris's wife and queen, gathered all of the parts of her slain husband to resurrect him with a golden phallus to sire a son, Horus. And then it was *Horus* who was raised to avenge his father and take back the kingdom of Egypt."

Ali cut him off and asked, "Are you making this reference in light of your own son to avenge you and the loss of your wife?" The chief continued to be impatient, particularly in the midst of hostages and warfare. Who wanted to hear some ancient legend in the middle of disarray? But the other men were interested in hearing how all the dots connected to the present.

Mohd answered, "Indeed. My son only recently changed his name to Ra-Heru, which is referenced as the Egyptian god of war and vengeance. But the name has its roots in *Horus*, who would avenge his own father."

The commander of the UDF soldiers nodded, understanding his own ideas of the story to be correct. "But Egypt is a *Muslim* nation now. You are our *brothers*."

Mohd smiled and shook his head. "This is where our true conflict lies. Egypt was *never* a Muslim nation. Nor was it *Christian*. So although I now carry the name Mohd Ahmed Nasir from my *own* father, it was my Nubian Egyptian *wife* who understood *more* of the country's history. And she reminded *me* and all of her five children that Egypt had been invaded by everyone, including Romans, Greeks, Persians, Turks and finally the Arabs. And each invading nation would force themselves and their cultures on Egypt in an attempt to change the beliefs, the language, the customs and the most elaborate *history* of mankind.

"So as I reveal *more* of the legend of Osiris," Mohd continued, "we find that he was from the *true* lineage of Egyptian ancestors, where *Set*, his jealous brother, was linked with foreign invaders, who became his army. And when Isis was made to gather the slain parts of her husband's body, she did so with the *allies* of Egypt, who would later help her son *Horus* to overthrow Set and his army of foreigners."

"But we're not *in* Egypt," Ali argued. "That was all a long time ago. Your son is now holding hostage *hundreds* of innocent tourists and their families who have *nothing* to do with Egypt or Osiris."

Mohd stroked his chin as he prepared a measured but stern response.

"That is where you are *wrong*. We are *all* in Egypt, my friend, and this has *everything* to do with Osiris. Just as the nomadic Arabs have now occupied lands that they build on and call their own, it is only through European investments in *oil* and more recently in construction, real estate and foreign trade that your so-called royal 'Skeikhs' mean *anything*. It is all stolen land and stolen wealth, where the arrogant Arabs now mistreat the Indians, the Africans, and the Asians, who are the true builders of these *new* Egypts around the world.

"So as I was first conflicted by my son's mission to remind us all of our need for human *justice*, the present day *Osirises* are the true ancestral people of peace, who continue to be plotted against, slain, enslaved and shipped around the world to work and appease the greed of *nomads*. I have now realized that today was my son's *fate*. And who else would be more qualified to remember this than the thousands of terrified tourists and their families, including thousands of more immigrant laborers who will all be affected by what happened here today at the International Suites?"

Even Ali fell silent. Suddenly Mohd's story of Ancient Egypt made perfect sense. For what was the city of Dubai but a modern showcase of Arab wealth and amateur relics at the hands of cheap and foreign laborers? Even their building of man-made islands could easily be said to be inspired by the greatness of the Egyptian Pyramids. The whole *world* had been inspired by Egypt—Italy, Greece, Persia, Russia, France, Israel, Spain, Great

Britain, India, China, Japan, Mexico, and the North and South Americas. It was not even an argument.

Mohd cut through the brief silence. "That is why the ancient Egyptians' bloodline continue to have a chip on their shoulders, knowing that they are the *true* royal people of this earth, no matter how much the nomads from the North, the East or from the West continue to amass their stolen wealth. And even Egypt fell from greed."

None of the men inside of the armored truck were from royal lineage, so they could all relate to the rich and wealthy of the world who had often used the ideas, the land, the labor, and the hope and dreams of everyone else to build their riches.

Tariq, an Oman immigrant with Ethiopian and Somalian blood in his own ancestry, finally ended the long-winded history lesson and brought everyone back to the tragedy at hand. "So how many immigrant men does he have?"

Mohd took a breath and knew that it was over. "Not enough to win. He only has enough men to make his point. And even some of those men are still loyal to me."

"And do you feel this all will be worth it?" the UDF commander questioned. Even he realized that Mohd would be put to death by the Emirates.

Mohd exhaled and answered, "*Life* is always worth more than death. So my heart aches for him. But if it were not for the untimely death of my wife, none of us would be here today."

* * * * *

As Mohd finished his historical conversation inside the armored truck headquarters with the UAE authorities, more than a hundred reinforcement soldiers were flown into the downtown area with more on the way.

Ra-Heru watched from the window of the twenty-seventh floor of the building as a dozen more helicopters flew in. He understood that the end was near. Not only had his men lost the surveillance room, but they had now lost half of the bottom floors to the Union Defence Force as more hostages continued to flee.

Heru then called his lieutenant on the bottom floor of the lobby to check in without his surveillance team.

"It's Heru. How are the men doing outside in the crowd?"

Down in the lobby with nearly a hundred hostages, the imposing lieutenant peeked outside to see what he could report without catching a sniper's bullet in his forehead. But the dozen or so immigrant men from the ambush had already been chased down and killed.

"They are no longer in commission," he reported back to Heru.

Heru nodded and paused. "Okay. It is time for phase three. Let's stall the soldiers for as long as we can, and let the people all know our mission."

"Yes, I agree," his lieutenant commented. And he immediately began to shoot into the ceiling to gain everyone's attention.

"AAAHHHH!" the tourists and their families screamed. None of the men had shot a gun in the lobby for the first thirty minutes that they had arrived there. They wanted the hostages to feel safe. But now the lieutenant needed them to listen while being well guarded by his men to prevent any attack.

"To all of you who are here, whether you are from America, Britain, Australia, France, Russia, Germany, Japan, China, India, South Africa or wherever, we mean you no harm. You have only been detained here today because the United Arab Emirates have *refused* to give us the young *Emirati* developer Abdul Khalif Hassan and his wife, Hamda, who have allowed *many* atrocities in their labor workforce. And not only them, but *all* of the *Emirati* developers of Dubai.

"We, the laboring immigrants from all around the world, have been the nameless and faceless builders, workers and dreamers of everything that is here. Yet the ruling class continues to ignore our cries for fair wages, health, housing and more humane conditions and respect on the job. And yet they have *refused* to negotiate with us on these most important issues."

"And this is how you respond, by taking innocent hostages?"

an Indian traveler yelled from the crowd. "And people have been *killed*, whether it was your intention to kill them or not."

Inside the basement staircase, Gary waited with a fully loaded assault weapon and an automatic pistol while listening to it all. He still needed his own education on the revolt. And although Johnny had already told him plenty about some of the conditions in the UAE for workers, it was indeed more informative to hear it from the angry workers themselves.

The lieutenant responded, "It was not *us* who harmed *any* of you. It was the *soldiers*, the *police* and *vigilantes*, who attempt to distract us from our goals."

"Nooo," the Indian man cried out. "It was *your* men who shot and killed some of us."

"Yeah!" a few of the other hostages chimed in.

"Which men?" the lieutenant asked.

A few of the immigrant gunmen grew nervous inside the room as the Indian man looked around for them. Finding the angry immigrant from Palestine, the Indian pointed and said, "Him. He has been very forceful with everyone."

Without hesitation, the lieutenant fired his gun into the chest of the defiant gunman. Again, there were screams from the shocked hostages.

"If we were interested in harming you, it would be as easy as that. But as it now goes on," the lieutenant said, "we doubt that the *Emirati* rulers have reported *anything* of your situation to the public of Dubai, Abu Dhabi, Deira, Sharjah or the over provinces and cities of the Emirates. *Why?* Because they are stubborn with the local news, and they do not want you to be afraid of coming back, and more importantly, they do not want the world to know the conditions under which we are forced to work here. But after today, they will have no *choice* but to listen to us."

Gary was ready to react immediately after hearing the gunshots, but he composed himself and continued to listen while hoping and praying for the best.

I just have to wait. I have to wait for the right moment, he convinced himself. The lieutenant continued, "Our Egyptian leader, Ra-Heru Amun, has organized us here today to *die* for our cause. And some of you may indeed die along with us, not by design, but by happenstance."

The lieutenant waited for their collective moans to die down before he continued. "I too am an immigrant with dreams from the lower class of Yemen, one of the oldest civilizations in the Middle East, which long ago became the stomping ground for the *new* civilizations. And I do not expect you all to sympathize with my cause and that of the other men in this room today, but I *do* expect for you to remember, and to do your own research, so that you are better prepared to know the true histories of the world."

* * * * *

Inside the armored truck headquarters, Mohd, Tariq, Ali and the UDF officials listened to the lieutenant themselves through high-technology microphones that were able to pick up all of the sounds inside the lobby. And they all agreed that the incident would pose a *nightmare* for the *Emirati* businessmen, who had begun to bank on the UAE as a safe haven location for much of their new economy.

Ali looked at Mohd and asked, "So their plan now is to converse with the world media?" Before he even posed the question, he understood that the Emirates would have no choice but to expose themselves to an international conversation about the practices of their construction workforce.

Tariq grinned, shook his head and stated the obvious, "The Emirates are not going to like that." The investigator had an acute understanding of how proud and determined the ruling class of the United Arab Emirates was to exert their will on their own society. But now the immigrant workers were forcing them to play a more compromised hand of cards.

In the meantime, the intelligence officials quickly looked up the meaning of the name "Amun" and reported their findings to their commanding officer.

"So, Ra-Heru Amun is the defender of the poor, and comparable to Zeus in Greek mythology?" the commander asked Mohd.

Mohd grinned, loving their sudden focus and respect for the ancient world history of Egypt. He then nodded with his answer. "Even today, in the Christian societies around the world, the masses of their poor call out to *Ah-men* after every prayer, the God of all gods."

The commander nodded back and was satisfied with their present grip on the situation. And he had heard enough. They could not possibly allow the immigrant terrorists to dictate their terms for world media coverage. It was impermissible. So the soldiers were forced to move faster and stronger to take out the head by any means necessary: Ra-Heru Amun, who was previously known as Talib Aquil Nasir.

The commander told his second in command, "Send all of the men to the top floors to terminate Ra-Heru. That is our own chance to avoid more of an embarrassment for the Emirates. And tell them to continue to move out the hostages."

Mohd overheard the command to terminate his son, but there was nothing that he could do about it. However, he understood that their task would not be easy, for even with a thousand men against him, Heru believed that he was right, and in his righteousness, he would continue to fight them until every drop of blood in his body had been spilled for the love of his mother, the vengeance of his father and as a champion of the silent people.

Chapter 32

THE SHOCKING NEWS FROM the International Suites had begun to reach the cities, provinces and the Palm Island fronds, through phone calls, texts and pictures, including the gas station convenience store where Basim worked.

"What?!" he responded to the news from his co-workers and manager. Basim had still not heard a peep from his cousin, and he had called and texted her several times before even hearing the news. He ran toward the front door and told his boss, "I dropped my cousin Ramia off at the International Suites earlier today, and she has not called me back yet."

The manager ran out behind him, not only concerned about the young man's beautiful cousin from Jordan, but about Basim's safety in trying to drive to the hotel.

"Basim, surely the traffic is backed up. You will not be able to get in through the commotion."

Basim ignored his boss and made his way to his car in the parking area beside the gas station.

"I must try anyway. *En sha Allah*," he responded anxiously while climbing behind the wheel. Basim was also secretly upset with the manager for not agreeing to hire his cousin. She could have been working there with him that day instead of downtown searching desperately for a second job.

Merciful Allah! Basim thought to himself as he drove recklessly through the traffic. Every light and slow-moving car ahead of him had quickly become a nuisance.

* * * * *

Back at the hotel, Ramia and Johnny were now accepted by the UAE soldiers and the police as they continued to walk the tourists, families and children out of the hotel. Ramia's gentle, kind and compassionate presence was indeed an enhancement to keep the hostages and children calm throughout the process.

"It's okay, it's okay," Ramia said, hugging a crying daughter. They had worked themselves up to the eleventh floor, and as she continued to think about the American tourist, her duty for the safety of the people had become her first priority. She only hoped that the handsome and courageous American would survive.

Johnny continued to watch her while he carried children and babies out of the building. He could not believe her energy and nerve to help so many strangers regardless of her own safety. His apprehension of her actions had turned into awe. Not only was she beautiful, she was worthy of his utmost respect.

She is so amazing! he began to tell himself, changing his earlier opinion of her. And he was glad that he had decided to help her.

* * * * *

Gary remained conflicted about his next move inside of the staircase to the lobby. He understood that charging the room full of hostages and more immigrant gunmen could only cause more harm than good. That was why the UAE soldiers and police had not attacked them again from outside. Heru's lieutenant had successfully fortified their position at the entrance of the hotel, where they were obviously now beginning to plead their case to the world. So instead of forcing himself to be a foolish hero who endangered more lives, Gary returned to the surveillance room to figure out his next move to save lives.

While viewing the many cameras throughout the building, he looked first for his Pakistani ally, who was climbing on top of the service elevator on his way up to face Heru on the top floors. He then looked again for Ramia and Johnny, who continued to help hostages out of the building down the left staircase. The soldiers and the police were helping them now.

Instinctively, he wanted to see them and thank them for their bravery. He did not expect it from them, but he respected it and wanted to help. But then he thought again about the embattled revolt leader, Ra-Heru Amun. Despite the man's noble mission, Gary realized that his extreme ideas had to be stopped. They involved too many innocent people. He also admitted to himself that he craved to see the man in action before he died, as if it was a creed of warriors.

Gary had often thought in his restless dreams and nightmares about facing the Colombian man who had killed his best friend in Medellín. And as he had faced the surviving West Virginia fugitive who had murdered his mother, he felt that by facing Heru and surviving it, he would make himself stronger. So he took off running for the left staircase to see Ramia and Johnny before helping the Pakistani and the UAE soldiers with Heru.

* * * * *

On top of the service elevator, Saleem first planned to avoid the many soldiers who might have confused him for the wrong side, so he was very careful to avoid them when he finally arrived at the top of the building. He even put on some of the soiled and bloody clothes of a gunman who had been shot and killed inside the service elevator below him. The stench of murder was everywhere.

As Saleem climbed out of the elevator shaft and into the hallway of the twenty-seventh floor, he could hear the furious sounds of the helicopters and the gun battles that were taking place on the roof. And there was a hallway full of dead men.

Saleem then dropped to the hallway floor to crawl forward while peeking underneath the locked room doors for the unfortunate hostages. He could see under the door as a lone man tiptoed from the bathroom, too fearful to flush the toilet and bring too much attention to himself and his woman inside the room who he whispered to upon his return.

"These people will never forget this when it is finally over," Saleem mumbled to himself.

The next minute, three immigrant gunmen ran down from the staircase that led to the roof and started grabbing loaded guns from the dead men who lined the hallway.

"Hurry up! Hurry, hurry, hurry!" one of the men shouted. But it was not the voice of Heru.

Quickly deciding to play dead, Saleem closed his eyes and remained still on the floor while one of the men attempted to pull his own assault weapon out of his hands, like they did with the rest of the men they presumed to be dead.

Surprising him, Saleem shot the man several times in the chest. He then aimed up the hallway and shot the others before they could realize what was happening and recover.

* * * * *

Heru heard the gunshots right above him from an empty room on the twenty-sixth floor. When he heard them, as he had for the past three hours, he grabbed his weapons and left quickly to investigate.

Heading to the staircase, he first wanted to check in on the positions of the soldiers below, and he found that they were getting closer, but not close enough to panic. So he continued on his way to help out his men on the roof.

* * * **

As soon as Saleem heard the footsteps in the staircase down the hall in front of him, he played dead again with his gun.

Heru looked up the hallway and saw nothing, but he remained suspicious. He continued up to the roof and decided to stop and wait inside of the staircase.

All the while, the furious battle continued on the roof, where the helicopters had to refrain from using heavy artillery out of the fear of killing hostages in their rooms on the top floor. And as more of Heru's men retreated from the roof to retrieve more guns filled with ammunition, when they spotted him waiting inside the staircase, Heru quickly signaled for them to be quiet in their work.

"Go," he said quietly, and pointed to the twenty-seventh floor.

His men obeyed him nervously, afraid that their fearless leader had caught them in a retreat, but Heru was more concerned about the gunshots and the silence inside the hallway. So he listened again and waited.

On cue with new gunshots, Heru leaped into the hallway and fired at everything within earshot. Expecting as much, Saleem covered himself with the body of a dead man and fired back.

Heru jumped back inside the exit doorway as the return of accurate bullets just missed him. And he knew immediately that he was up against a more experienced foe.

"Another traitor," he told himself back inside the staircase.

He thought about helping his men back out onto the roof, but decided against it. He understood that his new foe would be too dangerous to leave behind, so he retreated to the lower floors.

Saleem continued to listen to as much as he could through all of the gunshots on the roof, but as more of Heru's men continued to retreat to the twenty-seventh floor, he continued to shoot them down.

Meanwhile, Heru made his way down to the twenty-fifth floor and ran to the right staircase of the building to double back up to the twenty-seventh floor from the opposite side. This new traitor was in his way and stopping him and his men from securing the roof. But by the time he had made it back into the hallway, the man was gone.

Heru proceeded back up the hallway of the twenty-seventh floor cautiously and back toward the exit door to the roof. However, as he neared it, he could no longer hear the sounds of battle up on the roof, which was surely a bad sign. He knew that he had finally run out of able men. Not trusting the prospect of stepping back through the exit doorway, he picked up one of his dead men from the hallway floor and pushed the body through the exit. Shots rang out immediately and riddled the body.

Determined to win, Heru leaped through the doorway right afterward and fired several accurate shots up the stairs, hitting several UAE soldiers who had barely made their way into the building.

Heru dove down into the staircase right onto the backs and bodies of more of his slain men as he continued to fire bullets upward at more of the soldiers who were entering the building from the roof. And as he dove there onto the backs and bodies of the dead men, one of them moved and aimed to shoot him.

The traitor! Heru told himself.

Close enough to grab the gun, he pushed it away in close range as more bullets riddled the staircase wall.

Heru then attempted to aim his own gun at the traitor, only for his foe to grab it and push it away as well, with more bullets ricocheting up the wall.

Realizing the soldiers were far too close for comfort to tussle with a skilled traitor, Heru dove down another staircase to retreat to the twenty-sixth floor. And to his surprise, the traitor followed him. Heru then smashed the man into the exit doorway before pulling out his pistol, which was much better to use in close range. But again, the traitor countered and grabbed his arm away, causing the pistol to shoot into the hallway ceiling.

Finally, Heru was able to get a good look at him.

"I know you. You are the construction worker recruited by Father."

Saleem, the taller and stronger man, responded, "Yes. Mohd is a good man, and he will be brought down and killed because of the ideas of his *mad son*."

"He is an *old* man who was taken advantage of by the Emirates," Heru told him with a right knee to his ribs.

Saleem took the knee, leaned forward and attempted to headbutt him but missed as Heru fell backward with a trip move and the Pakistani's heavier weight, slamming him headfirst into the wall.

With no time to follow-up and shoot the traitor, the UAE soldiers were right on top of them as Heru fired several shots into the exit doorway.

He leaped back to his feet and ran down the hallway, continuing to shoot at the soldiers who pursued him. The reinforcement soldiers wore thick black helmets with shields and bulletproof vests, so Heru aimed for their necks and knees, injuring three of them in the front.

* * * * *

Back down in the thirteenth-floor hallway, Gary caught up with Ramia and Johnny, who were overjoyed to see him.

"Gary!" Ramia let out, hugging him instantly. "I was so worried about you." She squeezed him as if attempting to push all of the air out of his lungs. Johnny squeezed him as well to make it worse.

"Hey, *easy*," Gary whined, cringing. His ribs and arms were sore from so much diving, rolling and fighting earlier. But he was still ready for more, if needed.

"I was concerned about you two. I saw you on the monitors in the basement. What are you doing in here?"

"The same as *you*, man. We're trying to be *heroes*," Johnny quipped.

Gary grinned and shook his head. "You're unbelievable, man." Even in the middle of turmoil, the guy was full of jokes and positive energy.

"No, *you're* unbelievable!" Johnny said. "We saw how you got in here. *Everyone* saw it." Then he whispered, "So, are you a secret agent?"

Ramia slapped Johnny on his chest. "Stop it. Even if he was, he could not tell you."

Gary noticed their short but important work together had given them a chemistry, as if they had known each other for years. And it was good.

"I'll tell you both later. But how did *you* get in?"

With the soldiers passing by them in the hallway with more hostages, Ramia answered, "We'll tell you that later," and grinned, mocking him.

Gary chuckled. "All right, it's a deal. We'll trade secrets later. But I just wanted to let you guys know that I was all right."

Ramia became concerned again. She grabbed on to the hem of his shirt and asked him, "Where are you going?"

Gary took a deep breath. "To finish something."

Stealing the moment, Ramia pulled him into her and kissed his lips, forcefully.

"You come back in one *piece*, Mr. Stevens. We want to know who you are."

Gary nodded thoughtfully. "Okay. That's a deal." But as he ran off through the exit door and back down to the lower-level floors to avoid the soldiers, who he assumed would stop him from going up, Gary was concerned about facing Heru with a gun in hand.

That guy seems lethal, he mused as he hustled up the hallway of the eleventh floor toward the service elevator.

What if that tough guy can't take him? he thought of Saleem. The two of them still hadn't exchanged names. And although Saleem knew that Gary was obviously an American, Gary had no idea what nation Saleem was from. He looked like a million other men from the Middle East, with added height and ruggedness.

Nevertheless, the Egyptian Ra-Heru Amun appeared to be an expert assassin on a serious mission to kill as many UAE soldiers as one man could.

When the service elevator arrived, Gary quickly stepped inside with the dead bodies and climbed to the top as his ally had done earlier. Only he didn't know how to get off when it reached the top faster than he expected.

Gary jumped clumsily onto the wires beside him and nearly fell to his death.

"Shit!" he yelled, holding on for his life. He then swung his legs back and forth until he could reach the elevator doorway and pull it open.

After climbing into the hallway of the twenty-seventh floor, Gary dove to the ground in a pile of dead men as he spotted more UAE soldiers up at the opposite hallway. They looked down in his direction but failed to check it out.

"It was probably one of the guests at their door," one of the soldiers commented. "But we are not to help them escape until we find and kill Heru. That is the commander's direct orders. It is too dangerous to be concerned with the tourists at this time."

Nevertheless, they kept two men on the floor to watch over it, forcing Gary to inch his way toward the nearby exit staircase until he could make it out unnoticed. But once he had made it, he froze. Someone was hustling back up the staircase straight toward him, and it was a lone man and not soldiers. With more dead men inside of the staircase, Gary thought of blending in and playing dead, but the man was too close to him, and Gary was certain that his white skin and light-brown hair would stand out too much amongst the brown immigrant bodies on the floor.

With fight-or-flight instincts, Gary rolled back into the exit door and dove through it, returning to the hallway with the soldiers. But he remained low to the ground, climbing over the dead bodies. It was a perfect move that saved his life.

Ra-Heru Amun burst into the hallway shooting straight at the soldiers down the hall. He had a much stronger assault weapon that blew them backward like toys. Realizing how fast he had to move, Gary had already grabbed a weapon from the floor and fired back in Heru's direction. But he did it too fast to aim correctly, with bullets flying overhead into the ceiling.

Heru dove back from the fire and repositioned his big gun to shoot at the unexpected assailant with white skin and light hair.

That must be the American! Every thought and recognition was lightning fast with Heru.

Before Heru could aim his powerful weapon and return fire, Gary shot at the guestroom door to his left and broke inside like an American football player sacking the quarterback. He planned to apologize to whoever was inside the room, hoping that they would not be injured by him, but when he flipped and rolled over into the bedroom, he found that the room was empty.

Gary quickly looked over to the wall behind the bed as a buffer for a possible shootout with Heru, and he spotted a wall full of black bombs.

"Oh, my God!" he whispered to himself. Heru's final plan unfolded before his eyes. "He's gonna blow up the building from the top and let it burn down."

A memory of the Twin Towers in New York rushed to mind, where two airplanes had struck the top floors with tanks full of flammable fuel. And with a highly flammable explosion at the top floors of a building, because of the obvious height and the dangers of collapse, it was nearly impossible to put out as opposed to battling a bomb from a lower floor.

Heru was making *certain* that the world would not ignore their revolt. And as the thoughts of paranoia ran rapidly through Gary's mind, he felt fortunate that he had found the bombs before the plan was set in motion, but he also realized that he was trapped inside with him.

"I don't know who you are, my friend. But you just involved yourself in something that you will regret from your cremation," Heru spoke into the room from the hallway.

Gary responded, "I don't know who you are either. But it looks like you haven't set your bombs yet, unless you planned to have them all in one room."

He was assuming the room was a distribution point, but Heru laughed at him.

"You are wrong, my friend. Those are only the *leftovers*. But too bad you will not be able to tell anyone before you die."

Gary looked and thought of jumping out of the window with bedsheets. But while on the twenty-seventh floor, he would need to shoot his way back into a lower room, where he would surely endanger a family.

That's not gonna work, he told himself. *These sheets will only reach about three to four floors down.*

Fortunately, Heru had more soldiers to deal with as he began to fire back down the hallway at more men, so Gary seized the opportunity to shoot his way back out, aiming at the walls of the room where he felt Heru would be standing inside the hall.

Heru responded by shooting through the room's walls, forcing Gary to crash to the floor. But he was determined to blast his way out with the help of the soldiers.

Just keep shooting, he told himself. *He can't afford to stand there in the hallway. We all have to force him to retreat.*

Gary continued to fire up through the hotel room wall until he ran out of bullets. But his calculated hunch was right. Heru could not possibly hold his position for long. The soldiers would all know his position.

In fact, Heru had already remained there too long. And by the time he had returned to the staircase to escape from the twenty-seventh floor, the stairs were flooded with more soldiers behind him. Undeterred with his powerful assault weapon, Heru cleared a path with bullets that tore apart the staircase, forcing the surviving soldiers to retreat again.

* * * * *

Back down at the armored truck headquarters at the hotel's entrance, the commander of the UAE Defence Force was incredulous. He couldn't believe the continued reports.

"You mean that *one man* continues to rebuff you? *Ludicrous!* You are an *army!* So act like one!" he yelled at his men through their hi-tech military phones. The communications scramblers had no effect on them.

But as the commander of the Union Defence Force stepped back out into view, along with his second in command, Chief Ali Youssef and Tariq Mohammed, another secret plan was being hatched. Just as it was the UAE Defence Force plan to take out Heru as the head of the immigrant rebellion, Heru had a plan of his own to take out the head of the army. And out of the crowd, a woman wearing a full white burqa dress with a fully covered headdress, aimed a pistol and shot it at the commanding officer.

Tariq saw the assault in time and reacted quickly enough to push the commander out of the way. But Ali and the second in command officer were both hit with bullets before the police and the UAE soldiers could shoot the woman down.

Realizing that his good friend had been hit, Tariq quickly moved to him to lift him up. But without a vest and several shots to his chest and neck, Ali's death was imminent.

He then jabbed his friend Tariq in the chest with his finger and in his dying breath told him, "You're the new chief. *En sha Allah.*"

Tariq cried out loud, while cradling his dead friend. "AAAH-HH! Merciful Allah! Merciful Allah!"

The commander of the Defence Force was incensed as his men tended to his second in command, who was also dying from bullet wounds. The commander then shouted to his men in reference to the dead assassin, wearing the white burqa, "Take it off! Take it off!"

As the largely Muslim crowd watched in alarm, the soldiers found a scarred-face man under the clothing.

"Merciful Allah," some of the men commented and cringed at the sight of the severely burned face.

The commander had a look of his own and immediately understood that a full covering was the only way the man could hide his hideous face. But when Tariq saw him, he knew exactly who he had been.

"He was the accomplice with Heru two nights ago in Deira when they slit the throats of two elders who knew of their wicked plans. One of the attackers was hit in the face with hot fish oil.

And it was *him*."

The commander nodded, increasingly impressed with the investigator and private counsel. "You know your work well, my friend. And I thank you for saving my life."

Tariq nodded soberly. "If only I could save everyone."

Chapter 33

INCENSED NOW HIMSELF, TARIQ rushed back into the armored truck headquarters where they continued to hold Mohd, and the private investigator and counsel pulled out his pistol to point at the Egyptian's right eye. His friend Ali was already headed to the hospital, but only to confirm the obvious.

"You tell us what the plans are, right now!" Tariq shouted before the commander and his soldiers could stop him. "Right *now*," he repeated, "before more people *die*, starting with *you*!"

Mohd refused to even blink while waiting for the bullet to end his life. He repeated the words that he had told Bakar earlier. "I am already dead. And my spirit died long ago with my wife. This is why I have no control over my son.

"What he does now is of his own mind," Mohd continued. "I can only imagine, like you, what he will do next. And whenever I was able to find anything out, Heru killed them."

"How much didn't you come forth to tell the proper authorities then?" the commander asked him.

Mohd breathed deeply and felt guilty. He answered, "He is my son. So I prayed to every god of mankind that he would not go through with this. But Heru became his *own* god, and he would not be denied by his father."

The commander nodded and pulled Tariq's gun away. He told Mohd, "You are definitely going to die. But you're going to die after court in the *Sharia* law. That is the way of the United Arab Emirates."

"Do what you will with me," Mohd said. "I only pray that you are able to stop my son with the men that I have planted amongst him."

Just then, there were new reports from the soldiers that had finally secured the roof of the building:

"The American helped us to find a room full of bombs on the top floor. But he said Heru told him that there are more. So we have no choice but to evacuate the rest of the rooms to find the ones with the bombs in them on the top floors. That is why Heru has spent so much time protecting the top of the building."

Tariq's and the commander's eyes widened with fear. But they refused to panic. They were forced to figure it all out.

"What about the lower floors?" the commander asked his men.

"We found nothing in the rooms and only security men and shipment workers locked up in the basement."

"Well, continue to look," the commander ordered. "In the meantime, get rid of Heru! And then we will deal with the lobby."

When the commander ended his call, he looked at Tariq and asked, "Who is this American? Give us a search using his face."

"We tried earlier, but nothing came up but his school information. He is a graduate from the University of Louisville, with a double degree in Business and International Studies. And he was kicked off the lacrosse team at Duke for low grades in his freshman year. It also said that his mother, Gabrielle Stevens, was killed in a carjacking incident five year ago and that his best friend was murdered by unknown men in Colombia, South America, in that same year. So, he's sympathetic to those in tragedy."

"Yes, but he has nothing of a military history?" the commander questioned.

"Nothing that was reported. It says he owns a record store in downtown Louisville."

The commander chuckled and said, "This American is a total mystery man. But he has helped us several times today."

Tariq walked back over to Mohd and asked, "What of these loyal men that you have planted to stop him? Are any of them good enough?"

Mohd breathed deeply again and thought only of Saleem. He had a good feeling about the rugged Pakistani's potential in warfare. But it was only a hunch. And even Saleem was a longshot against the determination of his son.

Mohd said, "What of this American tourist? If he was able to speak to my son and live, then he may have a chance."

"Yeah," the commander grumbled, "we'll see."

* * * * *

As the time approached four o'clock, Basim had parked his car and started to run through the crowded downtown. Despite the Emirates disdain, even the restrictive news stations were beginning to report some of the story. But they were only allowed to call it a "disturbance." However, Basim thought better of it, and he was not going to wait to find out more, hours later, that it was much worse than what was first reported.

He also thought that he might be ready to send his cousin Ramia back home to Jordan or maybe move to America with her where the culture would be less restrictive and more of her liking. But America and its large urban cities, where the majority of the jobs were, could be dangerous too. Or maybe London could be an alternative.

All of those options crossed Basim's mind as he continued to run through the crowds for the International Suites. But none of his new ideas would mean anything without Ramia still being alive.

* * * * *

Not only was Ramia still alive, but she continued to help hundreds of others to survive the nightmare in broad daylight.

"We have only twelve floors to go," she told Johnny on the fifteenth floor of the building as they continued to move their way up after the soldiers secured the safety of each floor.

"Yeah, I'm gonna need the longest full-body massage in the *world* after this," Johnny complained lightly.

"Yes, but think of all of the beautiful women of the world who love a real hero," Ramia teased him.

Johnny paused and had a thought. "You want to take a picture of me on my cell phone inside the hallways."

"No!" Ramia snapped at him candidly. "This is not a time for pictures. So keep your mind on the benefit and welfare of the families that we are helping to escape."

"Yeah, I know, I know. I'm still here, aren't I?"

Ramia grinned while still thinking and worrying about the mysterious American traveler, Gary Stevens.

* * * * *

Back on the twenty-sixth floor, Gary worked his way down behind a group of new escaping hostages from the top floor, who were mostly the wealthier bigwigs with few children. And as they worked their way down the staircase, Gary noticed that soldiers had captured his ally.

Saleem sat in the floor between three armed men who were still trying to figure out what to do with him.

Gary saw him and went into acting mode. "Hey, that's my partner, Muhammad. We're working together."

The men looked at Saleem and then back at the American.

"He was knocked out while trying to fight with Heru," one of the men commented. "And he was lucky that we found him when he did. He was well on his way to being murdered. But he told us his name is Saleem, not Muhammad."

Gary thought fast and said, "Yeah, Saleem Muhammad. He's probably still a little dizzy, that's all. We all can forget our last names sometimes."

Saleem eyed him and was not at all amused.

"And what is your name?" the men asked Gary. They all continued to call him "the American," even their head commander.

"I'm Gary," he answered, "Gary Stevens from Louisville. Now let me get my partner back. We work much better together. Did you guys see us in the lobby earlier?"

He was hamming it up to get Saleem out of there. And it took awhile, but it eventually worked.

"You two need to go back down and let us professionals handle this," a more confident soldier boasted.

Saleem nodded in submission, as if accepting it all, but only until he could walk alone with the American down to the twenty-third floor.

"We need to get back up there and try him again," Gary whispered. "Maybe you and I both would be able to deal with him."

Saleem nodded, still massaging his aching forehead. "He's indeed a tough man to take. And he used my own strength against me, knowing that I could overtake him."

As they slipped onto the twenty-third floor, Gary asked, "So what's his weak spot?"

Saleem thought about it and said, "The bombs. That is his ultimate goal here. So he will continue to fight the soldiers to protect them."

As soon as Saleem said that, powerful gunshots began to ring out at the higher floors of the building again.

"Let's go," Saleem said. "You go back up with the soldiers, and I'll take the opposite stairs."

Neither one of them had a gun, but with so many dead bodies with guns on the top floors of the building, they didn't need to carry one. They only had to grab another one from a dead body.

By the time Gary had returned to the twenty-sixth floor, the tough-talking soldier was pulling a knife out of his neck while bleeding profusely.

Jesus! This guy is good! Gary told himself as he proceeded back into the hallway of the twenty-sixth floor. New dead of the UAE soldiers were everywhere, like plague. Heru was a serious one-man army.

Gary then heard more shooting and soldiers running on the floor above him. Grabbing another assault weapon and a pistol, he ran up the stairs and back to the twenty-seventh floor, where he arrived just in time to catch Heru climbing up into the ceiling.

Gary aimed and shot at him immediately, just missing his foot. Not wanting to chance him getting away again, Gary ran up the hallway after him and continued to shoot, forcing Heru to jump back down from the ceiling and shoot back.

Gary was forced to dive into an open room for safety. But as Heru ran to the opposite end of the hallway to take the staircase back down, Saleem charged through the exit door and cracked him with the butt of his assault weapon.

He now realized that it took too long to aim a heavy rifle inside of a small hallway. And you could never be slow against a man with the speed and anticipation of Heru.

Heru lost his gun from the hit and stated, "You again," and kicked Saleem in his chest to create distance. But Saleem grabbed on to his right leg, only for Heru to whip around his left leg and send the Pakistani face-first into the wall again. However, Saleem would not let his right leg go.

"Gary!" he screamed down the hall to the American to help him.

Gary jumped back out into the hallway with a gun, aiming to shoot, but knew that he couldn't fire with so many different changes in their position. He could accidentally shoot Saleem.

"Help me!" Saleem hollered.

Heru tussled with him and finally kicked his foot free while reaching down to grab his second blade from a holster on his ankle. Gary arrived down the hall just in time to distract Heru enough to swing his sharp blade in his direction instead of at Saleem.

"You missed," Gary teased. "And I'm not dead yet." He figured talking trash might be a way to throw off the Egyptian's concentration.

"Keep talking so I can hear you moan when I finally cut you," Heru said.

"Come on and bring it," Gary challenged him, bouncing on his toes with readiness.

Heru stood between both men in the hallway with his blade in hand, knowing that he could not afford any wide swings. Everything had to be quick and straight, which was more risky with two men who were also good at combat. So he was hesitant to strike, not wanting either man to get an edge on him.

Gary faked a jump forward to try and force a reaction, only for Heru to slice his right arm.

Gary squealed.

Saleem then made his move, only for Heru to whip his blade back around across his face. Saleem dodged it just in time. However, Heru caught his shoulder instead on the downstroke.

"Arrgghh," Saleem responded. But he remained hesitant to use his own blade out of fear of Heru being better with his.

Gary attempted to strike him with a fast elbow, only to catch the same right of Heru's blade in his arm.

"AAAHHH!"

"That's the scream I promised you," Heru teased him back.

On cue, Saleem decided to pull his own knife and jabbed with three moves that all missed. But Heru was able to slash him across the chest with his move, enough to make him bleed, but not enough to kill or damage any organs.

Frustrated by being too cautious with fear, Gary, in desperation, grabbed Heru's arm from which he wielded the knife.

"Get him now!" Gary hollered to Saleem.

When Heru went to punch him with his second hand to break free, Gary caught his fist in his palm, holding him two ways for Saleem to strike him. But Heru twisted his nimble body in the air and kicked Saleem's knife out of his hand, punching it deep into the wall. That forced Saleem into his own act of desperation as he tackled Heru's lower body to the floor.

Heru then switched hands with his knife, cutting the back of
Gary's wrist and freeing himself in an attempt to bring his blade
down on Saleem's back, but Saleem grabbed Gary's wrist just
before Heru could strike him. Gary helped to pull back Heru's
arm right as another round of UAE soldiers arrived at both sides
of the hallway with their guns drawn.

"Wait, don't shoot! We have him!" Gary screamed.

Saleem wasn't so sure. He felt that he and the American
might have to sacrifice themselves for the greater good of the
people. Heru was simply too skilled to be captured alive. But
as the armed men closed in on them, Saleem began to believe
that they could indeed capture Ra-Heru, the leader of the most
memorable labor revolt in the short history of Dubai.

Realizing that the soldiers were closing in on him with nowhere left to go, Heru dropped the knife and punched Gary in
the face with his free hand before rolling over, grabbing an assault weapon, firing it recklessly at the soldiers and diving back
into the room where the men had taken out the bombs earlier.
However, they hadn't checked under the mattress of the bed in
that same room. That's where Heru had hidden a parachute,
which he quickly slipped onto his back before shooting out the
window and jumping, all before Gary, Saleem and the soldiers
were able to get to him.

"Are you *kidding* me?" Gary commented as he and the others, having arrived in the room just a second late, watched the
Egyptian soar from the hotel room with a guided parachute.

Saleem took one of the assault weapons and started firing at
him to take him down. But Heru still had the gun with him as
well, spinning in their direction to clear them from the window
with a stream of bullets.

Unfortunately for Heru, the room faced the front of the hotel,
where the crowd, the police force and the soldiers were all able
to see him up high—an open target. Even the helicopters were
over top of them. But Heru shot the helicopters off.

The soldiers jumped on the military phones for the commander to order the snipers.

"Heru is flying away in a parachute right above you!"

* * * * *

Back down at street level, inside the armored truck head-quarters, the commander and Tariq heard the urgent report and ran out of the truck to get a good look at the ringleader flying through the sky.

"Horus or Heru was also know as half-human and half-fal-con," the commander commented to his intelligence force.

"Well, let's go shoot the falcon down," Tariq advised him.

In anticipation of the volley of bullets that he could expect while floating down in a parachute, Heru began to fire down on the armored truck headquarters and at all of the police and soldiers, forcing Tariq and the commander to duck for cover. But there were simply too many men outside with guns to miss a floating target, no matter how the ambitious Egyptian tried to maneuver around them. And after killing nearly fifty of their men by himself, the UAE soldiers and police finally had their chance at retaliation, more like a fifty-one gun salute.

Ironically, Ra-Heru Amun saw his death as an obvious need for an entire army to kill him rather than any one man or a group of snipers. So he accepted his death like a legend of war that he imagined himself to be.

The crowd watched it all unfold, including Basim, who had just arrived to witness the shooting by air, up close. Inside the truck headquarters, Mohd watched the camera monitor and heard all of the bullets being shot up into the air at his oldest son. He then closed his eyes to say a silent prayer, not only for his son, but for the souls of all the victims who died that day.

"Wow ... what a way to die," Gary commented from the window from the top floor of the building as they all watched the dramatic conclusion before them. Then Gary snapped them to attention. "All right, we need to find the rest of those bombs in the rooms and get the people out of here."

The soldiers moved fast as if the American was briefly their commander of the moment. But he was right—they had no time to marvel and gloat.

Saleem pulled Gary aside as the soldiers went on about their work. "It's been fun fighting with you, my friend," Saleem said, "but had it not ended that way with Heru, I don't know if either one of us, or both of us together, could have ever really beaten him."

Gary smiled and nodded. "Well, now we don't have to." He then wrapped several bathroom towels around his arms and wrists to stop his bleeding. Saleem did the same with his wounds.

"So, where do you go from here, my friend?" the Pakistani asked the American. He figured the man had come a long way that day. Maybe he would be ready for more antiterrorism.

Gary shrugged and didn't think of any missions as Saleem thought of them. He wasn't really a military man. So he answered, "Back home, I guess, after I spend a few more days in Dubai to heal my wounds. What about you?"

Saleem shrugged and didn't believe the American. He figured he was young enough to participate in a lot more dangerous missions. "I no longer have a home," Saleem said. "So I'll go wherever my next job takes me." *Maybe this is my best job,* he told himself without voicing it, *special mission warfare. It's much better than the disrespect of construction.*

"Yeah," Gary said, thinking of his own minimal ties back at home, "I know just what you mean." He still felt as if he would do more traveling ... *alone.*

Chapter 34

THE DEATH TOLL FROM the siege and battle was one-hundred and seventy-eight. It could have been much worse had Ra-Heru succeeded in his plan to detonate the top floors of the building. Soldiers found bombs on four of those floors.

Once the immigrant men inside the lobby found that Heru had been shot down and killed in his escape, several more of Mohd's loyal guard shot down Heru's lieutenant to take over the room. They were then able to release the rest of the hostages, but the damage had already been done.

The Union Defence Force took the heaviest loss with seventy-one killed, mostly by Heru, including his plan to assassinate the UDF commander. Sixty-four immigrant gunmen had been killed, along with twenty-eight UAE police officers, including Chief Ali Youssef. Of the tourists, fifteen hostages had been killed, including two elders who had died from massive heart attacks.

When Abdul received the final reports in Abu Dhabi at the home of his uncle Sheikh Al Hassan—where he and Hamda were ordered to remain—they were both devastated. Not only did Abdul understand that he had no right to fight his punishment of suspension of his construction and development licenses, he cried and prayed for hurt of the innocent families, the UAE police and for the Defence Force soldiers, who had lost their lives. He also hurt and prayed for his young nation and pondered what the fallout would mean for the future of Dubai. And he and his wife understood that they had a lot of amends to make in the country to ever regain respect for their good names.

As for Mohd and the rest of the surviving immigrants, they would have to deal with the *Sharia* law of the United Arab Emirates and the strong emotions of the people involved who had lost the lives of their loved ones.

* * * * *

After the dust had all settled that evening, the Prime Minister and the President of the United Arab Emirates met with the commander of the Union Defence Force, private investigator and counsel Tariq Mohammed, the American traveler Gary Stevens, the Pakistani Saleem, the Sri Lankan Johnny Napur, the Jordanian Ramia Farah Aziz, and several more of a large group of heroic men and women in the royal chambers to discuss honoring them all with a Bravery Medal, *Nut al-Shaja'at*.

Tariq was immediately considered to take over the UAE Chief of Police position, an honor that he asked to think about to discuss with his wife and children at home. The Defence Force honorees were asked to fill higher positions of command as well. As for the civilians, they were also to receive an undisclosed amount of "honor money," and their choice of a stay at the best hotel in Dubai, which was Gary's idea. He told the President and Prime Minister that he would offer any monetary award to the tourists and families, and that he would add a significant contribution of his own to the police and soldiers. He only asked that he and his new friends could have their private rooms at the famous Burj Al Arab hotel for the remainder of his stay there.

"I'll take the Burj Al Arab over a hospital any day," he joked.
"That can be easily arranged and granted," he was told.

* * * * *

That evening after midnight, Gary lay gingerly on a royal-sized bed at the seven-star Burj Al Arab hotel, an honor that billions around the world could only dream about. Words could not begin to explain the opulence of the room. But Gary felt that he actually deserved it, not through his inherited wealth, but through his selfless and heroic service to the people of Dubai who needed it. He had put his life on the line for them. However, his service did not stop there. He knew that there were many other places around the world that he could travel to, and many more people in need to help.

"Unbelievable," he moaned to himself as he nursed his injuries through a personal medical staff at the hotel. All he needed was to call them, like room service, to help change his bandages. The Emirates had even replaced his phone. However, they had no idea how complicated his broken phone was to replace.

I'll call Jonah in the morning, he told himself. He knew she would be worried sick about him, yet he did not have the same feelings of urgency to call his girlfriend, Karla, in Washington.

I guess that's my answer then, he thought. *I just don't have strong enough feelings for her.*

On cue, the doorbell of his hotel room rang. With the advancements of room technology, there was a camera at the peephole where Gary could immediately view his visitor on his large flat screen television that was high above the bed. He also had a remote control to open the door with. Such amenities were needed in a room the size of a public swimming pool.

Once Gary saw that it was Ramia, he quickly buzzed her in to keep her from getting into trouble with the Muslim nation's restrictive culture on open sexuality, particularly with Muslim women.

He sat up as she walked into the room and asked her, "What

in the *world* are you doing here? I thought you shared a double room with your cousin. He let you sneak out?"

She smiled and said, "I am a grown woman, whether my cousin accepts it or not. And I wanted badly to see you tonight. I could not sleep without it."

Her hair was out, clean and blow-dried, and she smelled of the exotic body oil and perfume that she had used after a long cleansing bath inside of a whirlpool. Her dress was nearly see-through under her robe, where she wore no panties or bra, like a liberated woman of the West. And as the beautiful Jordanian woman popped up on the bed with Gary, with her hazel eyes aglow, seeming to reflect all of the colors in the expensively decorated room, Gary took a deep breath and composed himself, realizing that he was in need of strong discipline. She then tossed her robe to the floor.

"So, who are you?" she asked him. "You still owe me plenty of answers."

Her beautiful, soft skin, with a natural tan that matched her eyes and hair color, was right there in front of him to touch and take advantage of. And it was what she wanted him to do, to possess her like a romantic American. Yet Gary fell back in his mountain of pillows and relaxed.

"I'm just a regular guy," he told her, "who's trying to figure out where he is in life."

Seeing him lying there with bandaged wounds and no shirt made Ramia feel comfortable enough to caress him softly and wrap her right leg over his.

"This does not hurt you, does it?"

Her body felt like another pillow, only warmer and slightly heavier, with a heartbeat. He felt like he had died and been taken to a Muslim heaven, yet he continued to feel uneasy about it. She was still so young, in a very expensive Arab hotel room with him where he was quite sure they had cameras. He figured that they could haul him away to jail for this.

But he told her the truth anyway. "No, it feels wonderful." And he wrapped his sore arm around her, tempted to massage her naked body through her paper-thin dress.

She asked him with her head in his chest, "Have you ever made love to a Middle Eastern woman before?"

"You mean a *Muslim* woman," he clarified.

"We are not all Muslim," she said.

"Well, I never have."

The heat from their bodies began to rise, but Gary continued to compose himself.

"How about we just hold each other while I tell you my story?"

Ramia closed her eyes, feeling sexy and womanly, but she was also exhausted from an extremely long day of walking up and down stairs. But she had what she wanted. She was finally able to relax without the anxiety of losing it.

"Okay," she moaned. And she slightly increased her grip on his muscular but injured body as if he were her pillow.

Gary began to tell her the long story of his life, knowing that she would fall asleep on him long before he would finish.

"I was conceived in a Jackson, Tennessee, hotel room, when my mother was fresh out of high school and not much younger than you."

Hearing another slight to her age, Ramia squeezed his injured ribs and was apparently not ready to fall asleep.

"Ahhh," Gary responded.

She looked up into his eyes with the fierceness of her recent experience. She decided that she would no longer allow herself to be denied of anything, otherwise she would have never been there with him. So she told him, "I am a *woman*. And you will *treat* me like a woman. Now continue," she added softly, with a gentle scratch of his abdomen.

Gary thought, *Oh, my God! I don't know if I'll make it out of this one.*

* * * * *

In the morning, Ramia returned to her room only to be confronted by Basim inside their foyer. He had been up all night, worrying and praying again, and he even wanted to send her back home to Jordan. But before he could get out a word, Ramia placed her finger to his lips and said, "Look, Basim, we now will have enough honor money from the Emirates to move and live the way we want to. But I no longer want to remain here in Dubai. So if you do not want to move with me to Britain, Canada or America, then I understand, and I will give you some of the money to make your own choice. But I am *not* going back home to Jordan."

Basim remained calm. "Fine, we can decide on it later. But where did you sneak out to last night until this morning?" He had a hunch but did not want to say it.

Ramia said it for him. "Basim, I am my *own* woman. And I will make my *own* decisions from this moment on and until I am *dead*. So if I want to see the American and talk to him, then that's what I will *do*."

Basim's eyes widened and his body tingled with tension as if he was ready to strike her. But Ramia's eyes looked fierce enough to kill him, and she had the favor of the Emirates and a friend in a resourceful American, so he fought to compose himself under the name of Allah.

But then he asked her cautiously, "You did not ... you only *talked* to him, right?"

"Yes, of course. And he was a complete gentleman. He only let me into his room because I would not leave his doorway until he would talk to me about who he is and why he did what he did. The man *inspired* me so I wanted to understand him. That is all that it was."

Basim wanted to trust her story with all of his heart. He felt that only the most honorable man should ever have her in marriage, and not some traveling American vigilante. So he took a deep breath. "Thank you. Allah is Magnificent."

Ramia grinned and told herself, *And I would never tell you more.*

"I love you, cousin. But you may need to allow me to become a real woman soon. Otherwise, some people may start to think of incest."

"Arrgghh," Basim responded and cringed. "What are you *talking* about? That is so *blasphemous.* Don't you ever say that to me. I love you as a cousin only."

Ramia continued to smile, knowing that she had shifted his mind away from the American on purpose. Basin was so defensive and embarrass-prone that she knew her slight could stick with him for a full day.

* * * * *

Gary allowed his friend Johnny to visit him for breakfast. They sat at a round and artistic table with tall designer chairs. And as usual, Johnny was bouncing off the walls with energy.

"Gary, this *unbelievable*! I couldn't even sleep in my room last night. I just kept rolling over and looking at everything and sitting on the sofas and looking out at the view at the window and touching everything and using the bathroom and the whirlpool. I swear to you, my fingerprints are on *everything* in the room. They could lock me in prison for reckless touching."

Gary smiled and shook his head. Johnny was indeed inspired by the wonders of the world. "I'm glad you had this opportunity."

"Man, I'm so glad I ever *met* you. I swear to you, this has been the *craziest* three days of my *life*. And my body is still *aching* me from walking up and down so many stairs yesterday, but I can't even feel it, I'm so excited."

"Yeah, Ramia gave you a real workout yesterday, right?" Gary hinted.

That changed the whole conversation for Johnny. His eyes grew wide as he responded wildly, "Man, she's like a *dream*! She's so *beautiful*! Where did you ever find her?"

"Out on the desert sand tour."

"*Yes*, and she even *looks* like the sand. Those eyes and the skin and the hair—it's like someone just *molded* her out of the desert, I *swear* to you. She's like an *oasis*, a *mirage*. And she's so *serious*! I can't *believe* I followed her into a building of terrorists!"

"And now you end up being much richer for it."

"Man, it's like, *unbelievable!* And you are so *lucky* to have her."

Gary shook it off and said, "No, it actually looks like she has chemistry with you now."

"No *way!* Are you *serious?* She thinks I'm a joke. I had no idea what to even say to her."

"Nah, you make her laugh. That's good. Women love to laugh."

"Yeah, but the ones I laugh with too much, they don't take you seriously."

"Dude, you just helped her to save a couple of hundred lives and will be honored with a Bravery Medal from the President and Prime Minister of the United Arab Emirates. Are you kidding me? Who's gonna have more juice than *that?*"

Johnny beamed at the compliment. "Yeah, you're right. But I'm no fool. She only has eyes for you."

"That was only temporary," Gary told him. "It was the heat of the moment. But I'm headed back home now to my own life. Whereas for *you*, you have a chance to take her to London and France and India now. She'll like that, and she'll trust you."

Johnny cringed and said, "Yeah, but her cousin, man, he's like *waaay* Muslim. I can't wait around five years for her. You know what I mean? I'm around far too many spontaneous women for that."

Gary chuckled. "Trust me, she's not gonna let her cousin in the way of what she wants to do. Remember, she just forced you to walk into a building full of terrorists, right?"

Johnny thought about that and said, "Yeah, she did."

Gary nodded. "So go for it. I think you two would be good for each other. And I know she won't stand for your nonsense."

Johnny laughed. "I'll think about it. But I don't know if I want a woman who can put me on timeout with the kids."

They laughed and waited for their big breakfast to arrive inside of the immaculate hotel.

* * * * *

By early afternoon, Gary received word at his hotel room that a traveling guest from the United States was there to see him in the lobby. Gary knew exactly who it was.

He got dressed and rode the elevator to the lobby to find Jonah waiting for him there in all black, including a pair of expensive designer shades.

"I see you got yourself into a ball of trouble again."

Gary opened his sore arms as a gesture to their surroundings. "And look where it got me," he quipped.

"Yeah, and it almost got you *killed* too. So when are you ready to go home?" she asked.

Gary looked down at his bandaged arms and hands. "I think I need to heal first. The pressure on the plane for a dozen hours would kill me."

Jonah shook her head. "Not on your way back. In the private jet you get to stretch out a bit. And the travel time is faster."

Gary thought about it with no comment. He couldn't believe his own life. Maybe he was a secret agent and didn't know it yet.

"I'll book my own room and be ready when you're ready," Jonah said.

"You're getting a room here?"

Jonah looked around and shook her head. "I don't want to get too spoiled over here. It makes you lose your edge. But we'll talk about that on the plane ride back." She dug into her small black carry bag. "By the way, here's a new phone."

She tossed it to him while Gary smiled.

"I guess I'll need to get used to this thing."

Jonah nodded and said, "Yeah. You do."

Chapter 35

THREE DAYS LATER, GARY stretched out next to Jonah on a private Gulfstream jet heading back to the Washington and Virginia area.

Jonah exhaled and took a sip of her orange juice before she asked him any questions.

"So, did you learn anything outside of how easy it is to die in the wrong place at the wrong time?" She didn't seem too concerned. Maybe she understood that he was well prepared to handle himself.

"I learned that the Middle East is very complicated."

Jonah chuckled. "I could have told you that without the trip. But you strike me as the kind of man who's determined to learn on his own."

Gary agreed without stating so. What was the use in living vicariously? "So, when is the big meeting with my father?"

"Next week. He's out of the country now himself."

Gary shook his head and grinned. "How convenient."

Jonah reached over and touched his arm before reclining her chair. "Don't worry. It'll happen sooner or later. In the meantime, I have some other people who would like to meet with you. And your father said it was okay."

Gary leaned his own chair back and asked, "What about?"

"We'll talk about it later. I need to sleep now."

"You didn't get enough sleep at your hotel room?"

Jonah leaned in his direction to look into his eyes. "After what you just went through, *no*."

Gary smirked. "I thought you weren't afraid of anything."

"I'm really not," Jonah told him. "But that doesn't mean I can sleep through it."

"I guess Dubai will have to deal with that stigma now for a while."

Jonah disagreed. "Nope. They'll drop the prices and the tourists will be back next month for their national holiday celebrations."

* * * * *

Two days after he was back in the States, Gary had lunch with his girlfriend at Po'boys restaurant in Washington's refurbished U Street area. But he was totally out of the conversation. Everything seemed to be moving in slow motion now at home. He felt like a swimmer treading water in an Olympic-sized pool and going nowhere.

"What did you just say?" he asked Karla, breaking himself from his daydream.

His girlfriend's style of hair and dress seemed extra conservative to him that day.

"I said, what are your plans for this weekend?"

On a whim, Gary thought of returning home for a while and showing it all to Karla, the place where he grew up. So he shrugged and said, "I don't know. You wanna go to Louisville with me this weekend? I still own a record shop there that throws parties every once in a while."

Karla looked stunned. "You own a record store? You never told me that. And I can't just fly out of town over the weekend. I wouldn't be able to leave until late Friday night, and I would have all kinds of packing and things to do."

Gary shrugged. "Well, do it then."

Karla looked at him and took a bite of her sandwich out of nervousness. She didn't like his tone. "Are you okay?" she grumbled through her food.

Karla knew far too many military men who were verbally and physically abusive, but Gary didn't realize his tone. He was simply bored with being back in Washington.

Feeling the obvious tension at their table, Gary brightened when his phone rang and he saw the caller ID number. It was Johnny. Gary excused himself. Karla was miffed, but Gary was already out the door before she could say anything.

As soon as he answered the call, Johnny's excitement rushed over the line.

"Hey, Gary, guess what, man? Ramia said *yes*. She wants to go with me back to London. But her cousin wants to come too. I don't *believe* this! How do I dump him? I don't want him around. All of my Muslim friends in London are *ten times* cooler than him."

Gary laughed out loud. "Maybe that'll be good for him. You can introduce him to a less-conservative Muslim in London to bring him out of his shell."

"Let me tell you, the Muslims I will introduce him to in London will do much more than just bring him out of his shell—they will give that poor boy a heart attack. I'm actually scared for his health over there."

Gary laughed good and strong again, and it raised his sullen spirit ... some. He felt as if he was having an international withdrawal. He couldn't take not thinking about going overseas again.

Then Johnny asked him, "So, where are you off to next, traveler?"

On a whim, Gary answered, "Shanghai. How about that one?"

"*Whoa*, you'll get in a whole lot of *new* kind of trouble over there. So you'll need to take me to drive you," Johnny offered. "I won't know where the hell I'll be going when we get there, but I can find out. You just tell me when you want to go."

Gary listened to Johnny's reckless energy while looking through the window of Po'boys. He was right there on the corner of 14ᵗʰ Street.

Oh my God, he told himself as he watched Karla. *I can't do this to her—just leave again, alone. I'll just have to tell her to move on.* He looked back at Karla and felt sorry for her. Like Ramia Farah Aziz from Jordan, he could no longer accept the restrictions.

He decided to be who he was ... a traveler.

CPSIA information can be obtained at www.ICGtesting.com
Printed in the USA
BVOW02s0833171013

334008BV00002B/3/P

9 781938 467493